LOVELIFE

*

George Kane: girl-chasing television director, on the run from domestic chaos. With him, his eight-year-old daughter whom he has kidnapped from his estranged wife as a grandiose gesture of 'emotional commitment'.

George Kane: Schizophrenic Man strikes again. George the Creep, George the Gambler. A man of obsessive drives and compulsions, seeing all life in terms of film. All life as a collage of past movie fragments. George Kane; sunk so deep in the medium that he can only surface, spluttering wildly, at intervals and despairingly note that 'real life' is just as fragmented and hopeless, before sinking again into his world of film and obsession.

George Kane: articulate man, with a precise sense of the ridiculous that makes this one of the funniest and most original novels about sex and sexual confusion. George Kane, who turns the intellectual scalpel on himself and peers fascinated at all the twitching, jumping emotional nerves as he parts the fat down to the funny bone.

Robert Muller

Lovelife

ARROW BOOKS

ARROW BOOKS LTD
3, Fitzroy Square, London, W.1

AN IMPRINT OF THE HUTCHINSON GROUP

London Melbourne Sydney Auckland
Wellington Johannesburg Cape Town
and agencies throughout the world

*

First published by
Hutchinson & Co (*Publishers*) Ltd, 1970
Arrow Edition 1971

*Made and printed in Great Britain
by Hunt Barnard Printing Ltd,
Aylesbury, Bucks*

ISBN 0 09 004960 8

For

BILLIE AND MATTHEW

One

THAT silver morning, squatting on a white-painted wooden seat outside the Martinez Hotel, I briefly tasted freedom. For all of five minutes I felt weightless. Floating. Disembodied after two nights without sleep. Might have prolonged the novel sensation by craning my neck and concentrating on the sun-flecked smoothness of the Mediterranean. Instead I picked up an abandoned copy of *L'Equipe*, began a systematic search for football results, found them :

St. Etienne 3   Rennes 1

Up in room 486 I had helped Leonore to undress. Tucked her into bed, drawn the blinds, brushed my teeth. By the time I'd quartered a nasty French apple for her, she was already unconscious.

During the night's flight, she had twice toddled along to the plane's lavatory to steal soap; I'd given her some sums to do; she had dozed off. In the bus from Nice Airport she slept heavily against my shoulder.

Cannes 0   Rouen 4

If we'd come a couple of days earlier, I could have taken her along to the Hesperides to see the débâcle. Might have provided both of us with a useful diversion.

The early sunshine prickled pleasantly over my skin. In the rush I had forgotten to pack sun-glasses. I squinted at the printed page, lulled my mind with the soothing order of league tables. When had I last seen a French football match? Must have been the winter Dick Bligh had first come down here to renew himself. Six years ago? Seven?

Great gleaming taxis were drawing up. Porters piled luggage on my seat, hemmed me in. Elderly, gabardened American males fumbled for money, paid off drivers, adjusted hearing-aids, turtled through swing doors. Somewhere down there, between the Croisette and the stretch of glittering water, beckoned a warm beach. No, mustn't stray too far from room 486.

My five minutes of freedom were already used up.

One of the deaf Americans loitered. His complexion brought Jack Pierce's Universal mummies to mind. Cocked his head in my direction. Flash of dentures. Yegods, was he going to engage me in footling conversation? My glare must have discouraged him; started chatting up a young *chasseur*: mournful discourse on a failed roulette system.

The youngster stared at the old monster, naked greed in his eyes, not getting the drift, but pretending to understand. Beautiful scene to direct. Why could I never get my actors to stand like that, do nothing except *listen*? At last the oldster ended his tale, tipped awkwardly, went inside.

Never heard of a more ridiculous system.

I wasn't going to play roulette this time, that much was certain. Not unless Dick came up with a Sitter; among other things. Never mind, done all that, over and over again, the whole grandiose ritual, with or (preferably) without Linda. Leisurely checking-in at the Martinez or Dick's Villa Rameau. Badedas bath. First Pernod. Trim and manicure. Second Pernod. Tense formalities over polished mahogany surfaces. Passing the scrutiny of the blue-chinned physiognomist to enter Josef von Sternberg-land, loser's paradise.

For me those rites were invented. Balm for the emotionally underprivileged. Knew that now, but could not enjoy insight as much as roulette. All gone. Every blowzy Soho alley promised a 'Casino'. The past. Tossed the paper aside, closed my eyes. Seen the Mediterranean before, too.

Yet how absurdly I warmed to that image of George the Gambler. Cherished it. With his stacks of coloured chips, soles sinking into high carpets, newly shined fingernails, endless columns of stupid numbers, inevitable domestic lies about 'breaking even'. Yet there was a sediment of truth, somewhere. Hadn't I lost four hundred pounds once, *in a single night*? And kept the truth from Linda?

But why restrict this image of self to roulette playing? Gambled my whole existence away. Investigate any phase of my life, what do you find? George the Gambler. Bridge-burner *par excellence*.

What concerns me is this: If George the Gambler is real, how can he bear to cohabit my soul with George the Creep, mean pettyfogger, Old Dependable of TV Drama, your one hundred per cent professional—in short: Linda's husband?

Dichotomy can be illustrated by what occurred at that precise moment. Lolling about on that white bench in the morning sun, having exploded his remaining bridges—*even then*, George the Creep was niggling away on a scheme to save the taxi fare to the Villa Rameau.

And this, mind you, with three thousand pounds of hard-earned cash locked away in Linda's personal account, our freehold house registered in her name, costly legal consequences of my flight looming ahead. Yegods, with all that *and* Leonore likely to wake up at any moment to ask inconvenient questions, I was thinking: maybe I should call the Villa Rameau, get Dick to pick us up in his car, thereby save eleven francs.

Must be the bloody German in me.

Don't need an analyst to tell me it's that atavistic Hun, Jerry, Fritz who controls The Creep. Diabolical Dr. Mabuse behind the projector, and on the screen: two ghost-white faces in a drab grey crowd. My father and mother standing behind an iron barrier, Platform 2, railway station, Bendabrück. Waving handkerchiefs. Drab grey crowd has assembled to dispatch non-Aryan offspring across Holland and the Channel to a place where they don't murder Jews.

In a night train ...

The recurring image (Camera: Karl Freund) reminds me that in that crowd were some who found ways and means to follow. My father and mother lacked those ways and means. But wrote to me to say they were trying. War started, they were still there; letters stopped. Silence. Must have expected me to do something. Maybe I should have tried harder. Fact is, I didn't try at all. True, I still wore short pants at the time, but did absolutely nothing. Not a bloody thing. Never saw them again.

Got around to doing something after the war. Searched for their names on much-fingered lists, badly typed, provided for Survivors by nice caring people in a Bloomsbury hotel converted into offices. Found them, both names side by side, page 87. While I was at it, also found the names of two uncles, one aunt, three cousins.

'Must get rid of that phony self-pity, George,' Dick would say. 'Didn't really feel a thing then, don't give a damn now. Until you come to terms with that, you'll always do second-rate superficial work. It's your alibi.'

Dick's wrong about that, of course, as he is about a lot of things. (I mean if *my* work is superficial and second-rate, cast your eyes over *his* crap some time!)

Still, leaning out of the window of that night train, that Children's Transport, seeing those handkerchiefs waving, I can't say I was consumed by any profound sense of loss. No. Was burning my first bridge, making a neat job of it. Escape!

No more pretences at school, no further need to explain away that Kahn was suspiciously like Kohn. (And to think Germany's best centre-forward at the time was called Conen! Conen of Saarbrücken. *Conen!* I ask you!) No more dreaming up excuses for not joining the bloody *Jungvolk,* either. No more bullying of cripples down at that tram depot: tomorrow it might be *your* turn. Because who was a cripple, or a Jew, was determined by my best friend Werner Lotz. Who hated me. No more Algebra under Dr. Wittens, incompetent sadist. No further cross-examination by Dr. Fontan, whose idea of Geography was to drum every existing church, farmyard, milestone on Bendabrück Heath into our heads. And, to be honest, no more moans from my father (can't remember his face, haven't looked at the brown photograph for years, where is it, anyway?) about his lost position as Chief Buyer, Men's Outfitting, in that department store in the Kaisterstrasse. No more arguments with aunts and uncles, that kept me awake at night, about consulates, and waiting lists, and affidavits, and guarantees, and emigration permits. No more letters on nice, thick stationery from distant relations and friends in the United States of America, insisting that if we could hold on just a little longer, things would surely improve. Hitler wouldn't dare to squeeze the Jews any tighter. Mr. Roosevelt would apply diplomatic pressure, because he depended on the Jewish vote, and not even Hitler would dare to defy F.D.R. So don't panic, friends. Keep your faith. Mind that *Angstpsychose*.

No more of that. Adventure lay ahead! Great houses in the country, Little Lord Fauntleroy. Hyde Park and Piccadilly Circus. Great Danes asleep in front of log fires. Arsenal versus Aston Villa. Ted Drake and Edgar Wallace. Breakfast-Lunch-Tea-Dinner-Supper. The English, it was well-known in Mabuseland, spent all their time sitting down to formal exotic meals. Fish and rice for breakfast they ate, and kidneys served in silver dishes by butlers.

Burn that bridge. . . .

Hadn't quite turned out that way. Never tasted any kedgeree until after the war. Wolfed down lots of Cadbury chocolate, was taken to see *Snow White and the Seven Dwarfs*. But no Lord drove up in a Rolls to claim me. The gentle people who journeyed to that converted holiday camp on wintry Sunday afternoons to pick out a kid that took their fancy, did not come anywhere near me. Maybe I had spots. Don't remember.

After three weeks in that teeming compound, drinking milky tea, learning English grammar, singing *Daisy*, I was securely labelled and sent off by train to a childless middle-aged couple who owned an electrical appliances shop near the Elephant and Castle.

Because of some clerical error they got me, Kahn Georg. Not the Kohn Alfred they had specified. Kahn Georg, it soon turned out, wasn't exactly what they'd had in mind. Wasn't orthodox, didn't even *look* Jewish. And they had particularly asked for a lad who was *froom*, and whom they could prepare for a decent Bar-Mitzvah. Hadn't they been assured, *in writing*, that Kohn Alfred was not only orthodox, but the son of a Cologne Rabbi? *This* boy, Kahn Georg, couldn't even read Hebrew. What sort of Jewish refugee was that, if you please?

Kahn Georg wasn't circumcised either. That grim truth wasn't revealed until a fortnight after my arrival, when for once I hadn't locked the bathroom door or worn football shorts in my bath to hide my shameful secret. Fortunately, they were kind people in that electrical appliances shop. You couldn't very well send a boy back and forth like a parcel, could you? So, allright, they kept him, though, with the grotesque evidence before them, more than likely his mother was a *Schickse*. (*Not so*. My parents were enlightened liberals. Had they stood by tradition, got a doctor to lob off my foreskin at birth, I could never have gone to that very good Aryan secondary school, to learn about churches and windmills on Bendarbrück Heath. They had left my foreskin intact for my own good.)

So I stayed where I was, swept out the shop every day, delivered radios and heaters all around the Elephant and Castle area, was enrolled in a technical school to learn electrical engineering. And the optician from next door came in twice a week to give me free Hebrew lessons, so that I might at least read prayers at table. And when I peed I kept the bathroom door locked.

One got by. Again. But by now it had got through to me that something must be very seriously wrong with my genitals to cause such a furore. A Jewish penis, which the Nazis deemed O.K., and the Jews recoiled from in horror, what kind of a misbegotten prick was that?

Started sort of playing with it in bed, found that if I rubbed it long enough, the tip would get moist, give me a lovely, itchy feeling. Soon discovered that this poor thing (but mine own) could fire sperm as efficiently as any other similarly-aged penis around, a fact I was happy and proud to demonstrate to any other boy in the street who might doubt my virtuosity in this field. *Mine was as good as anybody's . . .*

So the war, like separation from my parents, came as a relief. Escape! Our school was evacuated to Devon, another train roaring over a burning bridge: No more sweeping up shopfloors. No more sweating out Hebrew prayers. No more remarks about being the Dirtiest Boy in the street—just because the others got tired of competing with my firing power. Ahead of me: Country lanes and cows. Swimming in the sea. Conkers and rocks. Possibly even Kedgeree. . . .

Never wrote a line to my dear old couple of the electrical appliances shop, though their kindness had probably saved me from being sent to an Institution or a Concentration Camp. Or something. Tore up their letters. Burn that Bridge. They gave up writing to see me in the end, must have thought me a real ingrate. (Can you wonder, with *His* Upbringing?)

After I left school to earn a living, bridgeburning ceased to be imposed on me by circumstances, became a conscious *modus operandi*. Actually lit the fires, instead of watching the flames and scurrying for cover.

Stuck to my job as a costing clerk in a Wandsworth

ballbearing factory (for which my education had equipped me) for two long weeks, then packed it in, telling my great-aunt, Polish refugee of late vintage with whom I had found a home in Kilburn, what I was going to be: *Movie director.*

Every available sixpence, every furtive free hour, I'd spent on cinemas. Graduated from the News Cinema, Waterloo Station, through the Elite, Honicoombe, to the ecstasy-bringing four-hour double feature at the Trocadero. A life for Art!

Fantasying intercourse with Dorothy Lamour, I got myself a job as office boy with Paramount in Wardour Street. Burned another little bridge while I was at it: deserted my great-aunt, slept in tube shelters, which was not only safe, but cheap. Later, my great-aunt's flat was smashed by a doodlebug. Great-aunt killed. Might have been me.

My wartime career in films, fetching coffee for executives, sticking stamps on envelopes, firewatching on Tuesdays on the roof of Film House, was not thought sufficient contribution to the war effort, even from a bloody enemy alien. The war had to be got over with, so I retired from Paramount, grew tomatoes in a greenhouse in Enfield. This counted as a reserved occupation, was more agreeable than joining the Pioneer Corps.

Reculer pour mieux sauter. Burn that bridge.

Spent the next couple of years pottering about in an Enfield greenhouse by day, seeking out double features by night. Joined the New Metropolitan Film Society and other organisations devoted to the Art of the Cinema. By the time Labour got into power, I had seen *The Cabinet of Dr. Caligari* three times. Even sat through one and a half projections of *The General Line.*

I mention this fact because it was by walking out of the second showing of Eisenstein's legendary bore that I met Dick Bligh, who couldn't stomach *The General Line* either.

Dick had just got out of the Navy, was working in the story department of Gainsborough Pictures. A Professional Writer, who actually worked in The Industry, he seemed unimpressed by his good fortune. Bellyached because his talents were being wasted browsing through historical novels, which might yield parts for Margaret Lockwood.

Dick was tall, earnest, good-looking, sported a William Powell moustache. Knew everything, was not ashamed to admit it. Had an Irish father, who lived off shady business deals in Dublin. His mother had run off with a church organist when Dick was ten. Dick's closest relative and mentor was his Uncle Graham, film cutter at Riverside Studios.

Dick's Uncle Graham gave me my chance to burn the next bridge : wangled a Union Card for me. I got apprenticed to an assistant cutter, as *his* assistant. They never saw me again in Enfield.

So my friendship with Dick must be seen as being rooted in gratitude. He *did* get me started allright, no denying it.

We toiled together in The Industry, planned our luminous futures. Sat around in Dick's Bayswater basement, drinking my Algerian wine, smoking my Passing Clouds. Denigrated our employers, placed our faith in the *avantgarde* (David Lean, Peter Ustinov), attended double features. Also screwed or half-screwed a respectable score of typists.

I became a British subject. Burned yet another bridge : changed my name. Couldn't believe that Georg Kahn would ever become a household name. In homage to Orson Welles I now signed myself George Kane. Even had the *chutspah* to write to Mr. Welles about it, got a very nice letter back. But for the encouragement of that letter, stored in my wallet between Identity Card and Durex, I might have been frequently tempted to give it all up. Thank you, Orson.

Next Big Thing that happened was my chance to make a number of short Documentaries, raw and real, before their time. Scripts by Dick Bligh, direction, camerawork and hustling by George Kane. Uncle Graham did the cutting. Lindsay Anderson mentioned one of my early works in *Sequence*. Going places.

Intoxicated by success, Dick and I married a couple of serious girls who loved music, got taken to the Royal Albert Hall instead of being sensibly screwed or half-screwed in Dick's basement. I married Linda, our continuity girl, called Foxy Linda, because of her freckles and shiny, metallic red hair. Dick married Brenda, a thin dark graphics girl who designed our titles.

That was one bridge Dick and I burned together.

From force of habit rather than urgent need, we continued to bang an assortment of unmusical typists, until Brenda found out and spilled the beans to Linda, who instantly fled into an ice-cube, where she has remained ever since. Brenda, briefly saddened, *understood*.

In an effort to melt Linda down, I burned my next bridge. The documentaries weren't getting me anywhere. Didn't hesitate when the call came from Hollywood to direct some of the thirty-nine episodes of a crummy TV series called *Secret Doors*. Linda and I emigrated to California. I discovered, after hearing about it in three hundred and seventy-nine B-movies, what a raincheck was. And when they asked me nicely, I stayed on to direct some of the thirty-nine episodes of *Secret Doors'* spin-off, *Creaking Doors*.

We settled down in a so-called luxury apartment in Inglewood. It overlooked Inglewood Park cemetery. We rented it from a fat slob who'd amassed his stack running a hot dog stand in Santa Barbara, and was off now to splurge in Europe. The place was horrific, with imitation Second Empire furniture, phony Persian rugs, yards of bookspines without books. Amidst this excruciating clutter Linda and I debated the dangers of McCarthyism and

My Integrity. I acquired some kind of American accent.

It was Linda, to give credit where credit is due, who put the match to my next bridge.

We arrived back in London, disillusioned with everything, including our marriage (wondering whether to get a divorce or adopt a child) on the day Independent Television got off the ground. I had obtained real Hollywood experience, spoke mid-Atlantic, suddenly found myself in demand. I signed with the British Independent Network.

This happened twelve years ago, and facts must be faced. As a movie director, I've never made it. Whoremongers who make pictures these days have got me pigeon-holed as a Television Man. And I'm too old to wear hippy shirts and shoot modish bunkum with hand-held cameras.

But don't let me sell myself short. I may have let Orson down, but I *am* one of the most competent and, yes, *imaginative* TV drama directors in the country. Got three scrapbooks of cuttings *and* a Guild Award to prove it.

Which at long last brings me back to the puzzle that set off these ruminations: How can I reconcile these two conflicting elements? One: George the First, creepy Old Dependable, who has never taped a sloppy show, whose fetish for punctiliousness has been analysed by both the *Observer* and *Television Today*. And Two: George the Second, quixotic Bridgeburner, hero of some Abel Gance action sequence, his life a montage of destructive acts, always involving those he professes to love most.

To put it succinctly, where's the bloody synthesis?

Always had this obsession to make the definitive *Dr. Jekyll and Mr. Hyde*. Went down on my knees to Jack Martinsell, begging him to let me do a slapup TV version. Masterpiece. One day he'll let me do it. Just have to find the right slot. I'll direct the arse off that one. Ye-gods, *my* story ...

Must have dozed off, my left foot had gone to sleep. Opened both eyes, found myself sitting in a clutter of luggage. Forecourt of the Martinez teemed with more elderly Americans, just off some cruise boat, dazed.

I got up, waved my foot about, walked through the hotel's swingdoors, started to run upstairs, three steps at a time.

Free again! Set fire to that crumbling bridge! Strip everything down! Switch on the juice, let the tape speak for itself!

I am George Kane, formerly Georg Kahn, of 65, Blazers Drive, Kew, forty-one years old, married, 5 ft. 8 in. tall, weighing eleven stone exactly, colour of hair and eyes: brown, pale complexion, no special distinguishing marks. I am a television director by profession, and last night I kidnapped my only child, Leonore Gina Beatrice, aged eight, and flew off with her in a Trident to a secret destination.

I opened the door to our bedroom.

Leonore (named by Linda after the heroine of *Fidelio*, God help us all) was out of bed, leaning over the balcony railings, one foot off the ground, looking down at the Mediterranean, humming Burt Bacharach. Turned, reproached me. It was nearly eleven o'clock. She could tell by her wrist-watch. She'd finished her *Sparkie* and her *Beezer*, didn't feel a bit tired. And when were we going down to the beach to *play*?

It wasn't Dick who opened the pink portals of the Villa Rameau, but a mid-twenties brunette wrapped in a loosely-belted towelling bathrobe. She looked at the two of us balefully, then, with umbrage, glared at our suitcases. Her face was glazed with public despair. Tears had smudged the mascara around her eyes, flakes of pale rouge clung to her lips. I got the message: Current target for one of Dick's tactical exercises.

'When you're young, you're always prepared to rationalise your failures,' he'd told me more than once. 'I'm no longer prepared to lose, that's all.'

Tutored by two failed marriages, Dick believed in constant 'action' to achieve dominance, divided people into the fuckers and the fucked. To avoid being counted among the latter had become the prime object of his life. He spared no effort to implement his strategy, dismissed my charges of domestic fascism with a characteristically apologetic smile, probably caught the envy in my accusations.

Muttering inaudibly, the girl plucked protectively at her olive bathrobe. Had I peered? Surely not, with Leonore right beside me. Now I did take a peek. Nothing! As Dick got older, his girls got skinnier. Still, why look that particular gift-horse in the mouth? The fact that we never coveted each other's conquests (his preference being for keeping thin mistresses, mine for spontaneous cuddling with bosomy strangers), had helped to keep our relationship a going concern for more than twenty years.

'You like Mums,' was Dick's interpretation. 'I obviously like boys. Simple as that.'

The bathrobe girl had begun to irritate me, mumbling away in sulky, protesting French. I wanted to lie down, get Leonore settled. Didn't care to pay for another night at the Martinez. Dick, it appeared, had driven into Nice with Monsieur Raeburn to buy wine.

An unlikely activity if you don't know the painter and former account executive Charlie Raeburn. I'd known Dick's friend ever since he had moved into the top floor of the Villa Rameau. Driving to Nice to buy wine (in bulk, I presumed) was perfectly in character for Charlie Raeburn who was even meaner than George the Creep; more methodical in his meanness. Squandering time and energy on petty economies gave Charlie opportunities to dodge his empty canvases, indulge himself in the Moravian condition *La Noia,* which, he claimed, afflicted him. Others might have attributed Charlie's habitual despair to his conjugal relationship : Irene Raeburn was Charlie's senior by twenty-three years, and plain, irritable and exacting to boot. Not Charlie. He loved Irene. It had to be *La Noia.*

Leonore vouchsafed that she wanted to go to the toilet. I asked Dick's mistress if we might leave our suitcases, introduced myself as an old friend of Dick's. This here was my daughter.

The girl sniffled into a screwed-up paper hanky, searched her bathrobe for another. What she had previously endeavoured to conceal came briefly into view.

Yegods, would Dick never learn? Two broken marriages. Mistresses beyond count. And the best he could come up with : this flat-chested sniveller. Not friendly, either. While Leonore went to the lavatory, then stroked a cat, and I telephoned for another taxi, we were not even offered coffee, although the hall reeked of it, freshly made.

'Did you think that girl was pretty?' Leonore asked in the cab a few minutes later.

'Hideous.'

'Is she Dick's maid or his girl friend?'

'Did you brush your teeth at the hotel?'

'The cat was friendly, anyway. Pregnant, I think.'

'You always think cats are pregnant.'

'This one really was. Her titties were all hard.'

Leonore takes after me. That's why I had to do it. She's flesh of my flesh, blood of my blood. She's me.

'What's happened to whatshername then. You know?'

'Elsa— Ask Dick when you see him.'

'Elsa was nice. Tried to teach me the backstroke.'

The previous summer, when Linda, Leonore and I spent that Antonioni-type fortnight at the Villa Rameau, Dick was still playing house with a Swedish girl, whom Linda loathed on sight, but who 'loved children'.

'That girl had been crying,' Leonore mused. 'Why?'
'Dick probably beat her up before breakfast.'
'Oh, Daddy.'
'Some big girls like a good hiding from time to time.'
'I bet. Can we go to the beach now?'
'That's exactly where we're going, my love.'
'I bags the one with the blue and yellow umbrellas.'
'We told the girl we'd use the Martinez.'
'What colour umbrellas?'
'White, I think. And orange.'
'I haven't brought my spade, Daddy.'
'I told you to pack it.'
'Didn't fit into my suitcase. I've brought my bucket, but not my spade. Can we buy one?'
'Can't you manage with just the bucket till after lunch?'
'Suppose so.'
'You're a lucky girl, you know. A nice holiday on the French Riviera. And in termtime, too.'

Gave her a self-assuring cuddle.

She was burying herself up to her neck in sand, I was on my second Pernod, when Dick found us. He looked trim and bronzed in his teenage disguise, levis and T-shirt.

'You bastard. Might have let me know. Hello, Leonore.'
'I'm buried alive.'
'Stay that way.'

Though Dick made no pretence of liking children, Leonore was fond of him, held him in healthy respect for his worldly goods.

'I've finally done it,' I proclaimed, swivelling round on my bar stool, so that Leonore shouldn't hear me. Dick pointedly kept his own stool facing her, knowing this would place me in a situational disadvantage from the start. Dick, the tactician, attached great importance to such details.

'About time, too,' he said. 'Should have thrown that

.cow out years ago.' Waggled his fingers at the child. 'Your Mum allright, is she?'

Leonore shrugged, went on piling sand on her stomach.

'Told you I'd never leave her.'

'Where's Linda?'

'Bournemouth, I think. With her lover. Car-hire manager.'

'You realise this will be the first place she'll look for the kid.'

'It's only a temporary solution.'

'You're telling me.'

He snapped his fingers at a loitering waiter, who promptly turned and walked away.

'Bloody awful place.'

'Leonore had to get some sleep...'

'Going to let *her* run your life now, are you?'

'She's a *child*, Dick. For Christ's sake...'

'I'll drive you back to the house. Got a bit of a drama going on.'

'What's her name?'

'Janine. Not your type. Come on, we'll never get served in this sodding place.'

'The kid's enjoying herself...'

'I'm not.'

I called Leonore from her grave. She stretched out her hands, bared her bottom teeth, identified herself as Bride of Dracula. Told her all about Dracula when she was five.

Dick had driven up in his beige Buick, enormous, with stereophonic radio.

Suddenly Leonore was not at all reluctant to leave the beach.

After dinner, it turned cold. We tried sitting out on the terrace for a while, then gave up. Dick lay stretched out on a chaise-longue, hands folded behind his crew-cut, holding forth on my castration complex.

I'd known him to be better. His mind was probably distracted by tactics to be employed for the next round with Janine. The girl had left us alone after dinner to sulk in their bedroom.

As Dick droned on, his toes quivering nervously, I was reminded of the younger edition, the Bayswater Basement Dick, reclining on a creaky old divan, delivering lectures with that same languid certainty, half-challenging, half-apologetic. Linda's interpretation: Bloody arrogance.

Then as now he'd search for lost cigarettes, finally condescending to smoke mine. He had not yet become an expert in the psychology of sex, was still preoccupied with his ambitions, as I was with mine.

'That, my friend,' he would inform me, jerking a thumb in the direction of his utility bookshelf, sagging under the weight of Ibsen, Strindberg, Shaw, O'Neill, 'is the company I intended to join. The rest is just a waste of time.'

Having just read Clurman's *The Fervent Years*, I was drunk on the Group idea. My plan was to form a dedicated film-unit, producing small-budget movies of uncompromising realism. It boiled down to conning film technicians to contribute their services gratis to the Making of George Kane.

Dick, understandably, had a more flexible vision of the future. Didn't mind writing the odd script to help me out, but wished to leave his mark on the West End Theatre, which he condemned as corrupt, effete and decadent.

He managed to get some early work exposed in miniature theatres like the Chepstow and the Torch. Hungry actors performed Bligh for a fortnight, then dispersed. Critics came rarely, preferring corruption, effeteness and decadence to icy draughts and the terrible smell of failure.

Defiantly Dick papered his basement walls with rejection slips from West End managements. Our favourite was a curt note from an impresario (who ended his days

25

flogging land in the Bahamas), criticising one of Dick's early efforts for being too political, 'not suitable for an hall of entertainment.'

'Not suitable for an hall of entertainment,' we'd say during the next twenty years, coming out of *Last Year in Marienbad,* Stockhausen's *Gruppen,* Hochhuth's *The Representative.*

Dick's first marriage went sour on him long before I admitted the possibility of defeat in my endeavours with Linda. Brenda was making a useful living in advertising, but wanted children. Dick had no use for children. Read your Cyril Connolly. Children destroyed talent. Brenda, studious girl, adduced evidence that children were not listed enemies of promise. Dick could not be moved. After rows, Brenda came scampering over to our place for coffee, pour her heart out to Linda. Dick was an unfeeling, alienated brute. Lucky Linda, married to someone like me, normal human being, capable of relating to people. And Linda brewed more coffee for old Brenda, while I added my own mite of commiseration, luxuriating in Linda's approval, which even then was doled out only in public, and of which, therefore, I could never get enough.

After Brenda left to make it up with Dick (loved him), Linda picked up her magazine, crept back into her ice-cube, while I just sat there, feeling I'd betrayed Dick.

When I went to work in the States, Dick and I lost contact. Neither of us believed in writing letters. I did, however, get one picture postcard from him, mailed in Marrakesh. He was having fun, he claimed, seeing the world at a film company's expense. He had become a film publicist. I gloated briefly, went on directing *Creaking Doors.*

When Linda and I returned to England, we found the scene miraculously changed. Dick had become A Success. Brenda had been summarily dismissed from his life. A stringy Public Relations girl called Nancy shared his up-pity flat in St. John's Wood. He had slimmed down spectacularly, devoted ten minutes every morning to physical exercise, got Nancy to buy their edibles at the Wholefood Store in Baker Street. His hair, prematurely grey, was being crewcut for him at the Dorchester Hotel.

He was a New Man, he informed me. Success had severed him from his illusions. He was free. Truly *functioned* at last. (Still smoked my cigarettes, though). The catalyst responsible for this transformation was a shy publisher called Jeremy Shirlwell, on whom Dick had ruthlessly sponged for years, confident that Shirlwell ('my sycophant') would always come back for more punishment.

According to Dick, he'd got himself fired from his movie job for sticking a lighted cigarette in a vain male star's breakfast egg.

He had spent a restless night contemplating two alternatives: Eggs à la Hitchcock or the Cagney routine of grinding the grapefruit—what would make the more dramatic exit from the industry? Dick chose Hitchcock.

Broke and jobless, worn down by the steadfast courage of understanding Brenda, Dick had summoned Shirlwell, demanded a loan of fifty pounds to tide him over. One of his plays was on the point of being accepted by the Court. A film was in the offing. Desperate to please, Shirlwell proposed *giving* Dick the fifty pounds as the first half of an advance. There was a book he felt sure Dick could write if only he'd put his mind to it: a fast, sexy spy thriller for an exciting new publishing venture. Shirlwell's stuffy old firm intended to cash in on the James Bond boom.

Dick set about his assignment with contemptuous energy. Writing at great speed to finish the book and lay his hands on the other fifty pounds waiting at the end of the line, he invented a hero whose capacity for procuring simultaneous orgasms was matched by his ingenuity for devising methods of homicide. Villains were gouged, mutilated, electrocuted, drowned. Girls, all beautiful and in the throes of a jolly variety of nymphomania, climaxed with the noisy precision of cuckoo-clocks. To underline his contempt for his task, Dick tossed in two episodes of lesbianism, one of necrophilia, one of fraternal incest.

Shirlwell was so delighted, he published the book *hors series*, organised heavy promotion, reprinted before publication. At a press party, Shirlwell's publicity girl (Nancy) lulled journalists with cheap champagne, prompted them to invent The British Mickey Spillane. Dick got himself interviewed on television, said cunt, achieved celebrity status. Shirlwell ordered three sequels, which were optioned by American film companies before they were plotted. Dick had found his *niche*.

Brenda, meanwhile, had settled down to play her chosen role : childless victim of fate. Went on working after the divorce, moved in with Basil Tree, a misunderstood composer. Like Dick, Basil was poor, but enjoyed eating in good restaurants. Like Dick, he did not want children. Basil didn't even want marriage. Brenda kept up her friendship with Linda, came round for chats and coffee, lamented her life of self-sacrifice.

I felt sorry for Brenda, a mistake, as she had chosen the life that best suited her needs. I got the measure of this when I commissioned Basil to compose robot music for a Sci-Fi play I was directing for the Network. Brenda was furious. What was I trying to do? Turn her Basil into another tellywhore? She had cast me as Mephistopheles, also responsible for Dick's fall from grace.

Meanwhile in St. John's Wood, Nancy reaped her reward. Dick married her. I never got on with Nancy, breastless and ambitious, unappetisingly blending snappy superiority with archness. Back from their Jamaican honeymoon, Nancy started nagging Dick to give up dirty books and start writing plays again. Soon afterwards, Dick began to complain of claustrophobia, had to stay out of crowded rooms, tolerated restaurants only if he could sit by an open door. Nancy suffered the draughts in silence, continued to work, training Shirlwell's authors to say four-letter words on television.

The marriage never got off the ground. According to Dick, Nancy let him down badly. Just another bloody Brenda, only more so. Nancy moved out, Dick went to an analyst in Baker Street, and for a time became rather holy, gently plotting plays and hacking away at his neuroses. Nearly everybody was mad. He was one of the enlightened few who took action to cure his madness. He felt sorry for the others.

Nancy started to keep house for a fag film critic, and Dick served her with divorce papers, citing the film critic. Nancy convinced him that to be third party in a divorce case would be super for his image.

The analyst cured Dick's claustrophobia. Dick fired him. The man was a religious maniac, needed treatment himself. Dick had found his own diagnosis. All his life he had tried to compensate for his subconscious guilt-feelings about his mother's betrayal by allowing women to dictate to him. He no longer needed their approval. He stood Alone. Marriage was *out*. In the light of his insight, he prophesied imminent disaster for my own marriage. When Linda became pregnant with Leonore, he cut down my joy to size: the happy event could only be described as a catastrophe. Was I blind?

At this time our two separate careers began to interweave once more. Jack Martinsell beseeched the British Mickey Spillane to write a Series for the Network, Dick turned him down. Too busy. Writing a serious play. Television was *out*, too. Didn't need to sell his soul to the gogglebox. Look what compromise had done to *me*.

The Network kept on nagging Dick, Jack Martinsell whining away over fishy dinners about complete artistic freedom, the quality market, new concepts in mass communications. In the end Dick wilted (because he liked

29

Jack, he said), signed a contract to write six episodes of a Really Different Series called *Key Man*. I was touched when Dick made it a condition that I should direct the first three.

'We'll have fun,' he promised.

We hadn't worked together for a long time, smuggled a few good things past the Network's customs. Also screwed, or half-screwed, the odd typist. Made money. The Really Different Series (featuring a polygamous High Society detective with a yacht, a penthouse in Park Lane, and Royalty among his clients) topped the ratings. The Network sold it to the States.

Two years later, Dick was no longer writing *Key Man*. I was still directing it, and going through a nasty patch with Linda. She was threatening to leave me, taking Leonore with her.

Dick now decided the time had come to cut loose. He sold up in London, wrote to *The Times* that Inland Revenue was killing British talent, and flew off to Cannes for a last stab at self-fulfilment.

Escape to the South of France had long starred in our fantasies. (Dick's superhero had satisfied many a jolly nymphomaniac on the Cote d'Azur.) But Dick was nearly forty now; the South of France had become a pretty *passé* sort of fantasy. Younger and richer drop-outs were going to Ibiza or Barbados to fulfil their dreams.

Dick took his time settling in. He sank his capital into buying the Villa Rameau, a picturesquely run-down house on the Route de Frejus, with peeling stucco walls, marble statuary in the garden, a dilapidated swimming pool. He converted the top floor, rented it to the Raeburns, cleared a path to the beach, planted peach trees, renovated the pool.

I called him from time to time, and he seemed happy enough. No, he wasn't lonely—talent was thick on the ground. He was working, but slowly. He asked me to visit him, and quite frequently I did, losing at the Casino but getting tanned. In return for his hospitality, I did what was expected of me : I envied him.

Time passed. Dick built a garage, installed central heating, remodelled his terrace, so that he could work without getting sunstroke. The peach trees didn't work out; he tried lemons. He bought two electric typewriters, moved in a thin, moody German girl, who adored him. He threw her out a year later because she cooked fattening meals and called too many relatives in Düsseldorf. He traded her in for Elsa, Swedish, just as adoring but less domesticated.

I continued to fly down to Cannes to play roulette and get away from darkening domestic scenes. I found Dick becoming increasingly tetchy. He railed at the cost of living, the unreliability of local builders, acquaintances who descended on him in a conspiracy to stop him from working on his play. He also complained of recurring bouts of claustrophobia.

After three years of New Man-Mark II, Dick still hadn't finished a play. He derived some balm from the fact that the ex-advertising man upstairs hadn't finished a painting. He was also succored by the galloping deterioration of my marriage, and gave me much valuable advice.

Suddenly, Dick announced that he was Really Working. No, not a play; something he had to get out of his system; something that would finally clear his decks for action. On his remodelled terrace, he enthused over the project; another S. and V. thriller for Jeremy Shirlwell, but presenting a new hero : a Swede.

Dick stopped rebuilding the Villa Rameau, no longer complained of claustrophobia. Elsa approved of Dick's new hero. As for me, my only hope of salvation lay in ditching foxy Linda and, like him, become a New Man. If I agreed to join him, he'd feel no compunction about slinging the Raeburns out. They were getting on his tits anyway. I hummed and hawed. Allright for him, sitting in the sun, writing. Me, I needed people to direct. How was I going to make a living? What about my darling Leonore? Dick dismissed all objections. Neurotic quibbles. Bloody German Jew, who refused to be serious.

What could have possessed me to bring Linda *and* Leonore to the Villa Rameau for the aforesaid Antonioni fortnight? Seething silences, sterility, fingering of significant objects. The end of my marriage.

Leaving Linda to her ice-cube and large magazines, I walked alone round and round Dick's moonstruck swimming pool, giving birth to a few fantasy: Just me and Leonore and the Villa Rameau.

And patiently laboured to transform fantasy into reality.

'She's chopped it off,' Dick said, hauling a bottle of Stolichanaya from the tiled floor. 'That's what she's done. Connolly had the appropriate phrase for Linda: *eager to castrate everything but his cheque-book.*'

'He was referring to Zelda Fitzgerald ...'

'Look at yourself! A eunuch!'

Had I brought along enough underwear? Undressing for bed, she had placed her clothes over the back of a chair, except for her pants, stuffed under a cushion. Found them. Weren't very clean. Pretended *not* to find them. In the morning she would need a new pair. Must lecture her about wiping herself. Not yet.

'Why don't you answer me? What are you thinking about?'

'Underpants.'

'Jesus.'

'Leonore and I have this very special relationship ...'

'You and Linda had this very special relationship. Told me so a hundred times. Under this very roof. Still kidding yourself, George.'

She knew this was no holiday. Had accepted the situation. Trusted me. Was she awake and crying, wanting Linda?

'Casebook stuff. You need your living-in castrating

32

agent. You finally dump Linda, but you hold on to the kid. To fill in till you find a replacement.'

He poured himself another Vodka, stared serenely into the middle-distance, stylising himself the contented New Man, drawing strength from seeing me off balance.

'You're the sodding expert, Dick,' I said, and rose.

'Stop talking like a bloody poof. Sit down.'

'Haven't slept for two nights . . .'

'Relax, darling. One more cigarette.'

I sat down, tossed him my cigarettes and matches. My throat was parched. Let somebody else make the bloody decisions.

'What do you make of her?'

'What?'

'Janine. Talking about *my* little problem for a change. Been discussing yours for the last six hours. My turn. Fair's fair.'

Stylised languor. Not going to prompt you, Dick, you bastard. Take care of your own bloody pauses.

'If I keep up the tension for long enough, what do you bet she'll be moist?'

Groaned. Whether that bony French bit was going to be moist for Dick was hardly among my most pressing concerns.

'Didn't come home last night. Merely to let her imagination go to work. Shows I care. You don't like her then?'

So he still needed my approval. So they call me Concentration Camp Erhart. (*To be or Not to be,* Lubitsch, 1942.)

'She seems to have closed up shop,' I said.

'That's how I want her. Closed shop. Just open for me.'

'Why do you bother?'

'I happen to like working on my relationships. I'm in love with her.'

'You said that about Elsa. Another bloody sweetshop for your exclusive use.'

'Allright, but I'm still active. That's why I'll always be a better writer than you're a director.'

'Listen to who's talking. Bloody highpriest of the simultaneous orgasm! *Her opulent jutting breasts heaved, nipples straining against the thin fabric of nylon.*'

Old Joke. An Hall of Entertainment. He lit another cigarette. Instant revenge.

'And here's the pay-off,' I followed through smartly, 'you don't even like tits.'

'No, I don't, do I? But you do, and so do ninety-six million oedipal cunts like you. And that's why I'm here, living off the fat of the Cote d'Azur, and you—you're the uninvited fucking houseguest.'

Couldn't top that for irrefutable logic.

Dismissed.

I tiptoed to the side of the bed, peered at her face. She was sleeping on her heart side, knees drawn up, hands tight up against her left cheek, palms touching. Her mouth hung open. Snoring peacefully. I kissed her forehead, moved a twist of red hair from her eye. Curly, metallic hair. Linda's hair.

Jesus, how did I get myself involved in this Shirley Temple epic? *Why, Daddy, you're crying ... Curlytops!* Ludicrous! Aimed for Bergman, profoundly tragic predicament, ended up knee-deep in Allan Dwan.

Flung off my clothes, crept down into the cool side of our big double-bed, gazed at my sleeping-partner.

Her opulent jutting breasts heaved, nipples straining ...
Yegods.

During the semi-conscious half-hour before waking, George the Creep planned the day in detail.

Keep her so well entertained that she won't have time

to ask questions. An early trip to the harbour, watching fishermen sort and sell their night's catch. She'd pilfer a couple of sardines still quivering in the mesh. We could grill them for lunch. Fun. And instructive. Later, a swimming lesson. My siesta. Lingering golden afternoon on the beach. Marmite sandwiches at six. Story. Bed.

I pushed back the shutters. Rain was spattering down from a charcoal sky. Below, thousands of tiny expanding circles rippled the pool's surface. So much for the Creep's plan. Padded downstairs, made tea, buttered a few *biscottes*. Over breakfast, I read Leonore an entire *Beezer*, acting all the parts, until she complained that the crunch of her *biscottes* was blotting out my performance.

We got dressed. No sign of Dick and Janine. I found a lady's umbrella behind the refrigerator. Off we went in the pouring rain. Played Knights all the way to the bus stop. Leonore, doing her bossy chief knight bit, gave orders in a bass register. I, the assistant knight, did the actual slaying of the baddies.

Most shops had only just opened when we got to Cannes. We walked up and down the length of the rue d'Antibes, scrutinising cinema displays: dubbed B-Westerns; Jean Gabin, the white-haired gangster, quivering with rage; revivals of Fernandel.

We sheltered in Le Loup's, bought Wellingtons, woolly socks, several sets of underwear, rubbish for the beach. Leonore enjoyed that. George the Creep, thinking: Have to ask Dick to slip me some currency. Government was turning us into a nation of smugglers, fraudulent converters, tax evasion specialists. I ordered one set lunch at the Coq Hardi, split it between the two of us.

As we left the restaurant, a pain assaulted me, excruciating and beautiful. Wind and anxiety and a matured sense of fulfilment. I bought *Nice-Matin*, found the cinema page. *Mary Poppins* was playing in Grasse. Leonore said she didn't mind seeing it again, even if it was all in French. We hopped on another bus, drove uphill in the rain, fled into the cinema showing *Mary Poppins* in French.

Leonore was well occupied watching the screen and licking an *Esquimau Gervais,* when a grotesque thing happened. Sitting in that dank little cinema, my daughter crouched next to me, carrier-bag between my feet, damp ladies' umbrella soaking left trouser leg, I got this tremendous erection.

Couldn't get rid of it. The harder I stared at Julie Andrews, the worse it got. Great breakers of lust washed over me, *just a spoonful of sugar makes the medicine go down,* disturbing ocean-bed memories: squashy, itchy infant urgings; genderless, undiscriminating thrusts for satisfaction. How people like Dick sort about in this maw for memories that are safely heterosexual! As if it mattered. God knows I've lied myself, lied through my teeth, choosing to 'forget' those wrestling bouts with my mother, knee right up her crutch, schoolboy rope-climbing, lone investigations under the sheet, that first pleasurable shock of wetness in the hand, your own, someone else's, anybody's...

An ice-age of briefly illuminated darkness stretches between the womb and the touch of Jean's hand. If I settle for her as a beginning, it's to command a little order in the chaos of unselective recollection. Let Jean stand for the first spasm, the dirty poetry demanding endless repetition. Jean with blue eyes, straight blonde hair, red beret plus pompom, guffawing with sister Pam, often astride a bicycle. I see a back garden in the blackout, hear whispers, punctuated by bursts of high laughter, menacing, also full of promise. I was not inside that garden. Desmond *was*, tall, a prefect. No longer needed to do *that*, he said. As for me, why didn't I go out, get myself a girl? That's what one did, got hold of a tart, judy, skirt. Easier said than done, Desmond, not a member of that back garden mob. Besides, Desmond, big showoff, probably lied about what went on there, in the blackout. Bet he never even got off that bicycle of his, no more than did old Pam. You twerp, you must be bleeding blind. Pamela *did* it, the real thing. Properly. *In bed.* When her Mum was out fire-watching. And Jean? Did it as well. The *really* dirty bitch. Desmond knew, had been out with both of them. Heart thumped. '*Out*'. Magic. Bloody hell, you weren't allowed 'out', billeted on a retired, red-faced Colonel, with blood-pressure. Gave lectures to old ladies on First Aid, had you play the guinea-pig. Served on the Urban District Council, made you clean out his bloody hen-house, help the Mrs. with the washing-up.

Out. When you had to be in by 8.30, long before the back-garden orgies got going. Let you come into their chintzy sitting-room, listen to the nine o'clock news, read by Alvar Liddell. And when another German town had been bombed to bits, they brayed 'good' and stared at you, challenging, making sure you thought 'good' as well. Because you were still a bloody little Jerry at heart. Must be.

'Bet you people would be standing to attention with your arm stretched out and heiling, if you saw Fritz marching down the High Street.'

Or, chatting to a neighbour over the fence, while I mowed within earshot:

'Our little Hun can give you a hand in the garden after supper, Mary.'

Then one day, Desmond, who liked me well enough, even though I was a German *and* a Jew, *and* good at English, *and* sex-mad, Desmond, real friend, passed me a pencilled note:

Desmond thinks a nice boy like you wants a nice girl to go out with. My sister Jean will go out with you if you ask her but don't say I told you. Pamela Betts.

Two crosses.

On fire. I'd seen Jean, heard her whisper, and under her blue Mackintosh were breasts, real breasts. And hadn't

37

Desmond promised she was *dirty*? Oh, thump, thump, thump, how to get near her, and not muck it up?

While I plotted, Desmond lost interest, had done all he could. Took me another month to get in with that back-garden-and-bicycles gang, another fortnight, pretending to be indifferent to Jean Betts and her red beret, while she squealed under dark trees with other rotten sods. Then, one day: Met her in a High Street sweetshop, spending points on Milky Ways, hoarded under the counter. Made a proper job of it, as rehearsed, asked her *out*. No mucking about in the back-garden for me, with Desmond and the others hanging around all the time. Next Saturday, all day in the country. She could, she supposed, manage that. And in training for delights to come, I offered much sacrifice that night, breaking my own records, felt sick next day, stricken with this unique case of premature V.D.

Saturday came, it rained, *Chim-chiminee, chim-chiminee, chim-chiminee*. The day in the country was out, we jumped on a Devon-General bus to the next big town, boasting double-features galore. On the bus we shared a *Dailor Mirror*, commented on the merits of just-elected 'Stars of Tomorrow': Laraine Day, Rita Hayworth, Ruth Hussey, Robert Preston, John Payne, Jeffrey Lynn, Ann Rutherford, Dennis Morgan, Jackie Cooper, Ronald Reagan.

She knew them all. Intelligent. Couldn't possibly be dirty. Desmond, the liar, had set me a trap.

In the town we bought bags of cream buns and green apples, were refused admission to our chosen double feature: *Son of Frankenstein* (H) and *The Mummy's Hand* (H). She actually *admitted* she was only fifteen. God, was she unsophisticated! Desmond, I'll get you for this.

Managed to get into the Elite, round the corner, showing *Mr. Smith goes to Washington*, also *Tear Gas Squad*, plus Full Supporting Programme. Pocketing my glasses for vanity reasons, I manœuvred Jean into the back-row, had to screw up my eyes to get a clear image of the screen.

The cream buns and apples took some getting through. It wasn't until the climax of *Tear Gas Squad* that I could decently crunch up the brown paper bags. Flicked them, insouciantly, into the aisle. Debonair. Our hands were now finally unencumbered, I reached out for her, and, Christ, was she dirty, because no soooner did my hand touch hers, than she gripped my thumb, and turned her face towards me, and I was kissing her nose in the dark, and the red beret with the pompom fell off, and she bent down to retrieve it, and that gave me my chance to lay an arm across the back of her seat. Straightening up, she sort of lurched against me, I felt her elbow between my ribs, the screen swam in fragments before my myopic eyes. Long film, *Mr. Smith goes to Washington*; she never took off her belted blue Mackintosh. Very gradually, I succeeded in sliding my hand inside that Mackintosh, and under her sweater, and eventually inside the cups of her uplift bra, wrist aching. Oh, she knew what she was doing, keeping her Mac on. Nobody could detect my hand's progress, and she could pretend it wasn't happening. Real breasts she had, with nipples, and a humid cleft between rubber walls to accommodate my fist. Lovely.

I knew about French kissing, Desmond had recommended it; we did a bit of that, she still tasted of cream-bun jam. Then the miracle occurred. I felt the weight of her hand on my thigh, then finger deftly unbuttoning my flies. Never dared to hope she'd go as far as this. Filthy. Primly, she placed her beret over it, I had to whisper not so hard, not so hard, and she did it more gently, my way, never looking at me, and at the end of it, I was lost to the world, and she curtly asked me for a hanky.

Recovered, I thought fair's fair, and let my hand crawl up under the blue Mac's hem. Kept her legs crossed. Couldn't get between her thighs. Gone too far, I accused myself. Remorse. Now she'll get up, insist on going home. But she did nothing of the kind. Just muttered 'Not here',

39

nestled against me. Her duty done, she wished to see the movie.

Dusk when we came out of the cinema, but the rain had stopped. According to my calculations, there wouldn't be another bus home for an hour. I proposed a walk up to the cliffs and she agreed, but did not speak to me. Not a word. Didn't love me. Just dirty, like Desmond said. Like me.

Up on the cliff-path I made her sit down with me on a puddly seat, and started again, squeezing her breasts, more violently this time because I could open her coat: no audience. She clearly took this to be a signal, and silently and without undue effort repeated her ceremony of selfless gratification. On the way home in the bus, I fell asleep.

Next morning, entering Church with my Colonel, and his lady (went with them every Sunday, was a Christian too), I was suddenly assailed by a terrifying discovery: *Hadn't done it to Jean!* Worse: *Forgotten* to do it. What my brain had conjured up a thousand times, and Desmond had described in such loving detail, the celebrated sequence of moves towards completion—gone clean out of my mind in the intoxication of Jean's unquestioning generosity.

Ah well, next time.

Never was to be a next time with Jean. Wasn't nasty about it. Just busy. I hadn't passed the test.

We were on our way back to Cannes, Leonore and I, my arm protectively placed around her shoulder. She was still sucking her esquimau stick, needed it for tomorrow. Armour for her sandcastles.

In the eons that lie between two bus rides from dank cinemas, one in a red Devon-General, the other in a cream Rapide-Cote d'Azur, had I ever loved anyone?

Had anyone loved me?

Jean, with her deft fingers and utilitarian beret plus

pompom, had you given me that Next Time, how you might have transformed my subsequent lovelife . . .

By clinging to such brittle rafts of illusion, George the Creep hoped to survive life's tumultuous seas.

In the salon Janine sat upon Dick's knee, red-eyed and forgiven. They nibbled at each other, ignoring us.

On the way back to the Villa Rameau, we tried in vain to get Marmite and Ribena, ended up buying paté and flowers for our host and hostess.

I stood stranded in the middle of the large, unfriendly room. Leonore had gone directly to the indoor marble fountain, and turned on the water, which came splashing out of the mouth of a brass lion.

'Hey, stop that,' Dick said. 'Kindly control your brat, George.'

'Mustn't turn the water on without permission,' I told her. 'You're not at home now, you know.'

Leonore turned off the water.

'Don't know what to do,' she said, folded her arms.

'Where the Christ have you been in this weather?'

'To Grasse to see *Mary Poppins* in French.'

'Ah, Julie Andrews,' Janine contributed.

'We've bought you flowers and a sort of sausage,' Leonore said.

'For us?' Dick asked, spectacularly astonished. 'Aren't you nice?' He bounced Janine off his lap. 'Get the child something to eat.'

Janine obediently held out her hand. Leonore, trusting idiot, clasped it. They started for the door.

'And make us a large pot of China tea,' Dick called after her. 'And give that child a bath. She smells of mice.'

'*D'abord le bain?*' Janine asked demurely.

'*Non, le bain après. D'abord* some tea *pour tout le*

41

monde, et depeche-toi, poule du port.'

The door shut behind them, Dick grinned.

'Get away with murder, don't I?'

I sat down, wiped my glasses with Kleenex. Jack Martinsell had once told me I looked like Jack Lemmon. Just then I saw myself as early Emil Jannings.

'Works though, doesn't it? Been giving her hell all day. Result: Soft as putty, anxious to please.'

'I could have made the kid's tea . . .'

'Janine's not doing it for you, she's doing it for me. Makes her feel wanted.'

I threw him a cigarette. Then I got up to light it for him.

'Just think—if I'd treated Brenda like that, I'd still be married to her. Nauseating idea. Have to find you a girl while you're here.'

'In my state of health . . . with the . . . I mean . . . with . . . er . . .'

'Stop stuttering. You're dying for it, look at you. Think she'll love you more if you're deprived? Take you out to dinner. See what happens.'

'We'll need someone to sit.'

'What's wrong with Janine?'

'Isn't she coming?'

'What for? Had her around all day.'

He got up and switched on a lamp. Through the open windows, we could hear the croaking of frogs. In the kitchen Leonore and Janine were chattering happily. I felt some mild relief.

'Tell me something. Am I a bastard?' Dick didn't wait for a reply. 'You can't imagine what an effort it is, playing the Bastard. Much easier to be soft and pleasing, let them run the show. Trouble is, makes them so bloody unhappy.'

Janine came back with a pot of teabag tea. No China, she explained. Dick sent her out again to feed Leonore, and give her a bath.

'One thing about that girl, always ready when I am. When you're forty that counts.'

I poured out the tea. We drank in silence. Dick was giving me no cue to talk about myself. His self-absorption had reached a point where my curiosity was stifled. We were both glumly reading *Nice-Matin*, when Janine returned with Leonore, pink and fresh after a bath, wearing pyjamas and her yellow dressing-gown with the orange rabbits and carrots.

Dick ordered Leonore to sit on his knee. Janine slumped down on a cushion at his feet. I watched Dick and Leonore with some anxiety. He hadn't a clue where kids were concerned.

'You like it here, love?' he was asking her.

'Been here before, haven't I?'

'Rhetorical question. Just like your mother. Mistress of the *non-sequitur*, your Mum.'

Leonore squinted at me, pulled an embarrassed face.

'Tell me : you enjoy being with your Daddy?'

'Don't know what you mean.'

'Yes you do. You're not a stupid little girl. You're a highly intelligent little girl. I mean *living* with your Daddy. Without Mum.'

' 'sallright ... how do you mean?'

'Well, let's suppose for a moment that your Mummy and Daddy were to live in different houses ...'

Might have warned me. Talking to the child, but playing to me, and, in a more subtle way, to Janine.

'But they don't,' Leonore said. 'We all live in the same house. In Kew.'

'Yes, I know that, but suppose that your Mummy chose to stay ... in Brighton.'

Bournemouth, I almost prompted, totally detaching myself from the scene. Might be a couple of actors staggering through a first rehearsal. Sit tight, say nothing. See what *grows*.

'. . . let's suppose she's going to stay there for a while, and Daddy meanwhile looks after you . . .'

'*Here,* you mean? Lovely.'

'What? No, not just here. Anywhere.'

'Where then?'

'Somewhere. London, say.'

'Why?'

'What do you mean "why?" '

'Got a nice house already. In Kew.'

'Perhaps your Daddy wants to go and live somewhere else.'

'Oh.'

'Yes, and take you with him. Because your Daddy loves you, see?'

Leonore looked nonplussed, latching on to the idea that something *not nice* was coming up.

'You love your Daddy, don't you?'

'Hmm. Yes. 'course I do.'

I could see Janine drinking it all in. *Quel homme!* Guessed correctly: his performance was given strictly for her benefit. Sunshine pouring out of his arse.

'Well, then, let's suppose . . .'

'What's all this *let's suppose*? Don't know what you mean.'

'You just keep listening, lovey.'

Leonore grinned sheepishly.

'What I'm asking you is this: *If* your Mummy and your Daddy go and live in two different houses, and your Daddy takes *you* to live with him in *his* house . . .'

'Mummy wouldn't let him . . .'

'Well, that's up to your Dad, isn't it?'

'Only for . . . for a time,' I heard myself interject faintly.

'Shut up. Let's suppose . . .'

'Where's Mummy going to live, then? Somebody's got to live in Kew. Else all the milk will go sour.'

'Mummy might go on living in Kew, and you and Daddy could move on to this new house.'

'Why?' Leonore turned to me, open-mouthed. 'Have you and Mummy parted?'

Parted! Wherever had she heard that expression? Dick's script was taking an alarming turn.

'Yes, love,' I said solemnly, 'I think we have, for a while.'

She grinned, then bit her lip. Dick sat her round on his lap to face him.

'Now, lovey,' he instructed, 'there's nothing for you to worry about, see? You'll have good times, and possibly some not-so-good times as well. Not going to be all aeroplane rides and *Mary Poppins* and sandcastles. But it won't be all horrible, either. And that's what I'm trying to tell you, lovey, that's what life is all about. Good bits and bad bits. See?'

'I'm supposed to be at school,' she said.

Her eyes were beginning to swim. Dick had seen it, too. Alarmed glances met over Leonore's shoulder. Using the hiatus to slip off his knee, she came running over to me, stood between my thighs, hanging her head.

'It's allright to have a nice cry sometimes,' I said.

'Not crying.'

Her arms went round my neck, squeezing. Almost strangled me.

Dick turned to Janine. 'Isn't there some sort of fair going on?'

'Fair?'

'Roundabouts and things. That market square near the station.'

'*Ah, oui.*'

Janine rose for further instructions.

'Would you like to go to the fair, lovey?'

Instant recovery.

'Oh, Daddy, can we?'

'Your Dad will be glad to be rid of you for an hour. Come over here.'

She slipped off my knee, ran back to Dick to be cuddled.

45

Janine, uncertain about her next order, encompassed both with a look of stylised adoration.

'Blow your nose, lovey. Got a hanky? Give a good blow. I'll let Janine dress you and take you to the fair on one condition.'

'What?'

'Have to promise first.'

'Allright.'

'Say: My Daddy is always right.'

'My Daddy is always right.'

'Right. Off you two toddle, then.'

Janine closed the door. Leonore hadn't given me another glance. Dick lit a cigarette.

'I did that rather well, you must admit. Brilliant right up to the very end, when I made one mistake. Placated her. You'll probably still be paying for that bloody fair in ten years' time. Nothing one does is without consequences.'

'Thanks, Dick,' I said.

We went out to dine in style at Mère Besson. Afterwards we drove to the Casino. I borrowed money from Dick, won a couple of hundred francs. George the Gambler was back in control.

Everything was going to be allright.

A few evenings later, Dick gave a small dinner party for his friends Joe and Marion Leeds, passing through Cannes on their way back to London. They had been visiting Monte Carlo to watch location work on a movie Joe had rewritten.

Janine made *pot-au-feu*. Leonore spent the afternoon scraping carrots. The Raeburns came down from their upstairs flat to join us. We sat around the pool in wicker chairs, smoking Gauloises and drinking brandy, congratulating ourselves on talents which enabled us to enjoy

46

the scented calm of a Mediterranean autumn evening.

It had been one of those muted October days that dissolve into night without apparent transition. A full moon flooded the garden with a gothic kind of luminosity. Later on, a breath of wind would rustle the leaves, and blow them one by one into the pool, but for the moment the air was intoxicatingly still.

Janine lay curled up like a cat on Dick's lap, now and then licking his ear. Their public demonstrations of affection distressed the Raeburns acutely.

They were an odd couple : Irene a well-preserved sixty, with short grey hair, a crumpled face, the cheerful exasperation of an overworked headmistress. Charlie, tall, thin, wispy-haired, suffered from a weak heart, had nervous hands and a stare of constant alarm. He was devote to Irene.

'What do they actually *do* ?', I'd once asked Dick.

'Lay eggs,' he'd replied.

He was presently engaged in stroking Janine's lean thighs. It wasn't enough to embarrass the Raeburns. They had to be tormented.

In an effort to ignore her hosts' portable eroticism, Irene addressed herself to the visitors. I knew them both by reputation. Joe, a short, bald writer in his forties, had once been a rather fearsome book and theatre critic, now wrote unsuccessful novels, subsidised himself by re-writing rewrites of lousy movies. His face, with its sunken cheeks, deep-set eyes, pinched mouth (features almost totally obliterated by huge black-rimmed glasses), made me think of a spaceman from one of Léonore's comics.

Irene was politely asking him for his opinion of a recently published novel. Vigorously brushing ash from his thigh, Joe told her he hadn't read the book, had no intention of doing so.

'One of your sensibility merchants,' he fumed. 'Bonedry old literary ladies of both sexes collecting tributes from bonedry old literary whores.'

I recalled something Dick had once said. Just as no one would denounce Communism as vociferously as your disabused ex-Communist, so you had to turn to an ex-critic like Joe Leeds for a really blistering exposure of the stupidity and venality of reviewers.

'They're just too bloody lazy to re-evaluate properly.' he thundered. 'Doddering, from-my-cottage-window poof publishes his new book. Out comes your lavender-smelling Sensibility stand-by. Means you're uninventive and un-readable, can't think up a plot, haven't had an original thought for thirty years. Endless descriptions of pallid tea-parties, with your elderly hero mincing down the Old Brompton Road, sniffing after the lost glories of Henry James, and probably waxing nostalgic for a bit of public-school sodomy. Who needs a story, dear, your tight-arsed mandarin style will carry you through . .'

'Do you ever regret giving up criticism?' Irene asked him solemnly.

'No, I don't,' Joe bristled. 'Only worthwhile thing I did in my entire life. Eunuchs and charlatans.'

While Irene looked vaguely intrigued, Marion had been listening to her husband's tirade with attentive ardour, though she must have heard it all many times before. She was a pretty actress in her thirties, dark and petite, with a compact body, fervently concerned brown eyes, and some facial fuzz which signalled sensuality. She tried to radiate a sort of generalised warmth, which didn't quite come off, too obviously projected and unspecified. Jewish, I guessed. Never played leads, specialised in abused foreign sluts. Made a mental note to cast her at the next opportunity.

Next opportunity? Dependable old George had walked out of his contract, let the Network down, betrayed Jack Martinsell's trust. To cast Marion in anything, I'd have to throw myself on Jack's mercy, claim personal disaster, take Leonore along to make the story stick . . .

Thought I heard a cry. Got up, hurried inside, up the

flight of stairs to our bedroom. Leonore was fast asleep. Must have been an owl. In the closeness of the night she had kicked off her bedclothes. Carefully tucked her in, kissed the tip of her nose. Returning to the garden, I found myself in a bubble of silence. Talking about me in my absence.

'How *is* your little girl?' Marion Leeds asked, projecting passionate curiosity. 'I think it's marvellous for a father to take responsibility in such a situation . . .'

'Come off it, Marion. If I buggered off with Barry, you'd be after me like a bloody Valkyrie.'

'Right,' Marion agreed tentatively, anxious to avoid public controversy with her husband. To jam home the Married Bliss image, she placed her left hand on her husband's shoulder. Pudgy freckled hand. Made me think of a Dalmatian puppy. My loins felt a slight electric current.

'Children are such delicate little instruments,' Charlie said faintly.

'How long you been married, George?' Joe wanted to know.

'Four hundred years.'

'Must be a bloody anxious time for you. Could I have another shot of brandy, Dick?'

'Oh, *awful* . . .' Marion seconded, big brown eyes searching for mine. (Was she looking for work?)

'Liberated,' Dick told her. 'Like Joe, after he gave up writing reviews.'

'Marvellous,' Marion breathed.

'What about the technicalities?' Joe leant back, sipping brandy. 'Let's get the story straight. How did you smuggle the kid out of the house?'

'Picked up her passport, packed a bag, ordered a mini-cab.'

'Didn't she try and stop you, your wife?'

'Linda's sister had been looking after Leonore. I'd been away on location, my wife . . .'

'His wife's been chopping away at his peter for twenty years,' Dick elucidated.

What surprised me was that I wanted to jump to Linda's defence, not my own.

'Now he's got this idea that he can't live without Daddy's girl. Dragged her along to make sure Linda won't be far behind.'

'So what did you tell your sister-in-law?' Joe asked.

'Told her I was taking Leonore for a holiday . . .'

'Which is exactly what he *has* done,' Dick said. 'Sits there, hugging this gangster fantasy, *kidnapping* yet . . .'

'Give me at least credit for *abducting* her.'

George, the Creep. My eyes panned along the faces of my inquisitors, outlines slightly blurred in the moonlight. Enjoying my discomfort, or merely bored? Marion was crossing her legs. Miniskirt. Endless thighs. Trapped a tiny triangle of panties. White.

'Intend to send the kid to school in Cannes, do you?' Joe asked briskly.

'He can't stay here,' Dick volunteered on my behalf. 'Boy's got to make a living.'

'You poor man,' Marion commiserated. 'You must be in a state of shock.'

'Don't want to alarm you,' Joe said, 'but your wife's bound to go to court. Get the child restored to her. That's the form.'

Caught me eyeing his wife's panties?

'Surely you took legal advice?' Charlie enquired. 'I mean before . . .'

'Haven't even got a lawyer, Charlie.'

'I'll give you the name of my solicitor,' Joe offered. 'Fellow called Tetheridge, good man.'

'Told George what he's got to do.' Without warning, Dick opened his legs. Janine slumped to the ground, gaped up at him adoringly. 'Got to throw the book at her. Serve a petition the moment he gets back. Charge adultery and neglect, make it stick.'

'Linda's not really a bad mother, Dick . . .'

'If you don't want to lose the kid, you throw the bloody book at her.'

'Perhaps,' Irene suggested, 'you and your wife could come to some amicable arrangement about the child . . .'

'Amicable arrangement?' Dick placed one naked foot on Janine's head, toes rummaging in her hair. 'When Linda finds out, she's going to take George apart. His balls she's got already. Now she'll go for the rest. Money. House. Kid thrown in for good measure.'

Was he talking about Linda? Making her out to be a monster. Somebody needed to redress the balance. We hadn't got on, true. I'd wanted to leave her for years, also true. I'd placated her for more than a decade, and she'd repaid me by giving me hell. Nothing but the truth.

Yet, as Dick was giving judgement, it was with Linda I identified: Linda returning home, Linda reacting to sister Elspeth's version of events.

What would ensue? Magnani screaming bout? Dreyer stoicism? Strenuous Ealing tea-brewing? I could see myself even now bringing Linda a tray of coffee and biscuits, comforting her, receiving the usual icy absolution.

What did Dick know, anyway? What he had witnessed last summer was a marriage's last rites, the final casting-off of masks. For many years those masks had fitted snugly. The irony about keeping up a front is that you forget it *is* a front.

Really have to hand it to Linda. Through all those betrayals, His and Hers, she played the public loyalty bit with true distinction. Turned up regularly at every taping of every play, letting the actors kiss her chastely on the cheek, lucky George to have such a devoted wife. And then home, James, and back into the ice-cube.

God knows I'd given her good reasons for creeping back in there when we were alone, though being a perceptive girl she ought to have known what she had married. Must have had her suspicions about Mr. Hyde, *and*

George, the Gambler, *and* Dracula. Introduced Linda to all of them, casually, wanting her to save me from their spell. *There was something seriously wrong with me.* I had thirty-nine reasons to prove it. I say thirty-nine, because shortly after becoming serious about Linda I had started to make this list. *Thirty-nine* names: Typists, shopgirls, scrubbers Dick and I had found around the studios, girls picked up in trains and tube stations, not to mention a couple of anonymous silhouettes in dark cinemas, the hands of Jean, repeated thirty-eight times. For, to be absolutely truthful, Melud, only very few of those thirty-nine actually got screwed.

—Are you implying that your client's clandestine affairs were never consummated?

—Mr. Kane, into the witness box, if you please.

—Just a bag of old tricks, Melud. Playing with lights, gramophone records, giving my Bela Lugosi impersonation, my fingertips here, there, finding sensitive spots. With all due respect, Melud, the classic seduction scene.

—And how did your victims respond to these hoary blandishments?

—As you would expect, Melud. What's this in aid of? they'd ask, the appropriately genteel reproach of the forties and early fifties. Fingers down the blouse-front. What's that in aid of? I shall now sink my fangs into your lovely little neck. Oh dear, what's that in aid of, then? Little did these poor creatures know, Melud, that for the typist's Dracula, the sordid goal was merely to produce a verbal escalation from 'Oh no, you don't' to—if the court pleases —'Go on, then, stick it into me.' You follow?

—Quite. And then?

—And then, Melud, having achieved my modest aim, and being, as you might say, a Dracula-of-Honour, I'd beat the retreat, let them go home.

—Astonishing. In all my years on this bench, I have never heard anything as perverted or sickening.

—With all due respect, Melud, it makes my own flesh

crawl, too. Possibly it was self-disgust that originally caused me to identify myself with the aforesaid horror film figures of the thirties. Perhaps I ought to add that I did not always get away with it.

—With what, pray?

—Well, Melud, some girls would get shirty, refuse to take no for an answer. To do myself justice (if you'll pardon the allusion, Melud) I'd then be perfectly competent to yield to their requests. Then again, I'd occasionally meet a victim with proclivities similar to my own, who'd turn the tables on me, have *me* begging for a completion of the proceedings. What astonishes me on looking back on this scene, Melud, is that the vast majority of my victims actually *liked* this perverted or sickening approach. Not only came back for more of the same, but frequently deluded themselves that here was a man of infinite subtlety, who truly understood women.

—You may step down. Fifty-nine years' hard labour in Siberia.

Linda the Continuity Girl, seemed an unlikely candidate for Number Forty. Highly intelligent young suburbanite, read Byron, listened to the Art of Fugue, did a bit of wood-carving, too.

Dick and I had acquired a habit of likening the girls we met to animals. (Not just our own shorthand appraisal, but a tribute to John Steinbeck, who in *The Wayward Bus* had invented a character who always referred to girls as Pigs.) Dick specialised in cats, sleek, skinny and stubborn. I tended to vacillate between sheep and rabbits. Dracula got his best results with the drab, impressionable type.

In this zoo Linda could not be classified as a domestic animal at all. With her erect posture, metallic auburn hair (worn long, in abandoned Rita Hayworth fashion) and alert expression, she was clearly a fox. Sit bolt upright on her stool behind the camera, script on knee, stopwatch on a long chain around her neck, always quick to point out errors, ruthless in exposing shoddiness. Fancied herself the Gustav Mahler of Poverty Row.

After she had been working with us for some months, we started going to concerts at the Albert Hall and the Wigmore Hall, lavished money on heavy great record stacks of Haydn quartets, and *The Rite of Spring,* and even Berg's Violin Concerto, which, secretly, I hoped to use one day as a Dracula aid—change of pace from Harry James and Artie Shaw.

Linda was also a great Trotsky reader. Yegods, what an inflated bore! I was frequently taken to task: With my background, such political apathy was quite deplorable. For three months, I thought of Linda as a true friend, only one I had, apart from Dick. After a concert we would dine in Soho, I'd drive her to Leicester Square tube station, and she'd go home, on the Piccadilly Line, to the flat she shared with her sister Elspeth in Brentford. Her parents had been killed in an air-raid. Another spiritual bond between us.

One night, after being particularly scathing about a new English chamber work we'd just heard at the London Philarmonic Arts Club, she suggested going back to my place to hear some Stravinsky. To get the rubbish out of her system, she explained. Clean the palate.

I put on *Le Sacré*, and we settled down on my day-bed, and from sheer force of habit I started playing Dracula: Stroked her forehead, grabbed her tits, hoping for instant rejection. Nothing of the kind occurred. She got up, took off her skirt, pulled back the cover of my daybed, competently slipped inside, instructed me to switch off the lights.

Cold terror. Like losing my virginity all over again (an early production starring Paramount's deputy switchboard operator). Once her mind was made up, Linda was a determined girl, pulled me right into herself, no nonsense. I remember thinking as I pumped away, this is *not* the way I like it, she's too demanding, we don't *fit,* I've lost a friend.

Next morning I was desperately in love with her. Serious, music-loving, she hadn't stood for any half-assed Dracula stuff : only Linda could put me to rights.

To make myself worthy of her, I set out on a course of personal reform, endeavouring to put an end to the squalor of my love-life. Never occurred to me that the squalor was there because I liked it, as natural and necessary to me as Trotsky and Byron were to Linda.

What made interior renovation even more imperative was that, far from finding me a good lover, or even Understanding with Women, Linda was full of strictures for my performance.

'You make love like an old man,' she'd say. Knew what she was talking about, too. Confessed that she had been sleeping for a couple of years with a sixty-year-old cutter, Dick's Uncle Graham. Like Uncle Graham, I didn't seem to know about resting my full weight on my knees and elbows. Like Uncle Graham, I was too fond of lying on my back, waiting to be pleasured. With the spectre of Uncle Graham in the background, it became clear that not only I needed to be winged out of moral danger; Linda herself had to be saved.

We got engaged.

I forsook all others (for a while), took tea with Linda's sister Elspeth in Brentford. Elspeth's seven-year-younger husband had left her childless and embittered the previous summer, for a woman ten years older than himself. Nursing hatred of all men, she tried to infuse some of this loathing into her younger sister. Linda was, and forevermore remained, deeply devoted to her.

I even gave up my weekly football matches, which Linda (and Elspeth) didn't care for, concentrating all my energies on improving my screwing. Approbation was slow in coming. Linda was shy, she explained, about verbalising sex. Never asked myself (or Linda) why her shyness inhibited only praise, never censure.

The wedding should have warned me amply about

what awaited me in that safe harbour of married bliss: my twenty-years' flash in the pan, as Dick was to call it a generation later.

After signing contracts at the Town Hall—we'd installed ourselves in a two-room furnished flat in Paddington—sister Elspeth gave a reception for our friends (who arrived bearing dreadful utility-type presents), and a pretty shabby party it was, even for those days.

I remember two significant events concerned with that reception. First, the bloody row Linda and I had in the kitchen, while next door the guests tried to get pissed on Algerian wine. My complaints about Elspeth's meanness sent Linda into a state of high dudgeon. How dare I criticise her sister's generosity, when I hadn't even seen fit to buy her a wedding ring. No, *my* stinginess had forced *her* to go out and buy the ring, and I hadn't even offered to pay her back.

One act of meanness, I countered, didn't necessarily justify another. I was just getting going on my raw and real Documentaries, and some of the important people we'd invited wouldn't respond well to being fobbed off with cheap wine and home-made sandwich dainties. Elspeth's skinflint bloody reception was seriously undermining my career.

So it went on, with Linda, flushed with rage, informing me that she'd only bloody married me because I'd gone on insisting and pleading.

I had to correct that contention. I had actually proposed the marriage, true, but only after receiving that hoary old ultimatum: do something *decisive* about our relationship, or break it off. And how could I possibly break it off, when we were so busy reforming one another?

After that Linda turned her back on me, wept over the gas-cooker. I felt a louse, begged her not to make a fuss, they were all *noticing*. I loved her, didn't I? Didn't she love me?

No reply. I went back to the reception, tried to charm

our important guests. Linda stayed in the kitchen, comforted by Elspeth.

Second significant event: I began to notice an unimportant guest, wearing a green sweater. Reminded me of Landgirls. Had never seen this guest before, guessed she was somebody's gate-crashing friend; I was intrigued. She was dowdy rather than pretty, laughed a lot, had drunk enough of my new sister-in-law's rubbishy wine to confess her fascination for film directors. Before long we were in the corridor, necking—kisses for the bridegroom served as pretext—my knee wedged between her babywarm thighs. In the locked bathroom Green Dowdy became No. 41. Or as near as dammit.

Nor did the relationship finish in the bathroom. Green Dowdy, who turned out to be a remote cousin of Linda's, came along with us in the taxi all the way to Waterloo Station, wanting to know how one Got Into Films, kissing me primly goodbye at the end of the drive. That night, in Bournemouth when I had to make love to my wife, I was struck thoroughly impotent, thought, Christ, she'll never forgive me for this, finally had to summon up an image of Green Dowdy trembling upright against bathroom tiles. After which I performed quite adequately.

For a while we lived happily ever after. Damned lucky, I thought myself, married to such a very superior human being, whose generously exercised critical faculties were bound to aid me in my career. Despite my love for Linda, however, the virgin's vampire was soon at large again. Never imagined that my nibbling between meals could affect the high esteem in which I held the table d'hôte. Made certain that the girls after Forty-one were never exciting enough to invite serious comparison with Linda. Gambler kept driving to the brink, enjoying the proximity of possible disaster, Creep pulled up the handbrake.

Such conduct necessarily produced a confusion of identity. One day I would think of myself as a sharp seducer, practised, controlled, discreet; next day I'd see myself revealed a fumbling fool.

Confusion confirmed me as a compulsive liar. If anyone had good cause to lie, I rationalised, it was George Kane. Would I have lasted in my good Nazi school if I hadn't lied to my teachers? Might I not have been sent back to that camp if I hadn't fibbed to my foster-parents? Would Linda have married me had I told her the *whole* truth about Dracula?

My lies saved time and energy. Besides, where was the harm in telling Linda one had been rehearsing when one had watched a movie? Why not invent a pre-production meeting, when one had gone off to a football match?

Lie a little, and far from being exposed as George the Creep, you stayed intact as George the Gambler.

'You might at least listen when we're discussing your bloody woes,' Dick deplored.

'What you must do,' said Marion Leeds, 'you must bring your little girl to stay with us in Hampstead.'

Too kind. Too kind.

'At least till you get yourself settled, George.' She was leaning towards me, brown eyes shining, forward with the people, Marion Leeds sings Vanessa Redgrave. 'You just take that sweet little girl of yours by the hand and bring her to our house, and she'll come to no harm.'

Joe Leeds cleared his throat.

'Do by all means,' he amplified, then straightened his shoulders and sniffed, indicating that, as far as he was concerned, the topic of me and my little girl had run its course.

'It'll be super for Barry to have a little girl to play with. He's always wanted a sister.'

On that curtain line of Marion's the party broke up. Dick looked depressed, weighed down by a sense of anticlimax. Charlie and Joe helped Irene out of her wicker chair.

58

'What a lovely, lovely evening it's been,' Marion sang, and improvised a pirouette, profile raised in personal appreciation of the stars, 'Oh, Dick, what a lucky dear man you are.' She took my right arm and pressed it gently between pudgy, freckled hands. I caught a whiff of *Femme*. Linda's scent.

'You'll phone us the moment you get back to London. Promise?'

I promised. She executed an efficient stage turn. Joe placed a hand under her elbow, elegantly guided her out of our presence. Why, I mused, had I never cast Marion? She had talent.

Next morning Dick and Janine weren't talking. Dick worked for a couple of hours on revisions: Janine crept about the kitchen, sniffling; I washed out Leonore's smalls, furtively hung them up to dry in the garden. Later Dick and I joined forces on the terrace, watched Janine and Leonore fishing leaves out of the pool with a butterfly net.

'See what she's up to? What a game-player! Showing me she likes kids. The Elsa syndrome all over again. Had to toss her out of bed last night. *Forgot* to take the pill. How transparent can you get?'

'You have a gift for self-parody,' I told him.

'How do you mean?'

Leonore came scampering up the terrace steps, started to roll herself against my thigh. I gave her a hug, asked her if she was having a good time.

'Christ, George,' Dick complained. 'It's becoming literally impossible to talk to you these days.'

'Guess what? I had a funny dream last night,' Leonore announced.

'What about, darling?'

'Listen, darling. Your dear old Dad and I are trying to

59

hold a conversation. Hasn't anyone ever told you it's rotten manners to interrupt adults? Go on, sling your hook.'

'But I want to tell Daddy about this dream.'

'She wants to tell me about this dream...'

'Don't want to listen to any bloody kids' dreams. This is *my* house.'

'Oo-la-la,' Leonore said. 'Bad language.'

'Look, here's what you do, baby doll.' Dick produced a tiny spiral-spined notebook and pencil stub from his shirtpocket. 'Go away somewhere and write your dream down, and I'll tell you what it means. Can't do better than that, now can I?'

'Oh, thanks.'

She scuttled into the house with her booty.

'No idea how to handle children, have you, George?' Dick frisked his jeans for cigarettes. I offered him mine. He helped himself and kept the pack. 'Got a light?'

'Does it matter if I can't spell some of the words, Daddy?' Leonore yelled from the *salon*.

'Doesn't matter a bit,' I shouted back.

'I'm going to let her stew in her own juice for a bit,' Dick muttered, frowning. Another extended analysis of Janine's Syndrome coming up.

'Are Joe and Marion happily married?' I enquired hastily.

'I thought you'd get around to that.'

'Joe's got a touch of the classic *cocu* about him, you must admit.'

'Have you ever seen such an unconvincing performance of dejection?'

He pointed his toes in the direction of the swimmingpool. Janine was crouched on the ground, poking about in a pile of leaves with a twig.

'I thought we were discussing *my* problem for a change,' I said.

'If you want to be serious for once...'

'I was wondering whether to take up that invi...'

60

'No, you're not. You're thinking about getting your wick dipped.'

'How subjective can you get? Marion's your type.'

'Marion's got Mum written all over her. You were sniffing each other out like a couple of randy corgis.'

'Sleeps around?'

'Get a load of Mother Courage.'

Janine was now trudging up the garden path, wearily pushing a wheelbarrow piled high with leaves.

'Does she ...?'

'George, I'll discuss your chances of screwing Marion, but only if you don't nauseate me by claiming we're talking about Leonore's future.'

Leonore came running out of the house, flourishing Dick's notebook.

'Finished,' she said, looking expectant.

Dick snatched the notebook out of her hand.

'Let's have a look. My book.'

Leonore squeezed against me for protection.

'My Dream,' Dick read out. 'One rainy night my father and I were walking down the street when this Bady came up to us and said come with me. So the Bady whose name was Dick led us up to the head of the Badies but the head said put them all into the cave. But they didn't know it was a water cave. So one day we were walking round and round the cave when we saw five girls and went over to them and said are you traped in here ...'

'Trapped ...'

'... and the girls said yes. So my father told them his idea. He said when that water goes down then we can get out of the cave. Oh yes, oh look, the water is going down. So we all went out of the cave and my father said I am going to mary ...'

'Marry ...'

'... I am going to marry one of those girls. So my father married one of the five girls and when he was married we all went to Cannes ...'

'Very good, darling,' I said.

'So I'm a Bady, am I?' Dick asked her glumly. 'I'm not a Bady. What makes you think I'm a Bady?'

'I didn't dream you were the *Head* of the Badies.'

'That's hardly the point, lovey.' He was seriously disconcerted. 'I want to know why you make me out to be any sort of Badie. We've looked after you here, haven't we?'

'It was only a dream, Dick. You're not *really* a Badie.'

'No, I'm not. And I'll ask you to remember that while you're staying here.'

Janine was calling her. She looked confused, then turned and ran back into the house.

'She's certainly got *you* taped, George. Superficial relationships with five trollops in a water cave.'

'I marry one of them in the end.'

'She thinks you're going to marry Janine, obviously.' He got up and frowned up at the sky. 'I'm off for a drive. No doubt Janine will cook you lunch.'

'Oh, come on, Dick . . . Anyway, Charlie and Irene have invited me to share their Spaghetti Bolognaise.'

'Since when can Charlie afford mince?'

'He let it slip that mince costs sixteen francs a kilo.'

'It doesn't. Charlie drives his dilapidated old Consul all the way to La Bocca, where it's only twelve francs. Then he lopes off to a café and spends five francs on coffee and croissants to get his strength back.'

I'd turned Dick round again, thank God. Wasn't yet ready to leave.

'Still go to those funny old football matches of yours, George?'

After dinner we sat in the salon, drinking Pernod. He was playing games. Caution was advisable.

'Every other Saturday. Season ticket. Stamford Bridge.'

He looked pensive, tipping ash all over the marble floor, probably to annoy Janine, who'd been sent off to bed.

Still fairly presentable, I thought. Tries a bit too hard to come the *jeune premier*, but then who doesn't? Whom would I cast to play him? Running a few agents' lists through my mind, I ended up with Peter O'Toole and Richard Johnson.

'Why do you do it? Going to bloody football matches, I mean.'

'I like it.'

'No, come on, be serious.'

'I do like it. Millions of people do. Fine sport.'

'All right, fine sport. So's polo. Egg and spoon race. You don't think it's odd for a middle-aged pseudo-intellectual Jewboy to go bollicking off, every other Saturday, rattle in hand...'

'No rattle.'

'Why not?'

'If you must know,' I said, 'I also spend at least one hour a week swotting up the league tables of France, Italy, Germany, Austria, and of course Czechoslovakia.'

'Czechoslovakia?'

'Ask me who's heading for relegation in the Czech First Division. Go, ask me.'

Anything you can play, I can play better.

'Allright, George, who's heading for relegation in the Czech First Division?'

'This may astonish you, Dick, but it's Slavia Prague. Grand old side.'

'I see. And you really don't think there's something a bit off...'

'Odd?'

'No, *off*, a bit *off* for a man who professes to be an artist...'

'Craftsman. I've never...'

'That's just psychological insurance against rejection. You think of yourself as an artist, ducky, kid yourself not.'

I had to smile. Those 1940'ish phrases. Kid yourself not. Get a load of this. Couldn't care less. Ducky. Lovey.

63

If Dick ever decided to go back to London, he'd sound from Neanderthal.

'Professor Ayer likes soccer,' I pointed out. 'So do Clement Freud and Hans Keller.'

'Well, none of those gentlemen happen to interest me. You do, George. Always have done. In a funny sort of way.'

He poured himself another Pernod, added water from a Picasso jug, watched the liquid cloud in his glass. I thought: I've left the lights on in our bedroom. Leonore had wanted to read herself to sleep with *Black Beauty*. I'd forgotten to go up and kiss her good night. By now she'd be fast asleep. With *Black Beauty* on the floor, and the lights full on. Unkissed.

'You first started going to football matches when, George?'

'Nineteen-thirty-five, thereabouts. My father used to take me . . .'

'Oh, your father.'

'Look, there's absolutely no Freudian bloody significance in . . .'

'Shut up and go on.'

'I didn't just watch, you know. Actually *played* soccer. Didn't know that, did you? Violet strip with white facings and looped stockings. Outside right. Scored a lot of goals.'

Dick's interrogation, I suddenly realised, was giving me intense pleasure. Was there some link between Dick's game-course and my automatic assumption that Leonore would be safe here?

'Funny old Jewboy,' he said.

'Look, Dick, if you're trying to make out that just because I like football I'm living in the bloody past . . .'

'I thought we could really *talk* for once. I see now it's hopeless to try and help you.'

'Don't get you.'

'It's allright, George. Marion will let you poke her.

64

We're agreed on that. Stick to fiddling with your twitchy Mums, swinging your rattle at football matches, directing your television slop . . .'

'Listen, Dick, when I get back, I won't *have* a bloody job! I've walked out of my contract. I'm on suspension . . .'

'So?'

'So I'll be able to concentrate all my energies on taking care of Leonore.'

He groaned.

'It's not going to work, is it? It's simply not going to work, George.'

'It's going to work, allright, Dick. This-is-going-to-work.'

I rose to take up an introspective stance at the French windows. Early Brando. The telephone rang. Dick got up to answer it.

Linda! Return of the Creature from the Black Lagoon. Chills galore. Yegods, how that woman could still scare me. Saw George the Creep's haunted face reflected in the window pane, went into a desperate final rehearsal. Taking a stand. Made my decision. Could no longer allow her to fit in our child between sessions with her lovers. Prepared to fight her through every court in the land. I turned to take the call.

Dick was yelling into the receiver, I could hear Jeremy Shirlwell shouting back. Dick had been called a Corrupter of Youth on some TV programme. Across seven hundred miles of land and water the two men were roaring suggestions at each other on how this triumph could be exploited.

I ambled down the steps of the terrace. A night train rattled past along the narrow strip that separated Dick's garden from the beach. Squares of light flickered in the darkness. The train suddenly jerked to a halt, a bridge of lights across the Bay. My eyes focused on one of the carriages, then on one window: silhouette outlined in a square of yellow light. Child.

Child?

Nineteen thirty-five or thereabouts. Violet jerseys. Children of all ages squeezed inside an airless third-class carriage, smelling of sausage (kosher?) and bananas and oranges and drying piss. Couldn't stand the stench and the proximity of strange bodies. Clawed my way out, which was forbidden, to stand alone in a corridor. Guards must have been asleep, no one stopped me from pushing down the window. *Nicht hinauslehnen*. Night breeze, the scent of steam. Bridges burning in the night . . .

All night I'd stood in that corridor, swaying with the rhythm of the train, trying to read the names of stations as they flashed past. Uelzen . . . Celle . . . Hannover . . . Minden . . . Löhne . . . Bünde . . . Osnabrück . . . Recognised those names; places with their own football clubs, some in the lower leagues. . . .

First of the burning bridges. Fires fanned by a night breeze, inhaled from the window of a third-class carriage. Exotic draughts of uncertainty, excitement, freedom. A lifetime of bridgeburning, and you could never get back there, never re-enact that one ecstatic sequence. Cut.

The train started to move again. Slowly. The last carriage rolled out of sight. I could hear Dick's voice yelling at his publisher.

Looked up at the moon, round and cheesy, exhaled breath. Narrow escape for Lawrence Talbot, doomed Wolfman. Survival.

Sunday. We drove down to the Croisette to get the Heavies. Leonore sat in the back of the Buick, contentedly sucking a Lollipop. We parked the car in the driveway of the Carlton and went inside. In the lounge, I bought a French comic; Dick bought the *Observer*, *Times* and *Telegraph*. We walked out onto the terrace to drink coffee and plough through the review pages.

Though he maintained that he had *jumped off*, Dick's Sundays were ruined if the English papers failed to arrive. His Sunday afternoons on the cross were essential to him. Sweet torture. Threats everywhere. In-Out. The de Rochefoucauld syndrome: To be happy it was not enough to succeed; one's best friends had to fail. Dick admitted it. I could never have felt at ease with anyone who denied it.

We drove back to the Villa Rameau through a beige afternoon haze. Leonore sat in the back amidst a litter of grubby newsprint. The dregs of Dick's Sunday horrors lingered. Driving, he resumed battle.

'Ever see any of the old gang?'

'Who for instance?'

Every relationship has its limited set of conversations. *Who For Instance* meant tossing back and forth the names from our scruffy basement days, invariably ending up with Roger Arnold. After becoming engaged to Linda, I'd once thrown Roger Arnold down the stairs. Caught her cooking supper for him. Wasn't having any of that. For that unique act of violence, she'd really loved me.

For an opener, though, we ran through the minor names in our dog-eared catalogue: Eric Dixon, abstract painter, now designed mass-produced furniture. Bob Bradford, eternal Fan of Creative People, who wanted to manage my Film Group, had struck it rich as a Chartered Accountant, and still handled my tax affairs. Ned Mills, distinguished poet, had dropped out for a while, gone to the Far East to train as a Buddhist monk. Back now, flogging art books in the Charing X Road. As for the half-screwed girls (their names mislaid), they must all be middle-aged housewives by now, for all we knew even grandmothers. We got around to Roger Arnold, un-

67

quenchable optimist and amateur, eternal thorn in my flesh, earlier than usual.

'Still loathe his guts?' Dick opened, aggressively direct for once.

I shifted in my seat, looked at my watch, extracted an orange from the glove compartment, used my fingernails to peel it for Leonore, felt the juice running all over my hands.

'Poor bastard,' Dick went on. 'Struggling away as an actor all those years. You might have given him a job, George, helped him up a rung.'

I halved the orange, pedantically handed Leonore the less drippy half. 'Say Thank You.'

'Thank you, Daddy.'

'Roger couldn't have acted his way out of a Kleenex. He's the Ur-incompetent. Even tried directing once. An unparalleled disaster.'

'You ought to get rid of that obsession, George. It's not serious.'

'What obsession?'

'About Roger Arnold. Bloody destructive.'

This is what Dick, during his analysis period, would have called 'projecting your bad objects into others'. I'd caught Dick bleeding on the envy rack at the Carlton. Now it was my turn to suffer.

'Seems odd that he finally landed on his feet.'

Alarm and despondency, orange-flavoured.

'Roger? On his feet?'

'Yes. Swinging photographer now, didn't you know? Works for one of the coloured supplements.'

'Oh yes?'

Relief. Bloody photographer! No threat there.

'Yes, called me. Flying down to take some snaps of me.'

'When?'

'Next week some time. Don't mind, do you? Talk to him.'

Panic stations.

'British writers in exile. The tax refugees. That kind of bumph.'

'Good for you,' I said. Creepily. Knew suddenly that our days with Dick were numbered. Where could I take Leonore next? Joe and Marion's? Jack and Eve Martinsell's posh house in Barnes? The Bahamas? Jamaica? *Anywhere*. Just Leonore and me. Only thing that mattered. Get her a tutor. Leonore and me, and a tutor.

As we drove into the forecourt of the Villa Rameau, Janine was hopping about in the doorway, wildly signalling, clutching the telephone receiver.

Oh no, not this time. Not going to get caught again.

Dick scrambled out of the Buick. Leonore and I followed.

'*C'est pour la petite,*' Janine stage-whispered, as I got to the door. '*L'Angleterre.*'

'I'll take it,' I said calmly.

'Is it Mummy?'

Leonore reached for my free hand. My mouth was a desert. Kingdom for a Pernod. Request Programme: Dracula meets the Creature from the Black Lagoon.

'Who's that speaking? George? Who's that girl who answered the telephone? What the bloody hell have you done with Leonore? Where is she?'

'Right here.'

'Why isn't she at school? I wish to speak to her at once!'

'Yes. Sure.'

Meekly, I handed Leonore the receiver, just stood there, rocking on my heels like an idiot.

'Mummy? . . . yes . . . Daddy's taken me on a super holiday . . . didn't you . . . Is Lucy allright? Is she going to have kittens? . . . What? I don't know, Mummy, why don't you ask . . . you'll have to ask Daddy, Mummy . . .'

Didn't wait to hear the rest. Oceans roared in my ears. Fled upstairs, three steps at a time. Closed the door, packed our bags. Smell of burning.

69

Two

SAT on a bar-stool in the White Elephant, munched peanuts, watched the ice chips dissolve in my Scotch.

Was this still the place to go?

I'd had a close shave, wore a freshly laundered white roll-neck sweater. Dunk-it-in-the-tank-man-and-see-what-develops. George the Gambler in poorish vintage Robert Mitchum.

After half an hour of getting my fingertips peanutty, I still hadn't seen Anybody. Worse, Nobody had seen me. The headwaiter tangoed up with the menu and bowed. I said no, later, maybe.

At half past eight people started to arrive, men with faces like glazed fruit escorting home-tanned girls with anxious eyes that begged instant approval. I envied them all, vaguely. Nobody knew the trouble I had seen.

First person I recognised was a fat publicity man who'd been with the Network once, now worked in movies. Coming through the doors with his *Evening Standard* tucked under his arm, he gladhanded me, dropped the paper.

One up to me.

Asked me what was I drinking, then neurotically dug into the peanut-bowl, grabbing nuts by the fistful, popping them into his mouth one by one. Sure enough the dreaded opener came trippingly off his tongue: What was I doing these days, oldson, followed at once by Self-answering Service: Still the old goggle-box, is it?

'How's the old praise factory?' I asked him.

'Great,' he said popping nuts through yellow teeth, hating me.

The barman placed the fat publicity man's Scotch in front of me.

I sipped. He looked at his watch.

'Harry's late,' he confided.

'Harry who?' I countered wittily. Two—one, read the score. Good enough to take me into the next round.

The fat publicity man was surveying his image in the pink mirror behind the bar when Dan Wymans came through the doors, bird in tow. The fat publicity man slunk off to await Harry's coming. Just as well. I hadn't been able to recall his name. No need to annihilate the poor sod.

Dan Wymans ordered Bloody Marys, ignored his bird, and placed his arm around me in a bear-hug, squeezing my shoulder. Called me My Old Love, was dressed up as Mao-Tse-Tung, all in white. Wore dark glasses and a droopy Chinese Warlord moustache. A contemporary of mine in Documentaries, Dan had made it in Features. Mazeltov. Could afford to tell me that he had caught my opening segment of 'Lunar Mission'. Dolly. Great. A real gas, man. But hooked on the whole series. Already I did not hate him quite as much as the fat publicity man. His bird had received Dan's instant signal: Don't hustle baby, Not Important. She didn't even bother to smile. Screw her.

In the time span between clasping the big menu to his Mao jacket and getting his Bloody Marys set up, Dan imparted the following unsolicited information concerning himself:

a) He had traded in his Lotus for an Oldsmobile, which was built like a brick shithouse.

b) He had loved every one of his five marriages and didn't care who knew it.

c) Paramount was paying him two hundred thou to make a war epic that had to gross fifteen million bucks to break even.

d) His last movie, a load of old codswallop, if you asked

him, had bombed in Britain but was smasheroo in the States.

e) He still remembered Those Great Old Days, my old love.

f) He could direct rings round any whizzkid, who couldn't tell an Ophüls 180 degree pan from a fucking hole in the ground.

Dan hadn't yet touched his drink, when he was encircled by a group of gross Americans, who wafted him away into the restaurant's interior on clouds of *Eau Sauvage*. The bird, who still hadn't been introduced to anybody, followed meekly. Dan, for that matter, hadn't introduced me to the Americans. No doubt he couldn't remember *my* name. The fat publicity man came back, glanced at his watch, pursed his lips eagerly, thrust a fist into the re-filled bowl of peanuts.

The assistant headwaiter was enquiring if I now wished to order. Turned my back on him, helped myself to a couple of gratis miniature pizzas. People kept coming through the doors, looking past me, the Invisible Man, before being shown to their tables.

I was Out. Yegods, was I out. Everybody swung except me. Linda's fault.

I slipped off my stool, flicked the fat publicity man's left shoulder with my right index finger to denote eternal affection, started to edge my way out into the hall. I was just being helped into my overcoat when the last person in the world I wanted to see loomed up before me: Jack Martinsell. With Eve, girl-wife of six months' standing. White-haired, short, avuncular, Jack embraced me with grave warmth. 'Gee, I'm sorry,' he mumbled, patting my back all the while. 'Gee, I'm sorry.'

Greasy white hair was bobbing about under my chin. Before I knew what I was doing, I'd started explaining my head off. Girl-wife handed her mink wrap to the cloakroom attendant, drifted off.

'It's all taken care of, sweetheart,' Jack assured me,

feverishly caressing my spine. 'Don't worry about a thing, baby. Look, call me ...'

I wondered who'd told him what. Who was directing the eleventh 'Lunar Mission' segment?

'No, wait,' Jack said, 'I'll call you. Jesus, what are friends for? I'll call you, sweetheart. If there's anything Eve and I can do to help ...'

'Is Francis doing the show ... I mean the one ...?'

'Don't even think about it. I'll call you. And, Jesus, if you think it'll do any good, I'll *mediate*, know what I mean? I'll call Linda ...'

'No, for Christ's sake ...'

'Look, *call* me ...' His eyes were straying wildly over my shoulder. 'No, wait, why don't you bring little Laura round ...'

'Leonore.'

'Yeah, well, what you do, you bring the kid round for tea on Sunday. Any Sunday. No, wait a minute, not *this* Sunday, gosh. Look, I'll call you ...'

I was thanking him profusely. I was quite distressed to have to let this nice man down.

'About our contract,' I mumbled, searching for, but not quite finding, Jack's eyes, 'The fact is, I've been meaning to call Bill Dodds ...'

'Naw, let it go. Look, I'll *call* you, sweetheart. I'll call you tomorrow.'

As he squeezed my elbows, a funny old sequence flickered through my mind. I was a baby, hardly more than a baby that is, two and a half years old, no more. My mother was giving me a bath in a big china tub, my father was looking on. I was trying to tell my father that I was caught short and about to shit in the bath. Or maybe it would just turn out to be a fart. My father smiled, fluttering fingers at me, wearing a broad gold wedding-ring. I kept yelling it was going to happen, I couldn't hold it. My mother went on rinsing my body with warm water, my father grinned. Then I did it, stood up, started to cry

Sure enough, little round turd swimming about in clouded water. My mother was slapping my bottom, reproaching me. My father, bless him, had fled. I was bawling. My mother was wrapping my wet soiled body into a big woolly towel. End of Flashback.

'I'll call you. Jesus, have I got your number? Where *are* you?'

'I'm staying with Joe Leeds. He's in the book.'

'Joe? Oh, wonderful, gee, Joe's a beautiful guy. Isn't that just like Joe? . . . Yes, dear, I'm coming. Call you, George. Wonderful.'

He was off, short legs stomping away over soft carpet.

I tipped the cloakroom attendant, buttoned up my overcoat, started walking up Curzon Street. Passing the Playboy Club, I felt a momentary urge to join. Yegods, I was so far Out I was almost In again. Jack, for all his West Coast *schmus*, hadn't kidded me. You walked out of a contract, that was that. In television that was that. Curtains. What had he actually promised to do, anyway? Buggerall. No, to hell with the Playboy Club. Women dressed as rabbits. With tits. Eight guineas a year for *that*? My gambling days were over.

I crossed Park Lane, headed for the bus stop. Take the 2a to Swiss Cottage, then walk up Fitzjohns Avenue, that's what I'd do. My Jaguar was in my garage at Kew, and there it would have to stay. Needed my head examining. The house was in Linda's name. Not only that, but Linda and her sister were sole directors of my tax-avoidance company. Less than two years ago, I'd borrowed eight thousand quid from this company as a down payment on the house. For the remaining £15,000 we got a mortgage. Yegods, totally out of my mind! £23,000 for a big house I didn't even want! Just another shot at melting ice-bound Linda, and here I was, rich houseowner, feeling I couldn't afford a taxi back to Hampstead.

Even our cash was evenly divided, £3,000 or thereabouts in Linda's personal account, the same kind of money in mine. *And* I was owing a year's personal tax. I'd taken out every possible kind of insurance against leaving Linda. George the Creep in control. George the Gambler ruined.

But I did have Leonore, I thought, jumping onto a 2a bus. I had Leonore. I'd told Dick I'd never let her go, my only child, great love of my life. Dick had contradicted me. You'll leave them both, he'd prophesied. Well, I hadn't. I had Leonore. I had my strength. I was intact.

Joe and Marion were watching television when I let myself into their flat.

'Would you like something to eat, dear?' Marion greeted me.

'Anything happen? Any calls?'

'Nothing,' Joe said. 'Not a thing. All's well.'

They were marvellous. At first they'd let Leonore sleep with Barry in the nursery, but Leonore hadn't cared for that. Barry, seven, snored. So now she slept with me in the spare room. Two single beds set side by side. Like an old married couple.

'I've got something warm for you in the oven,' Marion said.

Yes, marvellous. George had landed on his feet. I sat down in Marion's vacated swivel armchair, Joe offered me a cigarette. Thought I heard the telephone shrill in the hall. Was always hearing telephones ring. Morning noon and night I was hearing those telephones.

Joe offered me a light. I thanked him profusely.

I'd settled for Joe and Marion Leeds, not because it was the final offer I'd had. It was the only offer. Made sense. Hampstead is a long way from Kew. From my new hide-away, I could safely fight my private wars. As for Dick's innuendo about possible dalliance with Marion, nothing was further from my dazed mind, or, as far as I could tell, from hers. Familiarity breeds sexual indifference. At least with me it does.

Nothing was too much trouble for Joe and Marion. I

couldn't get over it. Yegods, they didn't know me from Adam. They put me to shame. And to think I'd initially questioned Marion's motives. True, she was out of work, but there had to be easier ways of courting a job than sorting out George Kane's domestic disasters.

Actresses aren't usually the most practical people, but Marion astonished me. Whatever new problem came up she dealt with briskly and efficiently. Sold Joe on helping me, that much was clear. Not a moment's irritation on his part, either. Maybe he was studying my psyche for a book.

Marion, I confirmed, *was* Jewish. This was never discussed—Joe *wasn't* Jewish, that's probably why—but it created a bond of sorts between Marion and myself. At least, that's that I thought at the time.

Marion's son, who used every available opportunity to leap on top of his mother, trying to get between her legs or nuzzling her breasts, showed some resentment at first, but after sizing each other up for a couple of days, the kids climbed trees together. Leonore also got hold of Joe's Monopoly set and taught Barry to play, even let him win a couple of times. That sealed their friendship.

On the third day, Marion took us along to enrol Leonore in Barry's prep school, musty establishment near Hampstead tube station, hardly more than a private house, mouldering away in Edwardian gloom, the front reception rooms used as the main teaching area, a far cry from Leonore's teeming, beautifully equipped GLC school in Kew (Linda and I objected to private education for political reasons). I expected trouble with the headmistress, a Home Counties horse with a mouthful of dentures, but Marion put it on the line to her, big brown eyes watering, told lies of a deserting mother, a loving Dad.

Some of Marion's instant emotionalism rubbed off on the Home Counties horse. She called Leonore in, asked her to read from a story book and add up some tens and units. Then told her to consider herself accepted. I got an impression that the Horse would have accepted anything that breathed, provided it was white and a term's fees were paid in advance.

I coughed up the cheque, we left Leonore in the Horse's charge. That afternoon, fetching her and Barry in Joe's Renault, I found her a bit monosyllabic. I comforted her with a Mars bar, explaining that she wouldn't be New Girl for long.

'What's Mummy going to say?' she wanted to know. 'She won't like that funny old school, I know she won't.'

This was the first time she had mentioned her mother anxiously since Linda's telephone call to Cannes.

'All that matters is that *you* should like that school, love,' I told her. 'Mummy won't mind. Not if *you* like it. And you do, don't you?'

'Not really a proper school, is it?'

'Of course it's a proper school. You even have to pay to go there. Barry thinks it's a proper school, doesn't he?'

'Barry doesn't know Kew Central, does he?' she replied with unassailable logic.

'Try and make the best of it, love,' I told her.

'When is Mummy coming?' she asked, after a short but ominous silence.

'She'll come and see you the moment she's less busy.'

'What's she so busy with?'

'She's trying to sell the house,' I lied.

'Oh, is she?'

Another long silence. Desperately searched my imagination for some device by which I might suck her evident pain into myself.

'Aren't we ever going back to Kew then? Ever-ever?'

'We'll sort it out when Mummy and I get together, love.'

'When will that be, then?'

'Soon, love, soon.'

I brought the Renault to a halt in Joe's drive.

'Mummy knows where we are, doesn't she?'

I was rescued by Barry, who wanted to play Monopoly. We went inside, settled down to play on the floor of the nursery, Leonore dealt out coloured money.

Looking back on this phase of my lovelife, I see myself on my knees, playing this never-ending game of Monopoly, driving anxiety deeper and deeper into my bowels, shouting lunatic queries and exhortations: 'Do you want to buy Pall Mall, or auction it? ... Your turn, Barry. If you suck your thumb, love, I won't play ... I'll do a deal with you, three hundred pounds and Marlborough Street for Fleet Street ... You've *got* to want to build houses on Park Lane and Mayfair ...'

I knew Monopoly to be the simplest way of diverting Leonore. She loved the game, adored instructing Barry, felt sorry for me when I lost. Above all, she wanted to count money. From counting coloured paper money, it was a short step to wanting to count the money in my wallet, in my pocket, in everyone else's pocket. Counting coins, dividing them into little piles, asking me to guess the totals, slipping a hand into Joe's trousers for silver.

Meanwhile I listened for the telephone to ring, suffered from occasional bouts of diarrhoea....

The mystery of Linda's apparent inaction did not greatly surprise Joe's solicitor, Mr. Tetheridge, plummy-voiced, pin-striped, with the face of an elderly baby. He took a poor view of human nature in general, of clients' wives in particular.

'I dare say your wife is simply waiting to see which way the cat will jump,' he pronounced after I'd given him a painfully detailed account of my situation. 'She may be more preoccupied with that man in Bournemouth than you imagine.'

Didn't kidnapping our only child qualify as cat-jumping?

'Well, clearly, Mrs. Kane doesn't regard your action in that light. If she did, we'd be sitting here, discussing a court order, wouldn't we?'

'Court order?'

'To have Leonore legally restored to your wife. I shouldn't think she'd have much trouble in getting that. Judges are notoriously soft on mothers in cases of this sort.'

He chewed his pencil for a while.

'Of course she may be worried that you'll slap in a counter-summons for negligence.'

'That's what we're going to do, is it? Slap in . . .'

'If you can adduce evidence that she neglected the child.'

Neglect? Negligence? Adduce evidence?

Lost.

'Surely, Mr. Kane, you were appalled when you found that your wife had gone off with her lover without so much as a by-your-leave?'

'Well, it did give me a chance to see a lot more of Leonore . . .'

'Oh dear.'

'Why oh dear?'

'Well. Mr. Kane, surely you must realise that if what you have just said is true, your wife has a very good case for contesting your adultery petition.'

'Adultery petition? Is that what we're going to . . .'

'On the other hand, she may get in first with her own petition. I understand there has been a certain amount of adultery on your part, too . . .'

'Well, yes . . .'

'. . . in which case we could cross-petition. What seriously worries me is that by failing to object to her trip to Bournemouth, we've laid ourselves open to a charge of connivance, haven't we?'

Cross-petition? Connivance? What had all this to do with Leonore? So much for Dick's facile advice about throwing the book at Linda.

By the end of the interview, I'd handed over a cheque for £300 to retain Mr. Tetheridge's services. We would have to take Counsel's advice before proceeding. If I decided to sue Linda for adultery, I'd have to give some thought to my own discretion statement, which, he sincerely hoped, would not be of an epic nature.

Didn't understand a word of any of this, which amused Mr. Tetheridge. He dictated a letter, informing Linda of our present whereabouts, and adding that, in view of her highly reprehensible behaviour, I would be taking charge of Leonore until such a time as arrangements for her care could be resolved by mutual consent, or the due processes of law.

'No we'll see which way the cat will jump,' Mr. Tetheridge vouchsafed, and dismissed me.

'Not to worry,' he added, showing me to the door. 'In cases like this, possession is often nine tenths of the law.'

Joe Leeds agreed. Tetheridge knew what he was about. First-rate man. Got him off a libel hook a few years back.

'He looks like a great big baby to me,' I told Joe.

Which reminded Joe of a critic. Also looked like a great big baby, had tried to destroy his literary reputation . . .

Marion rescued me from a lengthy paranoid tale, asking me to help her put the children to bed.

'You're such a wonderful father, George,' she whispered to me in the dark of the landing, placing a plump hand on my sleeve.

'*You're* a mother, Marion. Can *you* understand why Linda isn't doing anything?'

'Women move in mysterious ways when they're emotionally involved,' she breathed. 'One day, I'll tell you some things about me which may surprise you, George.'

Actress to her fingertips, I thought with rueful affection. Never at a loss to dramatise herself, or to shunt any subject back to her own person. For the moment she was content to be enigmatic. Took me by the hand, led me back to the sitting-room, where Joe was watching the Miss World Contest.

'Unspeakable,' he fumed, eyes fixed on the television

83

screen. 'Decline of the West in a nutshell, makes you want to vomit.'

We settled down to watch the contest. Not until Miss World had been crowned, and broken down to the strains of a Wesleyan hymn, was I able to steer Joe's attention back to My Problem.

'Look, George, I know women,' Joe said, darting a quick, enquiring glance at Marion. 'She's just letting you stew in your own juice. Thinks you'll tire of all that nannying before long. Have you back in Kew within the fortnight, tail tucked between your legs.'

'She's *involved*, Joe, she's an *involved* woman,' Marion said.

'Dick says she's a first-class bitch.'

Again this absurd urge to defend Linda. Yegods, why couldn't I hate her more? Those American years, despite my soul-destroying job and the awful Hot Dog Man's apartment, had begun promisingly. I'd worked hard to extricate Linda from that ice-cube of hers. Even laid off Dracula, though God knows there was no shortage of likely Brides.

In her own frosty way, Linda tried, too. What kept us going was fear. Shit-scared and together we were. Frightened of my employers, the Moguls. Of the Bomb. Of sterility. Of Senator McCarthy most of all. So many acquaintances got into black-listing trouble, Linda and I came to think of ourselves as alien Cryptos, secretly engaged in subverting the American Way of Life. It was a bit like being back at school in Bendabrück.

Why, with me churning out creepy rubbish for the box, and Linda devoting all her energies to keeping house and inspecting alternative accommodation, we should have thought of ourselves as political underground fighters I can't recall now, but that's how it seemed to us at the time. Linda hated America. I liked it, and felt too ashamed to admit it.

Lingering problems stemmed from Linda's decision to

give up work. For a couple of years she had carried on working as a continuity girl. Then, one lunchtime, she caught me making a date with a wardrobe mistress on the lot, and that was that. Linda abdicated. Wasn't ever going to expose herself to such humiliations again. If I insisted on conducting myself like an adolescent lecher on the set, she'd rather stay at home and not be a witness to my compulsive behaviour. She never did work again, found new outlets for her highly developed critical acumen : lavished it on estate agents, surveyors, builders and plumbers. We moved house half a dozen times before coming to rest in the Hot Dog Man's apartment.

There we nested. Linda had become pregnant. I became the exemplary husband.

We both badly wanted a child, convinced ourselves that it would solve all our problems. I saw to it that she got the most expensive medical attention, spent every evening at home watching 13-channel TV, got into the habit of bringing Linda dainty supper trays. When she complained of feeling sick, I did the shopping. Linda didn't want a third person in the house, a spy, so we managed without domestic help. After the seventh month, I found myself cleaning and scrubbing as well. All that and *Creaking Doors*. I didn't complain.

According to Dick, all my subsequent disasters were rooted in this period. Linda, he interpreted, had acquired a taste for castration.

I genuinely thought we were headed for calm waters. Home. Kids. Mum's apple-pie. There is something about West Coast life that makes you fall for propaganda like that. I kept knocking myself out at the studio, serving Linda at home, groaning about McCarthy, getting into a sweat about the Bomb.

What, you may ask, had happened to Dracula ? How was I keeping Mr. Hyde down ? For a long time I cherished the delusion that I had 'changed'. Having passed up a few chances to get laid, I certified myself mature.

85

Time came for Linda to be shipped into that expensive clinic in Beverly Hills. She went ten days early. Her pregnancy had been relatively uneventful, but after waiting all these years we weren't taking chances. I visited her every evening, bringing flowers and fruit, avid to prove I was a real human being. In refusing to give me credit for this, Linda knew what she was doing. Had she once let up on her icy reign of terror, I might have gone back to my bad old ways before I did.

The baby was born, a son, and Linda came through the ordeal with courage, looking rosy. We split a bottle of champagne by her bedside, held hands. After we'd finished the champagne, the doctor informed us haltingly that something about the baby's bloodflow was not absolutely O.K. Latin nouns, much polishing of eye-glasses. Dracula meets Dr. Kildare. The little fellow would have to be kept in isolation for a day or two.

Never even saw our baby. He lived for thirty-six hours. Fifteen hundred dollars they charged me for killing my son. At first we couldn't believe it. Then we wept. They gave Linda a jumbo sleeping pill. I went back to the apartment and calmly, methodically went berserk.

Nothing as positive or romantic as getting stoned out of my mind, or sueing the hospital, or shooting Senator McCarthy. To shield myself from my grief, I cleaned up the apartment, and then sat down to make a few calls.

There was this friendly small-part actress who lived in the same block, married to a middle-aged printer. A jerk. Had dinner with them once. I'd got her message under the table during dessert. I called her.

There was also this twitchy highbrow Assistant Casting Director, who beguiled me with her opinions about Albert Camus and Hermann Hesse in the studio commissary. She had recently divorced her husband, was playing the field. Everyone down to the clapperboy recognised a Sure Thing. I called her.

Then I remembered this nineteen-year-old blonde with

apple-red cheeks and rubbery tits, who worked in the Inglewood Public Library, Jean. She thought I was British and Famous. I called her, too. Then, like Linda, I took a sleeping-pill.

The bit-playing actress came over at noon next day, ostensibly to cook lunch for me and offer sympathy. Ten minutes after arriving, with her clothes still on, she was kneeling before me on the kitchen floor. An hour later she left, I had thirty minutes to get myself cleaned up for the Assistant Casting Director. Had asked her to confer with me on casting *Creaking Doors*. I plied her with Martinis, then suggested a shower. Before long she was in my bed, drunk and damp, sobbing with orgasms and gratitude. The apple-cheeked librarian with the rubbery tits came at eight, bringing toasted sandwiches from the delicatessen downstairs. Plonked her on the sofa, played Dracula for two hours. We sweated and struggled. Finally I capitulated, had her on the floor three times. By midnight I'd got rid of her. I called Linda in hospital to tell her I loved her. I was never again to feel so elated, so free, so completely in harmony with myself—until that night flight with Leonore many years later . . .

When Linda came out of hospital, I set out to make good my betrayal. I was even more considerate than before. Her convalescence dragged on indefinitely, I hurried home every evening to look after her needs. I never went out alone. I cooked. I washed the dishes. I redecorated the apartment. I placated morning noon and night.

If coming to the States had been an act of penance for old sins, my entire life now became dedicated to appeasing Linda. We were caught in a vicious circle. My tireless placations made Linda feel resentful and insecure. The more she resented, the harder I tried to appease.

Had either of us ever articulated this situation, we might yet have saved the marriage; I might still have made it as a husband. But we covered up, not only to outsiders, but to one another. We were polite to the point of imbecility. I placated. She retreated into her ice-cube, smoking, biting her nails, turning over pages of unwieldy, king-size magazines.

She became very slow and deliberate in her movements. It took her hours to complete the simplest domestic task. She rose late and retired early. She spent entire evenings in front of her mirror, applying make-up in slow motion. If I forgot myself sufficiently to draw attention to this, she slowed down her rhythm still further. Mysteriously, she was hoarding her energies.

Frequently, I'd come home after a day's shooting to find her sitting in a chair, back turned to me, head lowered over her hands, manicuring her fingernails. If I mentioned food, she would instantly change into slower gear, and enquire if I expected her to jump to attention the moment I came home? In order to avoid a row, I'd go into the kitchen, prepare a meal for the two of us. She would reward me with sulks: Why was I always trying to make her feel inadequate?

Through all this, our voices were never raised in anger. We never became violent. No quarrel was ever attempted, let alone resolved. Occasionally, swallowing mutual distaste, we made love, but even this constituted an act of appeasement on my part. I could only make the effort after hearing complaints of my emotional atrophy. Her own admitted coldness she regarded as an injury inflicted on her by my past conduct.

Gradually, I began to weave secret fantasies of reversal. I thought of staging a great vocal showdown, of beating the living daylights out of her, of leaving her altogether. I did nothing, however; merely tried to contain my mounting irritation. Her refined voice irritated me. Her slowness irritated me. So did her failure to arouse me erotically, her political pessimism, the glum criticism of everything she read or viewed. Her boredom with herself irritated me, and so did her sullen contempt for my work. Most of all I was irritated by Linda in bed, by the cosy, absent-minded way she crossed her legs behind me in coitus. With others, I couldn't have enough of little heels grinding into my back, especially if the heels were grubby. With Linda all sexual activity that did not confirm my diagnosis of frigidity I found aesthetically distasteful.

One day, she cut her finger on a carving knife. Anxiously, I set about bandaging her hand.

'Why do you always laugh when something painful happens to me?' she wanted to know.

I denied that I had been laughing.

'You laughed allright. What a charmer you are.'

The months passed by. We sat reading or viewing in our airconditioned imitation splendour, smog and irritation blocking our senses, furtively hatching tragedy for one another. I finally got to a point of such desperation that I decided a breath of honesty might clear the air. I confessed my attack of erotomania during her stay in hospital. That is to say, I told her about the Inglewood Public Library blonde. I might just as well have told her about the other ladies as well, because Linda's response was catastrophic. For two weeks she would not talk to me at all, though she did manage to sit up in bed to accept the breakfast trays I brought her every morning.

When my two weeks in Coventry were over, she informed me calmly that, as far as she was concerned, our marriage was at an end. Panic-stricken, I suggested that we should try to adopt a child. The damage might still be mended. And I still loved her. She retorted that only a raving lunatic would think of placing a child in the care of a psychopath. We dithered about a divorce, but came to no conclusion. Instead we returned to England and, by accident, begot Leonore.

'Don't you love Mummy anymore?' Leonore asked me as we trudged up Fitzjohns Avenue.

I said, come on, let's play knights, love, look for conkers. First one to bag a conker is chief knight.

'I bet Mummy still loves you,' she commented sadly, resting her mitten-bound fingers in the hollow of my hand. 'I bet you still love Mummy.'

, I told her I wouldn't be a bit surprised.

After making breakfast for the children, Marion usually locked herself in the bathroom to make telephone calls. She called shops, girlfriends, agents, friendly TV executives, neatly crossing each name off her pad as the call was completed. This, I gathered, got her through the early-morning panic of finding herself awake and well, and out of work.

Joe suffered similar morning torments; he was *in* work, re-writing a Rasputin movie. For The Money. At the stroke of nine, he disappeared into his study 'to do his stint'. Ninety minutes later, he came out again, despondent and green, to open letters and glance at the papers. Marion switched on the electric blanket, and into the warm, safe cocoon of his bed Joe crawled, turning on the Music Programme, waiting for noon, when his self-imposed working period was officially over, and he could face the world with an eased conscience.

Marion then brought him a large pot of coffee—I caught myself grimly comparing her conjugal solicitude with Linda's apathy—and Joe scrupulously avoided his study until dusk, when he cautiously approached his desk again to re-write what he had re-written in the morning.

Conspiracies were menacing Joe from all sides. The world was full of corrupt film producers, cheating publishers and venal newspaper editors, all plotting to deprive Joe of due literary recognition. Sometimes Joe affirmed that anonymity was a priceless privilege for an artist, especially when allied to a regular income, but such helpful theories never consoled him for long.

'My real problem is that I'm second-rate,' he confessed to me one morning, his Martian head peeping over warmed sheets. 'Any third- or fourth-rater they'll give the benefit of the bloody doubt. A genuine second-rater is never forgiven for getting out of Fleet Street. Turn your back on them, and you feel their knives between your shoulder-blades.'

When Marion had run out of calls, she often joined us at Joe's bedside. Did *I* want anybody rung? I badly wanted to call Dick. He'd accuse me of being inactive and superficial, and this would make me angry, and I'd feel better. I guessed that Joe wouldn't accept cash from me for making the call, so I refrained.

'I've failed Marion,' Joe said plaintively. 'Look at her. Only feels secure when she's got a bloody telephone receiver clasped between her hands. Put *that* through your Freudian mincer, George.'

Continued sitting on Joe's bed, consumed with morning anguish, while the daily woman started the housework. They were my kind of people.

To cheer me up, they decided to give an impromptu dinner party. Marion hurried out to fetch her pad from the bathroom; we discussed possible guests. Joe suggested Jack Martinsell, but I vetoed that. Jack hadn't called. I had mentioned running into Dan Wymans, so Marion put him down. He might have a part for her. Joe added Hammond Fraser, way-out, with-it, passé young movie director. He and Dan would loathe each other on sight. That, Joe thought, might produce a few welcome sparks. Joe insisted on Ellis Trawley, faded actor-friend from down the road. Marion explained that Joe needed Ellis the way Dick needed Charlie Raeburn. Joe agreed. Poor Ellis's haplessness worked on him like a tonic. Dan and Hammond would bring birds. The list was completed by Cara, friend of Marion's, who had just opened a super new boutique in Knightsbridge.

'She's marvellous, George. A lovely person. And beautiful A big girl. You'll fall for her. Everybody does.'

As an afterthought, Joe added his accountant, Fred

Flake. I'd told him that my own accountant was now out of bounds; Flake, like Tetheridge, was touted as a first-rate man, who knew his stuff backwards. Clearly Joe and Marion were determined to restaff my life.

Marion happily hopped off to the bathroom to make the necessary calls. Joe made himself miserable by reading his successor's well-displayed theatre notices. I went on squatting on the edge of Joe's bed, tentatively conjuring up the likely contours of Cara's breasts.

After eating Marion's buffet-dinner in the kitchen, plates balanced on their knees, the party guests climbed upstairs, muttering about age and calories.

'The same bloody meal,' Ellis Trawley bitched on the way up. 'I must have come here a hundred times, and it's always overcooked spaghetti bolognaise, frozen bird, served cold, gooey cake and dago cheese. Poor Marion. No talent for cooking at all.'

The ageing actor, who was practically blind but too vain to wear spectacles at a party, had clung to me all evening, after witnessing my skirmish with Fred Flake. The accountant, pale, thin and stooping, wearing a really awful brown suit, had a way of unexpectedly splitting his very English face into two unmatching halves by means of a sinister Conrad Veidt smile. Perfect casting for an undercover sex delinquent: no sooner had we started talking cars, than Flake glimpsed the boutique-owning Cara, stately maxiskirted Brunette. Wore a plastic fried egg tied around her wrist, which kept time; her face was made up to resemble death by starvation. With a hunter's instinct, Flake registered her as the evening's sole available prey. Deserted me, accosted Cara, switching on his alien smile. Worse, Cara actually took to the cube, ghastly brown suit, car talk and all. So much for Marion's matchmaking, I thought grimly, resigned myself to Ellis Trawley's company.

Poor old sod. The interior clockwork that had once galvanised 'that distinguished actor' (as *The Stage* still referred to him), had stopped long ago. He still walked very upright, his projection of confidence was intact to those who didn't look too closely, but as he droned on, it became clear that he moved the hands of the dead clock manually and in secret. I'd been told by Marion that he found it impossible to get work. He certainly was no longer usable on television; knew better than playwright or director, liked to improvise lines and moves as he went along. His memory had gone to rust with the rest of the clockwork. Erroneous show-biz gossip issued from his handsome lips in a constant flow. Unable to remember a single name or title correctly, he became infuriated if you did not prompt him. From a distance, his profile still resembled Ivor Novello's, but in close-up you saw sheer bloody terror blazing from his eyes.

While I looked around for escape, Ellis recalled the glories of Gielgud's wartime season at the Haymarket. That marvellous *Macbeth*, with whatshername as Lady M. No, I told him, *Macbeth* wasn't part of that season. He was thinking of *Hamlet*. No, no, no, it most certainly was *Macbeth*. Seen it a dozen times. Whatsit was in it, you know. Played Banquo. Macduff, was it? No, I argued, *Macbeth* had been performed at the Piccadilly, not the Haymarket at all. Wait a minute, he said, clutching my arm, you my be right. I was doing whatsit at the time, playing you know, er.

Against all expectations, Dan Wymans and Hammond Fraser had hit it off, the former still immaculately disguised as Mao, the latter wearing plum corduroys and a sweat-stained green shirt, Byronic brown hair spilling down to his shoulders. They were standing by the bay-window, having found common ground as Creators who were uptight. Dan had avoided me. I was bloody sure by now that he couldn't remember my name. His bird, and Fraser's, sat together on the floor, showing vast thighs and muttering about gear.

'What's a Creator to do confronted with this scene?' Fraser was shouting at Dan. 'Tell me the movie that cries out to be made, like I mean right now?'

'Gotta get your big audience by the balls, man,' Wymans yelled back. 'That's my bag, sweetheart, the big audience. All the rest is masturbation. Take your John Fords. Take your Howard Hawkses. Commercial! Don't make movies for no arthouses, that's for sure.'

'Ford's a gas,' Fraser agreed, snapping fingers in homage to the master. 'Jesus, like he makes me want to freak out, that Ford.'

'Right. So what's with Andy Warhol? You tell me. The Big Audience. Right?'

'Andy Warhol is going to direct the new Sam Spiegel picture,' Ellis Trawley interposed tersely, over-projecting certainty. 'Er told me. No, wait. Read it in whatsit.'

'Like everybody's selling out, man,' Hammond Fraser lamented. 'There's your hang-up, man. The fuckin' system.'

'Hammond, baby, like if Sam offered you two hundred thou a year to make movies, you saying you wouldn't sign? Come *on* . . .'

'If I could do my thing, sure, why not? You wanna make bread, man, you gotta hustle. Shit.'

Marion came up from behind, playfully rubbed herself up against my back.

'Darling, there's nothing in your glass. I'm going to fill you up.'

'You're nice and warm, Marion,' I said. 'And it's a cold, cold world.'

'Won't Cara play ball with George?' she asked with unexpected venom.

'Haven't asked her, love.'

'I'm stoned out of my Jewish mind,' she sighed, rub-

94

bing up some more. 'Oh, George, I feel so lost, so lost.'

A drunken confession coming up. When actresses wanted to confess, they first touched you up. I slithered away on the pretext of wanting to refill my glass.

Activated by the Fraser-Wymans alliance, the party had converged on the centre of the room to play Great Bores of the World.

'Dostoevsky,' Joe opened. 'All the Russians.'

'Too easy,' Wymans pounced. 'Jean-Luc Godard gets my vote. Couldn't make it directing *Coronation Street*, that phoney. Right, George?'

'Aw, you can't say that, Danny,' Fraser said. 'So Jean-Luc doesn't grab you personally. But he's a Creator. Committed.'

'May I put in a word for Proust?' Flake asked, fingers surreptitiously browsing between Cara's buttocks. 'Always found him unreadable.'

Marion had detached herself from the group. Stood by the window, striking a Chekhovian pose of unspecified isolation.

'Rainer Maria Rilke,' Joe proferred. 'Your original sensibility merchant.'

'Eisenstein,' I said. 'Abel Gance. The Japs.'

'Whatsit,' Ellis contributed. 'Er, you know.'

'All nineteenth century novelists, bar none.'

'Not Balzac, though. I mean like he's one of your all-time greats.'

'Shit, Hammond, when did you last read any Balzac, man? Come on, name me a Balzac you've read lately.'

'Max Reger,' I tossed in. 'Case of the classic nonentity.'

'Some of his chamber works . . .'

'Hum me some Reger, Dan baby,' Hammond challenged.

'Reger must go.'

'And Dvorak.'

'And Cui, above all that Cui.'

'Who's Cui?' Fraser's bird wanted to know.

95

'The Sonny Tufts of music,' Dan Wymans enlightened her.

I wandered out into the little television room, collapsed on a sofa. If I'd stayed any longer, I might have insulted somebody. George Kane was in no position to insult *anybody*.

I reached out and switched the set on, but kept the sound turned down. Yegods, Nelson Eddy and Jeanette Macdonald singing at each other's foreheads, with a mountain in the background. Such innocence, confidence, craftsmanship! Beautiful. If only I'd got off the ground twenty years earlier, I might have been working for Metro in its heyday, turning out great old movies. With Myrna Loy and Jean Harlow and Clark Gable ... The King ... Louis B. Mayer—now there was a man. Would have appreciated George Kane's qualities ... could have got along with him, too ... Many fine directors managed to get along with old Louis B ... My boy, he'd say, you're the only director on this lot I can rely on. Groom me to step into Irving Thalberg's shoes. I'd supervise five or six fine old movies every year. With Garbo and Groucho Marx and Robert Taylor and Karen Morley. I'd even have a shot at smuggling Orson Welles past the customs, make Louis B. *like* Orson. You've got that boy all wrong, L.B., Orson is O.K., wants to make good, clean family movies. Take *The Magnificent Ambersons*. A family picture, L.B. Did that boy toss Dolores Costello down the staircase? He did not. Ate his aunt's strawberry shortcake, every last crumb. A clean picture. And today I'd be sitting pretty on some ranch in Arizona, and Truffaut would fly in and interview me for a book, and they'd be revering me in *Cahiers du Cinema* as a bloody *auteur* ...

'Hindemith ...'

'I'll let you ditch Hindemith if you'll let me dump Rachmaninoff.'

'Make it Glazunov, baby, and you've got yourself a deal ...'

96

'Er, whatsisname . . .'

Jeanette Macdonald was being helped onto a horse by Nelson Eddy. Maybe I should enrol Leonore in a riding school. According to Tetheridge, the more settled she was, the less of a chance Linda had of getting her back. Was that the telephone? Was I pissed? Leonore adored horses. One of the reasons Linda had wanted to move to that £23,000 house in Kew was that it had a good riding school round the corner. Oh, she'd found some fancy reasons for moving house. Logical, irrefutable reasons. Linda's logic was altogether in fine trim when we came back to live in England, and I started to direct for the Network.

For a start, it was a logical proposition that I was a sick man. A husband v ho screwed librarians while his bereaved wife lay in hospital, who made *assignations* a few hours after the death of his first-born, was in need of treatment. If I was serious in my desire to save our marriage, the very least thing I could do was to place myself in the hands of a good psychiatrist. Since I had done even worse things than Linda imagined, I fell in with her plans. She even found the psychiatrist for me, and made the appointment, and in a further effort to placate her I lay back and confessed my sins.

Understanding soul, the old guy explained that it was quite normal for a man to want to fertilise every woman he met. He had similar inclinations himself. Unfortunately society wasn't organised to accommodate such prodigality, and what one did, one eschewed opportunity. Yegods, as if Dracula hadn't eschewed six thousand god-damned opportunities in his time! The psychiatrist then asked me how old I was, suggested that I might now be past the age of sowing my wild oats. He had talked to Linda, he said. Provided I was willing to turn over a new leaf, she would be a good wife to me, and try for another child. Then he asked about my parents. How did I feel about their death in the holocaust? I said I felt badly, didn't want to be reminded. When he realised that I had no intention of reeling off traumatic events, and couldn't fit deep analysis into my rehearsal schedule, he switched channels, told me about this idea he had for a series on TV about psychiatry. Perhaps we could collaborate. What with his special knowledge, and me having the 'in' with the powers that be . . .

'So like who was Bach? A hack, man, who kept the system going. J.S. was strictly commercial . . .'

'Aw, Dan, that cat wasn't pounding out those forty-eight Preludes and Fugues for bread.'

Only went twice to the psychiatrist. He was more excited about setting up his TV series than coming to terms with my labyrinthine psyche. Linda, her critical hackles roused by my reports, though the man should be reported to the British Medical Association for unprofessional conduct. (She was beginning to lose her sense of humour.) However, the psychiatrist wasn't all that useless because Linda consented, as she put it, to resume conjugal relations. And, in the fullness of time, became pregnant again.

Both of us were determined that there should be no foul-up this time. We moved house again. Linda engaged an old Nanny. Then she invited her ageing sister to stay with us. She was penniless by now and needed financial support. Like Linda, Elspeth enjoyed breakfast in bed. Linda pointed out that since I *liked* getting up early, it was petty to make breakfast for herself and leave out poor Elspeth. My responses were automatic by now. Every morning, before leaving for rehearsal, I carried one breakfast tray up to Linda, another to sister Elspeth.

Leonore was born without a hitch. I was dotty about her. We moved house yet again, required a lot of rooms, what with Elspeth and Nanny staying on, and Linda needing a bedroom of her own. She was running quite an establishment by now. I began to feel like a paying guest in my own house, and not a very welcome one at that.

Elspeth and Nanny were both devoted to Linda, tolerated me as an eccentric who mustn't be allowed to get out of hand.

The fact that sometimes I came home as late as nine o'clock (I rehearsed until seven) and wanted to eat, was suffered with barely concealed impatience. I'd spend my evenings with a tray of cold cuts on my knees, watching the telly, surrounded by three hostile females.

I didn't take this lying down all the time, once even dared to bring up the question of Elspeth's continued presence in our midst.

'I can't really expect you to feel sorry for a poor deserted woman, can I?' Linda bounced back. 'No doubt you sympathise with the husband.'

That, as far as Linda was concerned, was the end of the debate.

I stopped bringing people home, ashamed of nesting among all those disapproving women. Did invite Jack Martinsell once, though, and suggested to Linda that sister Elspeth might like to dine with Nanny beforehand, then get lost. When I came home that evening, Elspeth and the Nanny were glumly laying the dinner table.

'Don't worry,' Elspeth remarked. 'We know we've been banished to the kitchen. We know we're not wanted.'

In her turn, Linda began to complain that I was ostracising her from my social life. Yegods, I no longer *had* a social life! At week-ends I spent all available time with Leonore. In the evenings, I fled to my bedroom early to escape Elspeth's snores. She had a habit of falling asleep in front of the box, but refused to admit this. Her bedtime was midnight, saw no reason for going upstairs before.

Although the house was full of females, I could no longer get anyone to wash a shirt or even sew a button on for me. Watching me one evening, struggling with needle and cotton, Linda looked up from behind her large magazine.

'Are you trying to score a point?'

No, I told her, I was sewing on a button.

'You don't have to, you know,' she said. 'I'm perfectly capable of sewing on a button.'

'Why haven't you done it then? I did ask you.'

'I don't propose to leap to attention the moment you give an order,' she said. 'What's the rush?'

I came to two conclusions. One, Linda's life was now dedicated to paying me back for the sins of Dracula. Two, I deserved her treatment.

Whenever I pulled myself together sufficiently to make a complaint, she replied that I was hardly in a position to take exception to her behaviour. If I didn't like it, why didn't I leave? I would do so sooner or later, just as Elspeth's husband had done. I might as well get it over with while she, Linda, was still young enough to start a new life.

Need I add that if it hadn't been for Leonore I should have followed Linda's advice long before that night flight to Nice. The conjugal bridge was rotting at both ends, crying out for my kind of arson. I started taking Leonore to watch Chelsea on Saturday afternoons. Linda put a stop to that when Leonore went down with 'flu. The ladies of the house were unanimous in their opinion that Leonore had caught the bug at the football match. For a while I stopped going to soccer games altogether. Appeasement had become automatic.

I became aware that my domestic defeats were affecting my work. I turned down directing single plays, and volunteered for lousy series, because they offered opportunities for location shooting and brief escapes from Linda and her companions. This was not lost on Linda, who expressed her conviction that I was allowing my career to go down the drain. To the child she said:

'Daddy doesn't seem to like it much at home these days, does he?'

It's a well-known aspect of the placation syndrome that

the more hurtful the attack, the more desperate the attempt to appease the aggressor. One night, before going off on location, I went to Linda's bedroom, and overcoming distaste, tried to screw her.

She wasn't fooled. What's the point, she wanted to know? I'd never given her an orgasm in sixteen years of marriage. My passion was spent on teenage librarians, was it not? I protested that I had been faithful to her for years. She countered that she had no proof of this. I'd lied to her before, hadn't I? If I had stopped chasing librarians, it was probably because a) they resisted me and b) I was impotent.

She had a point there. Dracula had certainly lost the knack. Away from Leonore, I began to dislike myself a great deal. I had mislaid the courage, if not the taste, for unpremeditated sexual combat. I was even afraid to tease, and stop at the brink. I'd become a jerk. I caught myself touching up young actresses under the guise of paternal affection. I laid hands on thighs in cinemas. I nudged breasts in trains. I attended inefficient lesbian exhibitions in Soho. I obtained pornography and masturbated. In provincial hotels, I offered cigarettes to Irish chambermaids, moved up behind them when they bent down to make my bed. Once you become one of the sexually underprivileged, it doesn't take long to accustom yourself to the habits and manners of the slum. After one taping session, a drunken actor introduced me to an experienced call girl, and I let her go down on me in her flat. Once and never again. She was expensive and I liked her. My guilt vis-à-vis Linda's governessy image was by now so deeply engrained that I resisted anything that might offer me genuine pleasure or release. Linda, of course, guessed my condition, and saw no harm in referring to it. Making up the laundry one day, she held up one of my bedsheets for my inspection, passed comment on the stains. I wished I were dead.

Quite often now, she voiced rhetorical threats to leave

me. Leonore needed to be taken out of my evil orbit. I was a sick man, a most unsuitable influence on a little girl. Evidently I had no wish to effect a cure.

Linda was telling me the truth. I ought to have been grateful to her.

Ironically all this occurred at a time when my professional reputation at the Network was at its peak. Jack Martinsell thought of me as his Best Bet. A new series? Bring on Dependable Old George to direct the pilot. A tricky script? Reliable Old George would smooth out the roughnesses, get the material across allright to the fishmonger's wife in Rochdale.

But away from the studios, and Jack's approval, I fell apart. Headaches attacked me the moment I walked through my front door. As soon as Leonore was tucked up in bed, I'd swill down a couple of Scotches and, ostensibly watching TV surrounded by females, find myself fighting for breath. In such an atmosphere I was not surprised that the new set of pets, that came with every new house, died on Linda like flies. Often wished I could join those poor sodding animals. Listening to Elspeth snoring, my head pounding, my breath coming in gasps, gripped by despair, I was neither able to concentrate on the screen, nor gather the necessary energy to drag myself to my bedroom. Paralysis.

All these miseries I parcelled up in my mind, labelling the package The Dreaded Eight O'clock Blues. What kept me going was the fantasy of emulating Dick's escape. I'd just sit there, dreaming up reasons for my next visit to the Villa Rameau, to draw strength from Dick's evident liberation.

'That turgid *Ring*. All twenty-nine hours of it. Hitler loved Wagner.'

'Loved *The Merry Widow*, too.'

'Right. Put down *The Merry Widow*. Who needs her?'

I didn't imagine that Linda's condition was much healthier than my own. By now, her conversation was reduced to making financial demands, voicing general disapproval, registering specific complaint. Leonore was the good child. I was the bad one. Dick advised me to bring it all into the open, have it out with Linda once and for all, force the issue. I tried once or twice, but my protests emerged as moans of self-pity.

'You know what you've done, don't you?' I told her one evening, coming home more pissed than usual, 'you've put me in a sexual concentration camp.'

'What are you accusing me of now?' she replied icily. 'Don't stop you from making love to me, do I?'

'You said you hated it . . .'

'I dare say I lack the attractions of teenage librarians,' she countered.

'That was seven years ago, Linda, for Christ's sake . . .'

'How does that make your conduct less disloyal, George? That girl knew me. I often took books out of that library . . .'

As usual when I started launching a hesitant attack, I ended up abjectly offering peace tokens. Told her I wouldn't object if she took a lover. No doubt my motives were impure. Maybe I hoped that by giving her more freedom, I would secure some licence for myself. Linda certainly wasn't slow to place that interpretation on my proposal. She cried, then started calling me names. I'd offered her the greatest insult of which a husband was capable. But a month later our doctor told me that Linda was dreadfully run down and needed a holiday. I paid for a fortnight in Amalfi. She said she didn't really want to go. Why was I so anxious to get rid of her? Was there another teenage librarian in the offing? But she went, and stayed away six weeks, while I coped with Leonore and the two women.

A new phase began. Linda absented herself from home with increasing regularity. She was making new friends, she explained. I didn't bother to enquire too closely into her activities. When she was away, the Dreaded Eight

O'clock Blues eased considerably. In desperation, I started an affair with Jack Martinsell's married secretary. Had her once in my car, twice in the open air. A rushed, sorry thing it was, but it restored my confidence a little. Going through my wallet, as had become her custom, Linda found a half used packet of contraceptives. For three months, she refused to cook for me. Daddy, she told Leonore, had been naughty, and naughty people needed to be punished, even if you loved them. She relied on me not to confuse the child's mind by explanations or counter-accusations. Elspeth and the Nanny took their cue from Linda, treated me like a greedy boy caught at the jam jars, sent me once more to Coventry.

I didn't know it then, but the horror movie was grinding to its climax. Linda clearly had problems of her own. The Nanny was suddenly fired, departed in a huff. I guessed the reason. While I was at the studio, and Elspeth enjoyed a matinée, Linda had entertained one of her new friends at home. Nanny had caught her in a compromising situation.

Linda's social activity increased. She looked all the better for it. Her slowness became less pronounced. I heard her singing in her bath. She spent a great deal of time at hairdressers, went in for a rigorous course of slimming, even bought herself a face-lift. She also spent a lot of my money on swinging new clothes. At week-ends she let me look after Leonore, while she and sister Elspeth went off on undisclosed errands. No doubt she took Elspeth along to reassure her that what she was doing was innocent. Linda could not bear to appear anything but saintly in her sister's eyes.

After the Nanny's departure, Leonore drew still closer to me. I thought I could detect light at the end of the tunnel. Now was the time Linda and I might have sat down together to work out the terms of an amicable divorce. Instead she said she wanted to move again. I bought her a £23,000 house in Kew.

When we went away for that climactic summer holiday at the Villa Rameau, Linda seemed to be winning all along the line. She had a new house, maybe a lover or two, and a castrated husband hellbent on appeasement. She hadn't reckoned on Dick, though. To amuse himself, he got us to play the Truth Game. Pissed, we both admitted in turn that our marriage was a bloody farce. The bandages were ripped off, our wounds exposed. Once articulated in front of witnesses, the sham had no chance of continuing. I made my plans. If Melud pleases, the marriage had finally and irrevocably broken down.

Coiled in a foetal position on the sofa, watching Nelson Eddy ride into the sunset with Jeanette MacDonald, I hadn't heard Marion come into the room.

I smelled alcohol on her breath as she stretched out beside me, sighing a little girl sigh. The fine down on her cheek touched my face. Allo-Allo, I thought, *Watch it.*

'Oh, George,' she sighed again.

I lay quite still.

'I'm going to cry,' she said. 'I don't know why.'

'*All sensitive old pooves who write chains of boring novels about sensitive old pooves walking down the Old Brompton Road.*'

Thank God, I thought: Joe was still playing.

'George?'

'Yes, Marion.'

'I feel sickly. Why am I crying, George?'

I touched her cheek. Wet. Not just a stage-cry. The real thing.

'Have a cup of tea, Marion.'

'Don't want a cup of tea. That *bitch.*'

'What bitch?'

'George?'

'Yes, Marion?'

'I think I want a cuddle, George.'

One leg was laid across mine.

'There are times, George, when one craves a friendly arm to reach out for one . . .'

'Yes, Marion?'

'No, don't do that. Just scratch my back. Nothing sexual.'

She was straining her loins against me. I registered an erection.

'George?'

'Yes, Marion?'

'George, you don't really know me at all . . .'

I would be able to draw back, before it got out of hand. She was drunk: I was in control. No problem.

'George, are you my friend?'

'Yes, Marion, I'm your friend.'

'Do you find me attractive?'

'Yes, Marion.'

'Physically or spiritually?'

'Both, Marion.'

'But you think I'm shallow, don't you, George?'

'Shallow? No, not at all . . .'

'Yes, you do. Everybody does. No, George.'

'Hmmmmmmm?'

'George, I'm homosexual. There, I've told you.'

'Just move your . . . there . . .'

'It's true, George.' She cried another tear. 'I'm a bloody Les. I'm as dykey as old hell.'

'Yes, Marion.'

'You think I'm kidding, don't you? Or just stoned out of my mind . . .'

Her soft lips were very close, teasing my cheek.

'I'm telling you the truth, George, because you're my friend. I'm telling you a profound truth about myself.'

'Your leg. Just move it a little over to . . .'

'She actually kissed me, George. In the bathroom. And I liked it. Cara. Asked me to go back to her pad.'

'Just because she's a dyke, doesn't make *you* one, Marion . . .'

'No, but I *liked* it, I tell you . . . her hands all over me . . .'

Poor old Fred Flake, I thought.

'George, put your hand there . . . yes, there. Higher. That's nice.'

'Thought you said you were a dyke.'

'I don't know what I am. You tell me, George. What am I?'

'Like this?'

'I'm lost . . . I'm so lost, George. Still a bit higher up . . .'

'There?'

'. . . Yes . . . gently, not so hard, gently.'

Her own hand was becoming active, too.

'I'm probably a bit AC-DC, George . . . that's it . . . that's it . . .'

'Does Joe know?'

'What? About Cara? No, of course not . . . yes, like that. That's perfect, George.'

Oh dear God, I thought. Tomorrow, we'll have to move again. Oh Leonore, oh hell. Start packing, Dracula. Burn that bridge.

The doorbell rang.

'*Marion?*' (Joe's voice).

'It's allright, darling. I'll go.'

'*What are you doing in there, dear?*'

'I'm looking after George, darling. He's feeling a bit sickly.' Then, *sotto voce*, to me: 'Thank you for letting me talk to you so frankly, George. Oh George, I was feeling so mixed up. Do up your fly, darling.'

She was gone. David Frost was frowning at the Archbishop of Canterbury. I turned up the sound. David Frost was asking the Archbishop of Canterbury to prove the existence of God. I turned the sound down. The Archbishop of Canterbury smiled. I got up and shambled into the living room, acting sickly. Joe, face flushed, glasses steamed up, was holding the floor with a denunciation of the *Observer*'s literary editor. The others looked bored.

'Feelin' uptight, man?' Solicitude from a greenshirt. 'Need a joint?'

'George, er ...'

I turned. Marion was standing in the doorway, her face very pale. She wasn't acting. Behind her I discerned the outline of a woman in a fur coat. Looked like Linda for a moment. I started to tremble.

'Excuse me.'

Linda politely brushed Marion aside. She wore the mink I have given her two Christmases ago.

'Yes?' I asked distantly, aware that the party guests were held spellbound by the unannounced cabaret.

'Why don't we all go and talk next door?' Marion suggested helpfully.

'I take it you are Mrs. Leeds,' Linda stated.

'Yes, I am,' Marion agreed, desperately conjuring up hostessy warmth. 'I'm so glad to meet you, Linda. George has told us so much ...'

'Yes, I'm sure he has ...'

Foxy Linda. I felt like a trapped rabbit. We all trundled off into the television room. Marion switched on a lamp.

'May I offer you something to drink, Mrs ... er ... Linda ...?'

'I want to see my daughter, if you have no objection.'

Marion looked at me, I looked at my feet.

'Your fly,' Marion hissed, trying to mask me.

I pulled at my zip. If she smiles, I thought, I still love her. I looked up. Linda didn't smile.

'She's such a lovely little girl, so bright for her age,' Marion said, brushing a strain of hair from her forehead.

'I'm perfectly aware of my daughter's qualities, Mrs. Leeds. Perhaps you could arrange for me to see her now.'

Cut, I thought. Cut. Cut. Cut. *Cut.*

Marion was guiding Linda out of the room. I switched off the television set, and sat down on the sofa, knees quivering. Now they're all going to find out I'm not circumcised. Dick's right. She's destroyed me. I clutched my head.

Suddenly Linda and Marion were back. Linda was smiling. An inscrutable, foxy smile. I got up, stood to attention.

'She's allright, isn't she? In fine shape, love.'

'I have my car outside...'

My car.

'I propose to get Leonore dressed, and take her home, George.'

'That's not possible...'

'Not possible?'

'Look,' Marion proposed. 'Why don't we all sit down and have a drink and talk this over? I'll get Joe ... He's very good at this sort of ... and your little girl really is in good hands...'

'So I see.'

Marion adjusted her belt.

'Linda,' I heard myself say in a strangled voice. 'You take Leonore out of this house over my dead body. My-dead-body.'

'I see. Well, at least we know where we stand now.'

She turned briskly. Marion saw her to the front door. I fumbled for a cigarette and lit up. Presently I heard the engine of a car being started. Somebody closed the front-door. The car drove away. I hurried up to our bedroom to look at Leonore. She was fast asleep, breathing evenly. I tore my clothes off and crept between the sheets, drawing all the bed-clothes over my head.

Safe.

Next morning Tetheridge telephoned. He had just accepted a summons from Linda's solicitors. She was asking the court to order me to return Leonore forthwith. A great legal rigmarole followed, of which I did not understand one word, though the general drift was clear enough. Tetheridge had also been served with Linda's petition, asking for a divorce on the grounds of my adultery. With seventeen women. Tetheridge sounded quite cheerful.

'An opening shot,' he explained.

'Shouldn't we have fired ours first?' I asked, then cleared my throat.

'Not necessarily.'

'So what do we do now?'

'I shall need your instructions,' Tetheridge advised.

Joe couldn't understand why I wanted to leave in such a hurry. Just because Linda had turned up? Why that very day? Shouldn't I consult Tetheridge?

Yegods, there wasn't time. There just wasn't time. Mr. Roosevelt wouldn't permit it. *Angstpsychose*. All day long, Marion's treachery-inspiring *Femme* fragrance clung to me, compounded with the sweat of my own fear. Keep Leonore happy, keep her occupied. If I couldn't convince Melud that Leonore was a happy little girl, my goose was cooked.

Burn that bridge.

Joe gave me a couple of his green-black Libriums to help me get through the day. I borrowed his Renault, determined to find a new home by nightfall. Thirtyish Warner Bros. montage: Sleek agents and incompetent agents. Parking tickets and foul tempers. Slummy hell holes and vast luxury flats. Quick Scotches and curling pub sandwiches. To quote from the superb *Gold Diggers of 1935*, a wild duck chase. Mediocre television director found dead with exhaustion in fog-bound Hampstead alley. Wipe.

It had to be Hampstead, because Leonore mustn't be

made to change schools yet again. She had to be *settled*. One blessing : I didn't have to face Marion in the morning. She was out, acting in a commercial recommending a vaginal deodorant. Joe called a few estate agents on my behalf. He couldn't work anyway, he told me. Hated Marion doing commercials. How could anybody take a writer seriously when they knew his wife was flogging vaginal deodorants?

During the afternoon I called Joe from a public telephone booth, asking him to pick up Leonore from school. Joe agreed. Had to collect Barry anyway. I apologised for monopolising his car and his time. Not to worry, Joe said. Poor bastard, I thought, deserves better than Marion. (Had she told him anything?) Onwards...

By five-thirty, I had found our new home : a furnished garden flat, five minutes' walk from the Leeds' maisonette. Thirty guineas a week, a quarter's rent in advance, and a deposit of £200 against future service bills and possible damage. *The child*. The landlady lived alone on the first floor, had specified No Children. Finicky old dear, widow of an officer killed On Her Majesty's Service. A title too : Lady Whitestone. We argued about *the child*. I had rented our own house to some Arabs. The mother was undergoing treatment for dypsomania. Personal Tragedy. Lady Whitestone sympathised, accepted my cheque.

By six-thirty, Leonore and I were packing.

I'd called Tetheridge, advising him about my plans. He sounded dubious. Would have to inform The Other Side about the change. Had I thought of the cost? I would have to install a housekeeper. My actions must not be open to misinterpretation. The move had the appearance of unpremeditated flight. He wished I had seen fit to consult him first.

There you are, Joe said, listening on the extension, told you so.

Marion came back from doing her commercial, bright-eyed and elated. She had tried the product during the lunch-break. It was super. She promised Joe she wouldn't do any more commercials, went into the kitchen to fill a carrier bag with packets of frozen food and tins of soup, kissed me chastely, locked herself into the bathroom to make calls. Leonore absconded to the nursery and stole a drawerful of Barry's comics.

Joe was depressed. Marion really liked me, I was informed. He knew she *talked* to me. Had she mentioned anything the night before, anything he ought to know about? Not that he was asking me to betray a confidence, of course, but Marion showed symptoms of going off the rails again. What did I think was the matter with her?

Leonore came into the room with her stolen comics wrapped in old newspapers. I went on packing. There had been a time, Joe said, when Marion had tended to behave in a rather unstable manner. All that had changed after Barry was born, of course, but now he could sense the old restlessness coming back. Leonore listened, open-mouthed.

'Marriage is no picnic,' Joe went on, 'even a happy marriage like mine.'

'Yes, Joe.'

'Did she say anything about leaving me?'

'Leonore, get that bottle of Ribena from the kitchen.'

'I know she loves me, but she's got those two little devils perched on her shoulders. Did she talk to you about her two little devils?'

'No, Joe. Never mentioned any little devils. Ribena, love, I told you to get Leonore from the kitchen. I mean . . .'

'I'll come round to you for chats one evening, George.'

'Yes, Joe, do that.'

'She's a marvellous wife, George. Totally incapable of disloyalty, know what I mean?'

By seven-thirty, Leonore and I were installed in the garden flat. I heated some soup, fried four beefburgers. Leonore was excited about the garden. Wasn't it super,

I told her, all the fun we were having, one lovely holiday after another.

We unpacked. Leonore said she wasn't a bit tired. We played Monopoly. She yawned. I touched her forehead. *Hot*. I realised I didn't possess a thermometer, rushed upstairs to borrow one from Lady Whitestone. She was playing bridge with three zombies, but obliged. (*Sunset Boulevard*, Paramount, 1950.) I took Leonore's temperature. Normal. I took my own. Nearly a hundred. Ye-gods, if I went down with 'flu now . . .

Don't give up, George, you've got a child in your care. *Wish I were dead*.

No, George, don't die, not yet. You've taken a stand at last, you're *intact*, got everything to live for.

Took six aspirins, went on playing Monopoly. My little love, I love you. Your turn. Committed.

'Mummy? I mean Daddy. I dreamt about Mummy last night.'

'Did you darling? You threw a five. Move the Boot.'

'I dreamt she came and tucked me in and left me a Mars bar.'

'Well, actually, love, what happened, Mummy did come and visit us at Joe's last night. You were fast asleep . . .'

'But there wasn't a Mars bar there this morning . . .'

'That's the bit you must have dreamt. There. I'm on my own property. Roll dem dice, love.'

'Mummy *might* have woken me up.'

'Don't you want Regent Street?'

'No, too expensive. She woke *you*, didn't she?'

'I wasn't asleep.'

'Not fair. How is Lucy? She *is* having kittens, isn't she?'

'Mummy isn't sure yet.'

'Daddy, would you like to marry Marion?'

'Marion is married to Joe. There. Six. Move your Boot, there's a love.'

'I liked Marion. Who's going to look after me now?'

'I am. Later we'll get a nice Nanny.'

'Why couldn't we have stayed at Marion's? If Joe dies, will you marry Marion?'

'Joe isn't going to die, and I'm married to Mummy.'

'Whom do you like better? Janine or Marion?'

'Marion.'

'Me, too. She's more cuddly, isn't she? I like Janine, but she's not cuddly.'

'Electricity Works. I've got that already.'

'Daddy, do you mind if we finish this game tomorrow?'

'Why, aren't you well?'

'I'm a bit tired. You're *always* wanting me to play Monopoly.'

We went to inspect Leonore's new bedroom. She helped me make up the bed. I asked her to get washed. There weren't any towels. I gave her an old shirt of mine to dry herself on. Thirty guineas a week, I thought. Yegods.

'Will Barry mind that I pinched his comics?'

'I'll buy him some new ones, love. Don't you worry about it. Go to sleep.'

I kissed her goodnight, switched off the light. My body felt ravaged. 'Flu? Typhoid? Among Leonore's booty of comics, I found a *Radio Times* and a coloured Sunday Supplement. I settled down to read, drank hot Ribena, swallowed aspirins.

I read the *Radio Times* from cover to cover. Every other name I recognised, every third name belonged to somebody I knew personally. I investigated all the known names for possible exploitation. There had to be *somebody*, apart from Marion and Joe, who could help me in my predicament.

Leonore came back into the room, complained she couldn't sleep.

'What are you doing?'

'Casting, love, casting.'

'For a play?'

'Yes, love.'

'Funny or sad?'

'Both.'

'Use Marion, she's pretty.'

I sent her back to bed with an orange baby aspirin. Tomorrow, I promised, we'll hire a television set. I thought of writing out a list : Leonore's qualities. Underlining those which resembled mine.

She *was* like me. That's why I had taken her. Or was my choice as compulsive as the selection of any mate? Not possible. A *rational* decision.

My temperature was still rising. I could feel it. I started to read through the Colour Supplement, found a trailer, promising publication of Roger Arnold's photographs of Dick Bligh.

Rock Bottom. I got up to call Dick. At length I got through.

'You've gone raving mad,' was his initial reaction to my news.

I muttered something about emotional commitment.

'Get on with your work, you fucking idiot.'

'Haven't got a job.'

'Well, get one. You'll lose the kid anyway.'

Going to fight, I told him.

'You're screwing up your life, and the kid's as well. How much rent are you paying?'

I told him.

'Insane. Got a spare room for me?'

'Why?'

'Janine's getting on my tits, can't work. Roger Arnold sends you his love.'

'Bugger him.'

'He likes you, silly cunt.'

He sounded lonely, didn't seem to want to get off the telephone. Such gratification as I experienced through our courtly exchange was diminished by the thought of what the call was costing me.

Dick was asking why I had left Joe and Marion in such

a hurry. Had Joe caught me fiddling with Marion?

'Crude sod,' I remonstrated. 'Nothing like that. I'm ill. Got 'flu.'

Someone cut us off. Just as well. I put down the receiver, ambled out into the garden.

The tablets were at last beginning to work on my metabolism. I filled my lungs with draughts of November Hampstead air. Elation. The night was humming with promise. The London sky shimmered, a beautiful, all-pervading orange glow. So I faced financial ruin! So I would have to explain adultery with seventeen women! So they were threatening to take Leonore away from me! After all those years in prison I was finally free. On my own. Unassailable. Intact. Life was beautiful. An overflowing bowl of Ripe old Cherries. Directed by Vincente Minnelli. In his heyday.

I turned and walked back into the house. Tomorrow, I promised myself, I'll advertise for a Nanny. An old one. A really plain one. A bag.

Three

On Saturday mornings, Leonore and I did the rough housework. She dusted. I hoovered. She washed. I dried. It worked. Dick was wrong; Linda had *not* got my balls.

Produced by George the Gambler, directed by George the Creep, my life was galvanised by purpose, pregnant with meaning. Importing my studio methods, I kept meticulous charts and timetables, divided my week into days, my day into hours, each with a character of its own, each demanding a specific performance. Gambler and Creep in harness, we coped.

After breakfast, I took Leonore to her new riding school, then hurried home to interview prospective Nannies.

First came an eager German *au pair* from Regensburg, long black hair, thoroughly toothbrushed smile, miniskirt up to her elbows. She was very good viss children, she assured me, did not mind at all being ze only voman in ze house. She had left her present place of employment in Golders Green, because she just could not get on viss ze people. They were Chews, you know. Self-righteously she crossed her long legs, adding that she could start fenever I vished. Faint with lust, I thought: I bet you could, you anti-semitic, Bavarian bitch. Dracula might have pounced, if the doorbell hadn't rung, forcing me to get rid of her and admit the second applicant: Mrs. MacWhirter, sixty if she was a day, Scots by over-emphatic characterisation, expensive but experienced, and smelling of parsley. Her current employers were emigrating to Australia. She produced illegible, handwritten references, owned up to being a Vegetarian. Just what the lawyer ordered, I told myself, brain still wrestling with images of anti-semitic Bavarian thighs wrapped around my neck. Let me sit on you, Mr. Kane, it is better zat vay.

I showed the Scottish nanny a photograph of Leonore. She approved. I lied a little about the absent mother, we made a deal. She inspected her bedroom, promised to join us in a week's time. Before leaving she delivered a homily about the evils of alcohol.

I showed her out, and spent five minutes regretting not having asked for the Bavarian nymph's telephone number. I went out to collect Leonore from her riding school. She looked pink-cheeked and content. I whisked her by taxi to the Toy Fair at Harrods. By the time the store closed, I had bought her a load of clothes she didn't really need, and I certainly couldn't afford. Tetheridge's idea: If Linda's neglect was to be established, we should show vouchers to prove that I had found it necessary to restock the child's wardrobe.

Tetheridge had decided to play for time. The longer I could hold on to Leonore, the more the Court would incline to regard the present situation as the *status quo*. Joe, Marion, and Dick were swearing affidavits to say that I was the best father in the world, and that, under my supervision, Leonore was glowing with health and happinesss. Soon, Tetheridge threatened, we would have to sit down together and compose an Answer to Linda's Petition involving me with seventeen women.

Yegods, how had Linda got hold of all those names? She must have spent days and nights examining old diaries of mine. Some of the names she'd managed to dredge up from the past I could no longer recall. Was Linda's fantasy conjuring up seventeen middle-aged Mums (grandmothers by now, I shouldn't wonder) rolling up to Court for the prurient delight of *News of the World* readers?

Melud, is the Respondent seriously asking us to believe that his associations with these seventeen women were of an entirely innocent nature? It would appear, Melud, that my client was at this time given to the aberration of impersonating Dracula, a character of fiction. If Melud pleases, the Petitioner finds difficulty in accepting my learned colleague's somewhat unusual interpretation of these associations...

Tetheridge remained reasonably optimistic. Seventeen women? Hopeful shot in the dark. It should not be difficult to prove that subsequent to my, er, adventures with these ladies, conjugal relations had been resumed, in which case my alleged offences could be said to have been *condoned*. Meanwhile, Tetheridge felt, we should take Counsel's opinion. (He was to experience this feeling frequently; every time it overcame him, it cost me forty guineas.)

'Daddy?'

'What?'

'What are we doing this afternoon?'

'What would you like to do?'

'You decide.'

We were lunching in a little restaurant in Knightsbridge. The afternoon stretched ahead, grey and long. I was wildly turning over pages of *What's On In London*. Not looking for rare old horror films either, as had once been my wont.

What to do? Abbey Treasures. Chelsea Pottery. Mill Hill Canine Society Open Show. Late Apple and Pear Competition in Greycoat Street, S.W.1. Victoria and Albert Museum: 18th Century English Furniture. Natural History Museum: Water Insects. Too wet for the zoo, too late for the Changing of the Guards. Horse of the Year? No, that had taken place the week before. Toy Museum? Closed on Saturday afternoons.

The day had to be got through somehow.

'Got a brilliant idea,' I chirped idiotically. 'If we hurry up, we can still make it to a soccer match, love. Queens Park Rangers are at home.'

'Oh, Daddy, not in this awful weather.'

No? Right. What then? The movies? No, I couldn't

keep dragging the child to the movies. If Melud pleases, it would appear from the evidence before us that, while under the Respondent's care and control, this poor child's daily life approximated the *modus vivendi* of a critic of the Kinema. No doubt Melud will concur with our contention that stuffy, germ-infested Kinemas do not constitute the most congenial background for a girl of tender years...

'How about the dinosaurs, love? They've got those lovely skeletons at ...'

'Oh, Daddy, I've seen those rotten old dinosaurs a thousand times. Why can't we just spend a cosy afternoon at home? I'll try on my new clothes. And we can watch *Dr. Who*.'

At home, she'd said. *At home.* I love you, daughter.

Was she positive she didn't want to do something *active*?

She was positive. She was quite exhausted, she said. Didn't have a moment to call her own.

I watched her shovelling chop, mashed potato, and peas into her rather large mouth. *My* mouth. Linda had a rather pinched mouth. As mouths go.

'Do stop it, Daddy ...'

'Stop what?'

'Making that fish face at me.'

'Fish face?'

'Whenever I'm eating, you open and shut your mouth like a fish.'

'I don't!'

'Every time I put a bit of food in my mouth, you open *your* mouth as well. Like this. Like a fish.'

'I'm not doing anything of the sort, Leonore.'

'You are, too.'

I checked. I was, too. Every time she lifted her fork to her mouth, my own lips kept time with her movements. Significant. Over-anxious identification. Had to stop.

Still uneasy, I managed to persuade her to stop by the

local Adventure Playground on the way home. Two and a half hours of daylight to go: the child needed fresh air and exercise. Wasn't going to be caught napping by some idiot in a Gluck wig.

We travelled by bus. Silently I raged at myself for spending a fortune on Harrods clothes, then being too mean to take a taxi. Not that she seemed to mind. We sat upstairs, counting Butchers all the way to Hampstead Heath. I guessed twenty butchers, Leonore guessed twelve. In the end we counted fourteen butchers, so Leonore won, thank God. Meanwhile my mind was grinding away to find the causes of my monumental meanness. Maybe it was Linda's Trick of the Week, as told to Caligari Flake.

'They want you to repay the £8,000 you borrowed from the company,' he'd told me on the telephone. He had to be joking. I'd borrowed that money from *my own company*...

'Well, you may think of it as your own company, friend, but the directors are Mrs. Kane and her sister ...'

'But that was just a tax-dodge. All the money in that company is my own hard-earned cash...'

'Try telling that to the Inspector of Inland Revenue, friend...'

'But listen, hold it, I borrowed the money from my company to buy Linda that house in Kew...'

'The purpose of the loan cuts no ice, friend. You borrowed the money and now they want it back...'

It just didn't bear thinking about. She'd end up with the house *and* the money, no wait—she'd get the money twice over, *and* ...

Extortion. Blackmail. They were hoping I'd become so desperate, I'd hand Leonore back to them on a plate, if only to avoid bankruptcy.

As for my tax situation, Falke added, now that he'd had time to study it properly, here was a tangled web indeed. Even if my last two years' earnings were taken in conjunction, Caligari couldn't offer much hope that . . .

'Thirteen!'

'Where? What?'

'You missed that one. A Scanlon's. You can't afford to miss *any*, Daddy. You said twenty, remember?'

'Right. Right. Do stop digging your elbows into me, love.'

By the time we arrived at the Adventure Playground, they'd switched on the street lamps. I was laden with parcels, my fingers were stiff with cold. Leonore nipped off to the nearest swing to get warm. Give us a push, Daddy!

Place was deserted. Only stray dogs and sex maniacs with kidnapped children frequented fog-bound Adventure Playgrounds on frosty November afternoons. I rested my packages on a roundabout, sat myself down on the swing next to Leonore's, pensively munched a pink marshmallow.

'Come on, Dad, don't be lazy, give us a push.'

Looking up, I observed two huddled figures striding past us in the gloom, a large one and a smaller one, hands linked. Destination See-saw. Even in the half-light, I recognised the larger figure instantly. Wasn't dressed as Mao-Tse-Tung for a change, wore a belted Swiss racoon coat. Ha, I thought, even the bloody in-people have their domestic *zores*. I called out Hey, Dan Wymans stopped dead in his tracks, looking as if he'd been caught soliciting outside Leicester Square public convenience. He strolled over, grinning. We introduced our children. His was a raucous lout of twelve or thereabouts. The kids scowled at each other.

'This is the place, my lovely,' Wymans opened, struggling visibly to retain some shred of with-itness.

'Yep,' I said, 'this is the place, baby.'

'Been shopping then?'

'That's it,' I said, swinging. 'Have a marshmallow.'

'Christmas already,' he muttered, accepting the s
'Christ.'

'You said it, doll.'

Silence.

'Access day,' he finally volunteered, vaguely waving in
the direction of the see-saw. The kids were squatting on
it, see-sawing away. Dan had started skipping about to
keep warm. (Why didn't I have a Swiss racoon coat like
that?) Eventually he sat down on the adjoining swing,
vacated by Leonore. We chatted about Stanley Kubrick
for a while. Finally he said:

'Got to split, man. Meet up some time. O.K.?'

I suppose he meant the White Elephant. Quite a change
of scene. I invited him and the lout to have tea with us. It
would be company for me. He promised to come. Had to
buy himself some shirts first, he said. Darkness was setting
in. I called Leonore. I could make out a faint red blur,
stranded on the high end of the see-saw by the weight of
Dan's lout. She jumped off. The lout jeered.

When we got home, I noticed an old Rover parked across
the road. A man sat smoking at the wheel, reading a newspaper, or rather pretending to read.

Hello again. Noticed him before, reported him to Tetheridge, who agreed that Linda might well be employing
a private enquiry agent to check if I was bringing girls
home. If evidence could be adduced to this effect, Tetheridge warned, the result might be calamitous. I was a re-
formed character. That was my case. And to think that
bloody detective was being paid to watch me with my
own hard-earned cash!

As soon as we got indoors, I switched on all the electric
fires in the flat, then made a cup of tea for Leonore. While
she drank, I avoided her blue eyes.

Afterwards, Leonore unwrapped her new clothes, then
tried them on. We played models and buyers for a while.
That took all of ten minutes. As games went, Leonore

showed great inventiveness, but tired quickly of her own improvisations. Liked to pass on to new adventures, I suppose. We played snap. *Twenty minutes*. Despairingly, I switched on the television set. Obscene wrestling. We searched for crayons, found them under her bed. I commissioned a drawing of the Adventure Playground. To send to Mummy. *Thirty minutes*. (A success.) I realised that Dan Wymans never had the slightest intention to bring his lout to tea. Just as well I hadn't raised Leonore's expectations by telling her.

A familiar knot of pain was forming at the base of my stomach : recurring ache of emptiness, which prevented me from doing anything for myself. Preoccupied with keeping Leonore busy, I couldn't find the energy to read a book, or write a letter, or make out a shopping list. The nagging ache fitted me for one sole function: making myself available to Leonore. Waiting for her to express a wish so that I might try to satisfy it.

While she sat and watched Fanny Cradock prepare a chocolate mousse, I obtained mild relief by stroking her red hair. Linda's hair. Could that ache, that emptiness, presage a revival of the Dreaded Eight o'clock Blues? And to think that to eliminate those Blues I had sacrificed all worldly goods ...

The chocolate mousse was making me feel sick, the pain threatened to spread through my whole system, creating panic. Leonore was complaining of a toothache. I made a note to ask Joe for the name of his dentist. Was my position hopeless and untenable? Should I cut my losses, send Leonore back to her mother, attempt to make some sort of deal for Access? I made a desperate effort to gather my remaining strength. I'd committed myself—here was the one meaningful act of my life. Then, with a sudden onrush of rage, I remembered the detective in his car. I stood up and shook the child. Needed action. Now.

'Come on,' I said, prancing, 'forget TV. Stand up and fight. Go on, put up your fists.'

She liked that. Grimaced and started leaping about, got very red in the face as she pummelled me as hard as she could. I started hitting back, dodging her little fists, landing mock punches on her chest. Sometimes she swooped down and hit me in the crotch. I screamed, she roared with laughter. She imitated my prancing movements, kicked my shins. I squeezed her nose and tripped her. She was playing *The Avengers*. I was playing *Seven Samurai*, Kurosawa, 1954: Now she was rolling about on the floor, struggling, I was tickling her. She kicked me, then tried to bite me. I wanted to weep, turned her body over, smacked her bottom. Hard. This time she did manage to bite my leg. I started to tickle her again.

'Don't,' she yelled. 'I'll wet my pants, Daddy.'

I sent her off to the toilet, sat down, pressed hot palms against my temples, wished I were dead.

The afternoon was saved.

'It's allright, nothing happened,' Leonore announced, bounding back into the room.

I went into the kitchen, fried fishcakes, grated carrots. Screw Dan Wymans *and* his lout, I thought, grating away. Who needs them?

Later it was my turn to go into the bathroom. I ran a hot bath. No sooner had I got into it than she pounded on the door, wanting to be my bath attendant.

'For God's sake,' I remonstrated, 'can't your Daddy have some modicum of privacy? Get off . . .'

'Oh, Daddy.' (Shirley Temple rehearsing behind the door.) 'You always used to let me be your bath tender.'

'Well, you're too old to be my bath tender now.'

'Daddy, *really*! I'm not interested in *that* anymore.'

'What?'

'Don't want to see your Willie.'

Left me in peace, then went back into our sitting-room to catch up with *Dr. Who*. Later I read her to sleep with one of Andersen's fairy-tales.

Alone at last, I collapsed into an arm-chair, gazing at

the switched-off television set. *White Zombie*, Halperin, 1932. Ah, masterpiece. What I would give to see *White Zombie* right now ...

Got up to take off my clothes, swallowed two seconals. The telephone rang. Marion. Would I be interested in directing some commercials? She'd made some super contacts. All the best directors were making commercials. Might tide me over financially. Jack Martinsell hadn't telephoned, had he? I thanked her, did a bit of significant pausing. Not a word about Cara, or about our own sweet interval in the television room. She rambled on. How was darling little Leonore? Was I getting enough to eat? Did I possess a hot water bottle? Had I heard— she'd landed a job in a new TV serial? Super part. If I needed anything, *anything at all,* would I be sure to let her know? Was she calling me from her bathroom? I asked. No, she wasn't. Funny question, darling. Never mind, give my love to Joe. Good-night, George darling. Good-night, Marion darling.

Next morning, Leonore brought me tea in bed. She made very good tea. Gratitude so overwhelmed me that I took her into bed with me for a cuddle. We glanced through the Sunday papers together, eventually got dressed. I took her to Church. Tetheridge had advised it. The child was a baptised Christian, another act of placation on my part. Regular church attendance might impress the Court in my favour. Should I get a voucher from the Vicar, certifying our attendance? No, Tetheridge replied plummily, that would not be necessary.

Leonore contentedly mumbled through her hymns and prayers. I found myself going through the same motions, hoping to assimilate the service through her perception. Every television programme, every movie, every bus ride I was trying to experience through a child's eyes and ears. Identifying with Leonore's imagination to this extent meant that my own regression was inevitable, probably even desirable. Lost all savour for the present, the current of events hurling me back into adolescence, childhood.

The Reverend preached his sermon, my mind adrift among memories of cheap dance halls and odorous armpits, the velvet cover of the divan in Dick's basement, third-class train carriages rattling through the night, the first draughts of hot sweet milky tea, South London pavements encrusted with winter slush, evil-smelling dining rooms, frying tonight, Jean's sticky hands, standing in line for a sixpenny seat at the pictures ...

Anchored. The baroque glories of the Trocadero: four hours of stage-show, double feature, organ recital, community singing, Donald Duck. The Getty in Canterbury Road: mysterious fleapit, 'H' films luridly inviting from red and yellow posters. The Ideal Cinema: cheap and generous, double features changed *twice* a week. Claudette Colbert in *I Cover the Waterfront,* Ronald Colman as Bulldog Drummond, *Desire* with Marlene Dietrich, Gary Cooper as *The Plainsman,* all consumed in comforting darkness. Forbidden Bela Lugosi. Wurlitzer Organ. Two sleepy people with nothing to say. The taste of liquorice. Yearned to see every movie ever made. (Later longed to make every girl ever seen.) Still further back in time, over weed-covered rails, the night train roared. Another mystic ritual: violet jerseys dancing over a gravelly football pitch. Goals without nets. Daddy, give us a push. Did that ritual still take place, even without me? What was the name of that Club that performed in violet jerseys? My father had taken me to the Club secretary, my mother had bought me studded boots, didn't look too Jewish to join, thank God.

Sudden impulse: rush out, find a German newspaper. What *was* the name of that Club? Had been on the tip of my tongue. That time Dick cross-examined me. All those goals I'd scored, all those goals in violet jerseys. Prehistoric secrets ...

They're going to sing again. Get up, my love. If I

allowed my mind to drift back far enough, I might find the way to enter her world. Then she would love me more. In the name of the Father...

Get up, my darling, hymn one hundred and five.

Why aren't you singing, Daddy?

On Mrs. MacWhirter's first afternoon on duty, I hurried out to see Melvyn Douglas in *The Vampire Bat* and Boris Karloff in *The Ape* in a small cinema in Dalston. Then, changing buses several times, I proceeded to the Classic, Tooting, to see Bela Lugosi in *Frankenstein meets the Wolf Man*, and *The Body Snatcher* with Bela Lugosi *and* Boris Karloff.

Fleapit euphoria. Ate my way through two brown paper bags of buns and apples. If Jack Martinsell could see you now, baby. Dependable old George, Winner of the Guild Award. Linda would get me certified. What of it? If I wanted to catch up with Bela Lugosi in Dalston, Tooting and Timbuctoo, chewing buns through sixteen double-features, that was my affair. What good was an incomplete father to Leonore?

That evening we dressed our Christmas Tree: Leonore, Mrs. MacWhirter and also Lady Whitestone, who came downstairs to offer Leonore a segment of home-made lemon meringue pie. In the black-and-orange London murk outside, Linda's detective sat ensconced behind the wheel of his old Rover, reading newspapers and running up bills.

I watched my two ladies fussing around the tree, garlanding it with glitter, while Leonore brought up supplies of baubles and chocolate Father Christmases.

I was drinking Scotch. Coming home from Tooting, I had broken my journey in Soho to buy a pile of German newspapers. Wildly turning the sports pages in the tube, my fingers grimy with newsprint, I discovered the forgotten name: *Fortuna Hansdorf*...

The side existed still, suspended halfway up the table of some local League. Hansdorf: suburb of Bendabrück. More obscure than that you couldn't get.

What was happening to me? *Down, down, down.* No longer at home in a mansion in Kew, no longer a house guest on the Côte d'Azur or in an arty maisonette in Hampstead. Unemployed, living in furnished lodgings, once more encircled by old women!

After Leonore had gone to bed, and Mrs. MacWhirter retired to her room, I let rip: got out my German paper, scrutinising all the local league tables, my mind securely anchored among the shallows of village names, games played, goals scored. Had always kept up to date with the Federal League, but all these local divisions offered heady excitement, *recherché* distraction, novelty. *Fortuna Hansdorf.* A hard, grassless pitch, violet-jerseyed Georg Kahn running uphill, centering to his inside right, waiting for the return pass, all four foot ten of him. Changing and showering, sauntering home, mother's lemon tea and buttered poppy-seed bread waiting. Careful, boy, avoid that tram depot with its uniforms and jeering laughter...

Yegods, even Bela is better than this, I told myself, as less welcome pictures began to intrude: white faces behind a platform barrier, fingers turning the pages of a well-thumbed list. Now it was Leonore in that shabby office, a grown-up Leonore barely distinguishable from Linda, finding my name on the list, deciding to let it ride. Good for you, baby. Another Scotch. Picked up the paper, let the league tables come back into focus. Relief. George the Creep alone. Directed by Robert Bresson.

Both Joe Leeds and Ellis Trawley took to coming round on impromptu visits. The old actor arrived with little bags of expensive chocolates dangling from his wrist. Sat down on my sofa, spilled out inaccurate gossip, failed to remember a single name or date, alarmed me by dropping hints that Joe and Marion's marriage was heading for the rocks. All I needed.

Joe lent some support to the actor's wild-eyed confidences. Came bearing carrier bags filled with egg-slicers, thermos flasks, junior aspirins, teacosies; Marion thought we might need such comforts.

Cowering down in my deepest chair, little Green Man from Mars, Joe grumbled on about the treacheries of agents and film producers. I tried to keep my yawns in check. Couldn't even summon up interest when he suggested we might work on a treatment together, set it up with me as putative director. I barely listened, could think of no new film I wished to see, let alone direct. My own predicament seemed crushing, inescapable, Joe's constructions bloodless and irrelevant.

Often got the impression that these pseudo-professional chats were a cover for something else : Joe wished to warn me off Marion. Sooner or later, he would steer the subject back to her. Marion had this dangerous predilection for briefly attaching herself to human wreckage, her compassion causing havoc.

Heard about the blind pianist who needed mothering; the lapsed Catholic who suffered agonies of guilt; the epileptic painter who feared turning queer. Always it was Joe who had to step in to clear up the mess. Oh, no, he assured me, Marion wasn't as uncomplicated as I might imagine. Once she'd fastened on to the notion of being needed, off into the wild blue yonder she would go, and hang the consequences. Almost the last straw : that Lesbian, whatshername, Cara. Marion had actually imagined she might *cure* the dyke. And the less said about that little episode, the better.

Got the message. *Lay off*. Next bit of wreckage needing attention might be Married Man with Child. O.K. But how do you tell a nice man like Joe Leeds that you're not interested in his wife? Especially when you are?

Alone in the flat, doing nothing, delaying the writing of urgent letters, part of my mind *willing* Tetheridge and Flake to call with news of fresh disasters, another setting off on famished night train journeys to mystic destinations.

The front door bell rang. A slight young woman in a shiny black raincoat stood on the doorstep and smiled at me.

'I'm the demonstrator,' she said.

I asked her what she was demonstrating about. She was about thirty, I guessed, very pale and neat and ordinary.

'No,' she explained. 'From the Electricity Showrooms. You asked for somebody to demonstrate your new cooker.'

I had a vague memory of complaining to Lady Whitestone that I couldn't make the bloody electric cooker work. Nor could Mrs. MacWhirter. Oven was always turning itself on and off, sounding shrill and meaningless alarms. I asked the demonstrator to enter. She removed her raincoat in a very brisk, businesslike manner, asked to be shown to the kitchen.

'Could I have a coat hanger, do you think?'

I went back into the bedroom, got a hanger, cast a quick glance out of the window. For a change, Old Rover wasn't parked by the kerb opposite.

The girl wore a very short brown dress. Not as short as the Regensburg *au pair*'s, but short enough. While I carefully fitted the coat round the hanger, and hung it on the hook behind the kitchen door, she started to demonstrate.

'Now then,' she began, pointing stiffly with pink little manicured fingernails. 'Heat view controls for high speed rings, one, two, three, and that's the control for the grill and oven. Are you with me so far?'

I stood quite close behind her. Yes, I was with her. Thank you, Lady Whitestone or God (thought Dracula) for this lovely Christmas present. Just what I wanted.

'Each control,' she went on, 'is identified by that orange ring situated just below each control knob. See?'

I affirmed that I saw. Her smell pleased me: toilet water rather than perfume. Her hair, tied at the back by means of a neat green clasp, was freshly shampooed. I had already forgotten what her face looked like. Her dress, brown wool, home-knitted, had a zip-fastener sewn into the front. A large golden ring was attached to the top of the zip. She wore tights and shiny, round-toed patent leather shoes. There was a wedding-ring on one of her pointing fingers.

'Now then, as you turn the knob clockwise, thus,' she explained, 'you will see this sloping orange band moving gradually up in this little window above the knob. See?'

'Yes, I see.'

I had detected a slight Midlands accent in her voice. Touch of your Beryl Reids.

'Have you been experiencing any difficulty with this model?'

'Some considerable difficulty,' I agreed.

I stood so close behind her now that before very long she would be forced to take an attitude.

'Now then,' she was saying, 'this clock.'

'You have a very neat waist,' Dracula said suavely. 'This clock . . .'

I placed my hands firmly on each side of her waist. She paused in her demonstration.

'Do carry on,' I said, 'I'm listening.'

'Now then, this clock. Maybe that's been your difficulty. A lot of people experience some initial difficulty with the clock of this model.'

'I did indeed experience some initial difficulty with the clock,' I said. 'Please go on.'

'The clock,' she said, 'keeps correct time, provided you leave the cooker's main control switched on.'

My hands pressed her waist very slightly. I could barely believe my luck. I inhaled deeply without letting on that I was doing so : actor's basic breathing exercise.

Time passed. She went on demonstrating.

'You don't mind if I touch you,' Dracula volunteered at last, careful not to put the words in the form of a question.

'An interval timer operated by the white hand on the large clock is fitted on the same dial as the clock,' she rattled off defiantly.

My fingertips started to slide forward very gently towards their next target : the front of her thighs. Having got there, they halted. Disaster could still strike. Control and stealth were essential.

'This,' the girl said, pointing again with her stiff forefinger, 'is most useful to remember. That is if you want to time foods taking up to one hour to cook. The lady of the house...'

'No lady...' Bela vouchsafed gruffly.

'Ah.'

She evinced even more cunning and deviousness than her ravisher. Perfect casting for a Bride of Dracula. That one Nottingham-flavoured syllable 'ah' communicated to me not only sympathetic understanding for my masculine helplessness with regard to the cooker; it also tacitly approved, though without final commitment, the sexual assault in progress.

'Always turn off the knob clockwise to OFF when the clock has been reset, see?'

Her playful projection of the word 'see' I interpreted as a further token of acceptance. A new sense of intimacy was colouring my relationship with the demonstrator. Encouraged, my fingertips began to move again, very slowly, almost, I hoped, imperceptibly. Upwards they journeyed, until, after an eternity of suspense, my hands were securely hidden underneath her dress. This was the moment of truth. If she failed to acknowledge my intent now, she was clearly conceding defeat. My fingertips applied pressure. Continuing to point and elucidate, the demonstrator acknowledged nothing. The kitchen reeled a little; I had to close my eyes to retrieve my balance. Sensations of delight and omnipotence surged through my body, prodigal sons returning after long absence.

Dick and I had often discussed My Syndrome, as he called it. He just couldn't understand what pleasure was obtainable from an operation of this sort. Surely some vital factor was missing when the partner failed to co-operate, pretended that nothing was happening? How could I expect Dick to get the point that Dracula did not play to common rules? Physical obstacles, lack of time for execution, intensified the pleasure. Every delay, every moment of suspension, every risk contributed their particular note to the ascending scale of ecstasy. It suddenly occurred to me that Marion might understand. I chased the thought from my mind, concentrated on the delicate operation in hand.

'When at "O",' the demonstrator continued, 'the time sounds a continuous buzzer alarm.' Her voice, I noticed, had lost its edge of confidence. Also, her body had begun to tremble minutely. 'That's to remind you that cooking time is up, see?'

Far from accelerating, I now slowed down the rhythmic progress of my fingertips. She would now be given a fair chance to manoeuvre herself out of her precarious situation. By missing this opportunity, she would provide Dracula with the most rapturous thrill of all.

Very slowly, my hands slid downwards, and then up again, *over* an area of wool this time, while I turned the body slightly towards me. As expected, she averted her face, but made no protest when my grip became more purposeful. How could Dick possibly appreciate that Draculaism reached its apotheosis when no explicit admission was encountered, even as inevitable climax approached? I had once described to him a similar encounter on an aeroplane : on a nightflight from London to Nice, involving a nameless passenger.

'But nothing happened !' was his naive reaction. 'Nothing *could* have happened.'

What he failed to realise was that in such a situation, quite irrespective of the 'end' in view, one simply aimed to raise anticipation to a pitch of sublimity. Willingly risked exposure and disgrace, merely to reach the next minutely differentiated stage of the assault, and to test the extent of the silent partner's collusive responsiveness. Above all, what neither Dick nor anyone else could ever fully grasp was that one had no choice in the matter. One either was Dracula, or one wasn't. I was.

By now, I was holding the couth demonstrator in a loose embrace, one hand coolly brushing the surface of her clothed butt, the other pressing her head gently against my shoulder, thus sparing her the embarrassment of looking at me.

Having at last transcended the point of no return, the assaultee made no further overt attempt to demonstrate the cooker. Instead she offered a mild guffaw of submission. It now became imperative not to blunder into mistaking compliance for active participation. This was where non-Draculas tended to lose their heads, and ended up in court. Or even in bed, with a relationship on their hands.

I therefore quietly and uncommittedly continued to stroke her respectably married buttocks, gradually moving my fingertips round to her thighs again. Eventually, without ever hurrying, or anticipating reactions, the travelling hand reached the critical patch of nyloned damp between her thighs. This revealed that the operation had gone according to plan. The rest of the affair would be mechanical, almost superfluous.

'I've got another call to make,' my chaste partner pointed out, finding my eyes at last, and looking at me rather sternly, though content to leave my hand where it was nesting. 'Headington Gardens.'

'It's round the corner,' I told her, kissing her forehead. My free hand touched her cheek affectionately. She closed her eyes, and standing resolutely still, legs slightly apart, began to pant. My thumb moved across her lips. Rubicon. Lips parted. Crossed. My thumb invaded her mouth, and briefly collided with a soft tongue. Travelling hand, meanwhile, detached itself from its warm resting-place to guide the demonstrator's fingers to where their touch was most urgently required. We both swayed a little; she fumbled quite ably. No words were exchanged. Eyes shut, the demonstrator contentedly sucked my thumb, greedy baby at the nipple, while her hand performed as bid. Once or twice, she tried to say 'no', but with a full mouth it had become difficult for her to articulate even that one syllable. I shifted the weight of her body slightly, giving her the kitchen wall for support. Again, she began to say 'no', but made no real attempt to extricate herself. She was, in every way, delightful. Not quite as potent as Jean, but then who was? They were both treasures cast in the same golden mould.

Twenty-five minutes later, the demonstrator and I were enjoying a pot of tea together. She completed her lecture about the cooker. That's what she'd come for, after all. When using the oven manually, she explained, the pointer on the start dial must show the same time as the main clock.

'Ah,' I said, 'that's where I must have gone wrong.'

'Yes,' she agreed with an understanding smile, 'that *must* have been the trouble.'

I showed her out. Up to the very end, we treated each other with impeccable courtesy.

If Melud pleases, are we being seriously asked to lend an adulterous connotation to a demonstration of the Respondent's electric cooker? The Respondent does not deny, Melud, that in the past his behaviour may not have been, er, all it might have been, but, er. I put it to the Petitioner, that in her eagerness to discover sexual impropriety in even the most harmless domestic arrangement, she has surrendered to an *ideé fixe* . . .

I went into my bedroom, pulled back the bedclothes and fully dressed slipped between the sheets. Tomorrow, I promised myself, I shall call Crane, my agent, ask if there's any work going. Typical of Crane not to have tried to get in touch with *me*. The warmth of satisfaction absconded from my body; I felt a random rage building up inside me. Flinging the bedclothes aside, I walked over to the window. Old Rover was back in position. The detective sat behind the steering wheel, smoking and reading.

I decided to telephone Dick. The Saga of the demonstrator might amuse him. The part of the pattern that Linda had always complained about most emphatically. *My disloyalty*, she called it. But then no sexual contact was so pleasureable that its flavour could not be enhanced by embellishment, the act completed in the re-telling.

Dick's number was engaged.

I crawled back into bed. Mustn't go to sleep. My Schedule. Things to do. Days chopped into hours, hours into minutes. Responsibility. Trains roaring through the night. Carry me back to old Virginia. *Fortuna Hansdorf*. Sleep for an hour, have a bath. Remove Demonstrator's smell. No, first tidy up the kitchen. Then pick up Leonore from Barry's birthday party.

Wish I were dead.

When I called Crane, my agent, I was angling for an invitation to luncheon. Even lunch would have done. At your White Elephant as in days of yore. Was getting a bit chuffed with Mrs. MacWhirter's wholesome nursery goo, fancied a really good blowout. Felt too mean to invite him, however. Crane paid me back in kind, handed me the drinks-before-lunch-old-boy routine.

Crane, my agent, is a proper English gentleman. Puce-faced and Nabarro-moustachioed, and thirtyish for twenty years. Takes care of himself and plays golf. Is 6 ft 6 in. tall and carries himself like a bloody Hussar. Wears hacking jackets, and likes to organise chummy show-biz cricket matches. He chortles and grins a lot, and does this old act of regarding business as a bore to be fitted in between social engagements. Since he deals mainly with people like himself, or with American Jews, whom he gives an inferiority complex merely by chortling, grinning, and towering above them, he does pretty well for his clients. In the eyes of Crane, my agent, there is a look of total vacancy that is often mistaken for reticent wisdom. He is a bachelor, and probably a eunuch, but being an English gentleman, he never talks about his private life. He and Linda used to get on like a house on fire.

Except for the post-recording booze-up, I loathe standing about in pubs, preferring to do my drinking at home and in secret. Crane's favourite pub, moreover, is crammed at lunchtime with a hundred other Cranes, all chortling, grinning and towering, and lapping up large gins and tonics, a poisonous drink at the best of times.

Pinned down and vertical for the best part of an hour. My eyes were level with Crane's button-hole carnation, he burbled on about how well all his other clients were doing. I found myself creeping into a soundproof shell.

The worst thing that can possibly happen to a director was happening to me. I was shying away from people; they inspired horror. I didn't like their smell. So into my hidey-hole I crawled, while Crane chortled on, carefully avoiding the only subject that interested me: where my next bloody cheque was coming from.

Crane, my agent, sipped his poison, frowned thoughtfully. Hadn't been able to get hold of Jack Martinsell. Odd, that.

Bloody odd.

Hadn't my contract with the Network another year to run? He'd take a look at the files after lunch, get himself clued up on the exact position.

Boiling with rage, I felt like drawing colour-me diagrams for him: I've walked out of my exclusive Network contract, you great stooping English supernit! Astronomic outgoings! Couldn't approach another company until I'd sorted myself out with Jack! For Christ's sake, Crane, you poofy great Maypole, don't just stand there hawhawing, *do* something!

None of this was articulated, of course. He chortled; I grunted.

He knew the score allright, did Crane, my agent. But sorting me out with Jack Martinsell meant raising his long public-school arse off his revolving office chair; it also meant taking the risk of antagonising the Network. No doubt some administrative cog in Martinsell's machinery had given him the thumbs down sign on me weeks ago, and Crane wasn't letting on.

As if the agony of Crane, my agent, looming over me wasn't painful enough, I badly needed to spring a leak and suddenly felt the stab of a needle in my groin. Yegods, had that electricity nymph given me a dose? Supposing she had, and Leonore, using the same lavatory seat . . . Phantasmagoria. Lining up for inspection at one of those hospitals advertised over the urinals of public lavatories. Date and nature of your last sexual contact, please. Ask the little girl to wait outside and lower your trousers. Hellsbells, when other men got away with adulteries galore, why couldn't George Kane even frig an electric cooker demonstrator with impunity?

I made a quick mental note to ask Joe Leeds for the address of his doctor. Dear old Dr. Finsbury was out, swearing affidavits on Linda's behalf, assuring Melud that my actions had caused his patient to have a nervous breakdown.

Crane, my agent, mentioned commercials. (Had Marion been busy on my behalf? I only half-listened.) Might be a wise move, old boy, to fill in time while *we* waited for Martinsell to come to *us*. Very civilised chap, old Jack. Why was I so worried about him? No doubt Jack understood the position perfectly, was simply taking his time to come up with a mutually acceptable solution.

More diagrams needed: The Network's stopped my cheques, you lazy golf-playing hound! For once pull your finger out, you anti-semitic middle-class ponce! A thousand Old Testament curses on your sodomite old school tie!

Commercials, I mumbled. Yes, well . . . what about it then?

Well, there was this up-and-coming production company, had contracts with some of the best agencies, chap running the show was sort of a neighbour, had this place in Wraysbury, played golf with him . . .

Oh really? Sounds interesting . . .

My eyes were hypnotised by Crane's bouncing red carnation, but attention drained away. Hopeless.

That morning Tetheridge had called. Some News. He'd just had a long chat with the Other Side's managing clerk. (Twenty-five guineas, I interpreted.) Tetheridge had persuaded him (*conning* would have been my word for it) to agree to an adjournment of the hearing to decide Leonore's custody. We required more time to study the Other Side's affidavits. A very wise move, Tetheridge averred. As he'd told me all along, time was on our side. Of course, in agreeing, the Other Side had asked for their pound of flesh. On my behalf, Tetheridge had agreed to let Leonore spend Christmas with her mother and aunt in Kew.

To let Leonore go back for even a single day sounded

like ultimate betrayal. Besides, what guarentees did we have that Linda would let the child come back to me after Christmas? Hadn't Tetheridge himself pointed out that possession was nine tenths of the law?

That, Tetheridge admitted, was a calculated risk. At the same time, he had the Managing Clerk's written assurance—without prejudice, of course—that there would be no hankey-pankey. Following the seasonal cease-fire, legal battle would resume. Both sides had agreed to abide by the verdict of the court.

Didn't like the smell of it, said so.

He would of course have to accept my instructions, Tetheridge sighed, but couldn't I see that by sending the child back for Christmas, I was removing the taint of kidnapping from my past actions? Counsel (another forty guineas gone west) had fully endorsed the wisdom of the proposed move.

Still didn't like the smell of it, but in the end I agreed. To everything.

As now I agreed with Crane, my agent, that I might indeed shoot a few commercials while waiting for Jack Martinsell to show his colours, or the flag, or whatever it was that Crane wanted him to show. All I cared about was getting away from that odious pub, by now packed to the hilt with ten thousand burbling Cranes, all baying for gins and tonics, and plotting to unleash lovely Enoch Powell, Saviour of England.

But Crane, my agent, wasn't through with me yet. I'd got hold of the wrong end of the stick. Slightly. Wasn't actually expected to *shoot* any commercials. No, old boy, this Wraysbury chap had imported this American genius to do this series of commercials. Some Ministry of Labour red-tape merchant had refused to give genius a working permit. So here was the set-up: Wraysbury needed someone to stand by, *pretending* to make the bloody commercials, while genius went ahead and actually shot them. Money for old rope, old boy. Sipping.

I glowered at the carnation. Gangling twit. Next thing he'd be wanting me to send Leonore out to work, playing moppets in floor polish ads. *Over my dead body*. Squared my shoulders. Compact Cagney getting ready to land a punch on Edward G's nose. Alas, Crane was already in the process of backing away. Probably had a luncheon date at the Caprice. With Roger Arnold.

Alone at last, I wolfed down a liver sausage sandwich, then hurried off to the Gents' to examine my genitals.

Walking Leonore home from school that afternoon, I observed that she was sulking. Sulked over her fish fingers, too. I pressed her. She broke down. Only girl in her class without a proper school uniform. They were all laughing at her. It was bad enough being New Girl. Having no uniform was intolerable.

Ban all private education! Subscribe to the *Black Dwarf*! Another Oscar for *If*...!

I hugged Leonore, promised to buy her a lovely school uniform during the Christmas hols. Also, I had a nice surprise for her: We were going to spend Christmas Day with Mummy in Kew. Wasn't that nice?

Did we have to come back afterwards?

Have to? Didn't she *want* to? Hadn't we been having a super exciting time together? First that marvellous holiday with Dick in Cannes, then all the fun of living with Joe and Marion, finally settling down in Lady Whitestone's lovely garden flat...?

Leonore, undressing a doll, didn't have much to say for herself. Love-stricken, I stared at her. Panic. If she told her mother she didn't *want* to come back, no lawyers' scrolls could force Linda to let her go again.

'Now you listen to me, love,' I said, propping her up on my lap. 'Whatever happens, it's not you who needs to make a decision. Just remember that, my darling. It's your Mummy and Daddy who make the decisions in this family, right?'

Mummy and I would sit down, work it all out, do the best for our darling girl. She did appreciate that, didn't she? She was a big girl now, old enough to understand.

'I miss Lucy.'

Her eye muscles laboured, produced one perfect round tear.

'We'll ask Mummy whether *we* can look after Lucy, that's what we'll do.'

'Mummy wouldn't like that, Daddy. She'll never agree to let Lucy go. She's very fond of Lucy, and now that she's having her kittens...'

'Well, look if Mummy says no, we'll get ourselves a brand new pussy, and then she and Lucy can visit each other...'

'Oh, Daddy, can we?'

Turned her round again, thank God. Exhausted, I kissed the tear off her hot cheek. Try and shoot that, I thought. Only the bloody Japs would get away with an embarrassing scene like that.

'We'll get us a lovely new pussy,' I affirmed eagerly. 'Everything allright now? You happy?'

'A ginger one with white spots?'

'A ginger one with white spots.'

'Lovely, Daddy. Super.'

I let her jump off my lap, got Mrs. MacWhirter to take charge, sank back drained. Ginger pussy indeed. Hadn't fooled me for a moment. What that whole conversation had been about was my affair with the electric cooker demonstrator. Guilt was the name of the game. I'd played Dracula, and instant placation of the love object had to follow. Emigration to America, big house in Kew, ginger pussy. If I give you things, you'll love me more. Dick was right. It never worked. That ginger pussy would cost me plenty.

I drank some Scotch, then called Joe to let him know my life was falling apart. Joe was out. I spoke to Marion. Or rather she spoke to me. Couldn't get a word in edgewise. Darling, she confided, that new serial was a total shambles. The director was an absolute nutter. All he cared about were his shots. Pretty pictures. Never *talked* to the actors. No concern for an artist's emotional approach. Drew diagrams all day. The whole cast were on the point of walking out. Sounded like a pretty good director to me, but didn't tell her that. When I got my turn, I mentioned I needed a good dentist, also a doctor, and the name of the firm that supplied Barry's school uniform. And did she know of anyone who had a ginger pussy to spare?

Darling, she said, leave it all to me.

Guilt pursued me into the kitchen, where Mrs. Mac-Whirter was teaching Leonore how to make wholesome vegetable soup. The smell was atrocious, but I stayed and watched because Leonore asked me to. I was also suddenly paralysed with remorse over the shabby way I'd reacted to Crane, my agent.

Just how ungrateful can you get? The man had come up with the only possible solution. How could I even think of going out to work, when all my energies were needed right here? Crane had considered Leonore, I hadn't. Crane was a saint. Watching Mrs. MacWhirter and Leonore chopping cabbage and onions, I decided to send Crane a case of champagne for Christmas. He'd earned it.

Later Marion came round with names scribbled on little pieces of paper; also a plastic lemon squeezer. She asked to be shown round the flat. I let her see as much of it as was practicable: Mrs. MacWhirter and Leonore were asleep in their own rooms. A line of junior washing was strung along the length of the bathroom.

It didn't matter, because Marion took a fancy to my bedroom. Flopped down on the bed, announced that she had *snapped*, declared her intention to contribute no more energy to the serial until nutty director had sorted him out.

'Come and lie down beside me,' she said. I obeyed.

'Don't do anything, darling. I'll hold your hand. That will relax me.'

'Would you like me to stroke your forehead, Marion?'

'That would be nice,' she agreed.

We just lay there for a while. Harmless fun. Relaxing.

'You're such a marvellous father, I do admire you, George.'

I told her about our domestic arrangements over Christmas.

'I'll come and cook your Christmas dinner,' she volunteered.

'What about Joe and Barry?'

'I can cook two dinners,' she said. 'I'm a fairly capable person, you know.'

'That you are, Marion,' I concurred. 'Thank you.'

I stroked her cheek. Her skin was soft and furry, like an animal's.

'What with all your other troubles, George, how are you managing about sex?'

'It's a problem, Marion.'

'That's true, George. The older I get, the more of a problem sex seems to become. Now, you take that nutty director I was telling you about. Ignored me all day, then grabbed my arse in the canteen.'

'Did you mind?'

'Not really. Rather dishy, actually, even if he *is* a nutter.'

'Did you tell Joe?'

'About the grab in the canteen? No, of course not, darling.' She looked around for a cigarette, but seemed disinclined to shift her position. 'Joe is so involved with his own problems. He's terribly wise in his way. Trouble is, he doesn't understand women. That's where you and Joe are so different, aren't you?'

'You think I understand women, Marion?'

'Oh, George, darling, you *know* you do. The very first day I met you, that time at Dick's, I said to myself, now there's a man who understands women.'

'Really, Marion?'

'With you I get this feeling that there's nothing I couldn't discuss quite openly, not even the most intimate subjects . . .'

'For instance . . .?'

'Well, you see, George, I have this difficulty . . . you don't mind me talking quite frankly, do you . . .?'

'Go ahead, Marion. Shall I go on stroking your . . .'

'Yes, please. Trouble is, George, I don't find it easy to have an orgasm. Does that shock you?'

'It's a fairly common complaint among women, Marion.'

Dr. Bela Kane talking: Diagnosis. Suave Hungarian accent. Stroked Marion's eyelids.

'I'm not frigid, George, don't think that.'

'I'm sure you're anything but frigid, Marion,' I purred.

'It's just Joe. He's sweet, and I love him dearly, but well, no matter how hard he tries, darling, not a thing ever happens. With me, that is.'

'Have you discussed the problem with him, Marion?'

'Oh, I can't. He'd feel so hurt, poor darling. I pretend, and I suppose he believes all those moans and groans.'

'Do you experience difficulty with vaginal or clitoral orgasms?'

'Both really. No, vaginal . . . I mean, that's the point, isn't it?'

'Ah, you think it's more proper to . . .'

'Well, I've had this very suburban upbringing, darling. Golders Green.'

'There you are,' Dr. Bela Kane (Maximilian Schell) smiled reassuringly. 'You're probably the clitoral type,

148

Marion, but some puritanical control mechanism prevents you from ...'

'Darling, I think you may be barking up the wrong tree there. God knows I've tried everything. The lot.'

'With Joe, you mean ...'

'No, yes, no. I mean I wasn't really thinking of Joe, darling. Oh George, I was such a hopeless Lesbian.'

'It disgusted you?'

'Well, actually, it made me laugh.'

'You didn't find it agreeable?'

'With Cara? Oh, darling, it was *agreeable* allright, but she said such funny things while she was doing it. I mean I got the giggles.'

'Miscast?'

'Hopelessly. When we got down to it, it was dear Joe all over again. Just go, go, go. And all that verbalising. Now we'll do this, now you do that. I suppose I'm just shy sexually.'

'Yes, Marion.'

'I mean what I really like, what I really like, George, is *this*. Just lying quietly, doing nothing, letting things, well, grow ...'

'Me too, Marion.'

'Oh, darling, really? It's so rare to find a person who isn't go, go, go all the time.'

'Marion, do you mind keeping your voice down a bit? Leonore's next door, and ...'

'Oh sorry, darling. We'll just whisper then. *George?*'

'Yes?'

'George, I'm getting my dress all creased. Do you mind if I take it off?'

'No, Marion, do by all means.'

'You take off something too, darling. Then we'll just lie quietly, side by side, and you may stroke me very gently. Nothing sexual, I mean.'

'No, of course not.'

She was up, flinging off clothes right and left. She had

a strikingly lovely figure. Dressed, she looked appetising enough. Naked, she stood revealed as a curvaceous mini-beauty: bouncy bottom, slim, long waist, round brown breasts with big motherly nipples. The mounting pleasure of making inventory was curtailed by the sudden fear that Leonore might wake up, take it into her head to come in and ask for a glass of water ...

'George, *do* get undressed.'

'Yes, Marion.'

'Darling, do you mind if I switch all the lights off?'

'No, not at all.'

We slipped between cool sheets, her flesh burned into mine. I thought blissfully of Dick's dirty books, jutting breasts and all.

'As I was saying, darling ...'

'Yes, Marion ...'

'Just stroke me very gently ...'

'Do you know where I can dig up a ginger pussy?' (Urgently needed distraction).

'Leave it to me, darling, leave it to me. Oh George, this is so nice.'

'Isn't it?'

'George, I do like you. You understand me. My trouble is, I just want to be cherished, not all this go, go, go, which never gets me anywhere.'

'Marion, I doubt if *this* will get you anywhere, either.'

'Don't give it a thought, darling. You know, I bet all women basically want the same thing. You don't have to explode all the time. Bang, bang, bang. We're just not made like that, darling. Gentle creatures we are. There, put your leg between ... that's better. That's nice. Let me see, ginger pussy. George, you don't think I'm a horrid old tease, do you?'

'Not at all, Marion.'

'I mean, just because one feels the need of an occasional arm around one, because one wants the warmth of another body in a platonic, non-sexual way . . . Oh George, what am I going to do about Joe?'

'He loves you, Marion.'

'And I love him, I really do. But I can't go on deceiving him when we sleep together. The effort, darling . . . I mean, it's making me quite neurotic . . .'

'Listen . . .'

'What?'

'Just thought I heard a noise in the corridor.'

'It's nothing, darling. Probably a car outside.'

Yegods, Old Rover!

If Melud pleases, need I remind the Court that at the precise time at which this particular offence is alleged to have taken place, the Respondent's small daughter *as well* as his Housekeeper were present in the flat . . .

'What's the matter, darling? You've gone all cold. Isn't this nice for you, too?'

'Very nice, Marion.'

'You have such marvellous control, darling. I do appreciate a man with control, a man who isn't all go . . .'

'Yes, Marion I know.'

'Come closer, and get really cosy. Here, let me . . .'

'Marion, I don't really . . .'

'That feels nice, doesn't it?'

'Marion, have some . . .'

'Just lie still, darling . . . there . . . gently . . . sweet . . .'

'Marion, if you don't get out of my bed this very minute, so help me I'm going to fuck the arse off you.'

'But I don't want that, darling. Beside, I'm an actress, I can control my breathing. No one will hear . . .'

'If Leonore wakes up . . .'

'Darling, I've been very selfish. Forgive me.'

She was out of my arms and off the bed in a flash, projecting contrition. She stepped into her clothes. Adorably. Leant over and kissed me very gently on the mouth, told me she fancied a peanut butter sandwich.

'I do feel so much better,' she sighed. 'Really, George.'

'So do I, Marion.'

I held on to her hand, pressed it. Long enough for her to turn the simple act of withdrawing it into a five-act tragedy by Racine.

'Don't let's get involved darling,' she said. 'We mustn't.'

'No, Marion.'

'You've got quite enough on your plate already, my darling.'

'Yes, Marion.'

Linda came for Leonore at nine o'clock on Christmas morning, looking determined and self-possessed. She moved very slowly, holding a cigarette horizontally in her gloved hand. Where, she demanded to know, was this Mrs. MacWhirter, my so-called housekeeper. I told her Mrs. MacWhirter had gone to Motherwell to spend Christmas with relatives.

Delaying the moment with remarkable restraint, she finally embraced Leonore and without taking off her mink, helped to dress her.

I stood in the doorway and watched them: Linda, furry bear bent double; Leonore, confused rabbit clutching her mother's arm. Once more I wished I were dead.

'Daddy's going to get me a ginger kitten, Mummy.'

'I see.'

I continued to hover, overcome with helpless compassion for Linda.

'Let me drive you back to Kew,' I said.

'Don't bother,' she said. 'I'm sure you have more important things to do with your time.'

'It'll be a pleasure.'

'Why? Don't you trust my driving?'

'Just give me the car-keys, Linda...'

'*Please.*'

'...and don't argue in front of the child.'

'You can bloody well say Please.'

'Does it matter?'

'I'm through taking orders from you, you bastard.'

'Oh, Daddy, do say *please*. You're always telling me to.'

'Allright. *Please*.'

The car-keys fell 'accidentally' on the carpet. I bent down to pick them up, dropped them into my trouser-pocket. Throughout this little exchange, Linda had never once permitted her eyes to rest on me. I couldn't help but stare at her. Foxy Linda. Belinda Blue Eyes. Eighteen years? One tiny gesture, a hand on my elbow, a smile: Might have swept her up in my arms for a Culver City 1935 close-up and fade out. Might also have strangled her, of course. 'You two sit in the back,' I said. 'I'll drive.'

'If you insist. But you're not coming into the house.'

'I don't want to come into the house.'

'I don't care whether you do or not. I'm not having Elspeth upset by you.'

Thank you, I thought, thanks for being so ghastly. Now I won't have to burn up any more energy trying to love you.

Carried Leonore's suitcase downstairs, locked it in the boot. They both got into the back of the Jaguar. I started the engine. It was a pleasant feeling sitting behind the wheel of my own car again. As I moved off, I observed that Old Rover had been given the day off.

The roads were frosty and deserted. A ghostly metropolis. Beautiful. Why had nobody ever thought of shooting in London on Christmas Day? Unions wouldn't wear it. In the car mirror I could see Linda sitting very upright, stately and composed. Leonore chattered on about kittens, apparently unconcerned. I switched on the car radio. Christmas Carols from King's College, Cambridge. From time to time I heard snatches of my loved ones' dialogue.

'Daddy, I mean Mummy, will Lucy mind?'

'Mind what, darling?'

'If Daddy gives me this kitten? I'm going to call it Lulu. Lucy might be jealous.'

'I doubt it,' Linda said.

'Lulu might be a boy,' I contributed.

'I don't see what that has to do with it,' Linda snapped.

I searched the mirror for a glimmer of humour in Linda's eyes. She instantly averted them, and for my benefit retreated into stylised inscrutability. My Snow Queen. The silent reproach. I thought again of all those recordings she had attended. Frosty, foxy charm dispensed to one and all. If you say so, Mrs. K., that's praise indeed. And no sooner were we back in the car, than those great Sibelian sheets of ice descended. The evading eyes, the corners of the mouth turned down. Was I *that* bad a director? Had I shown too much joy getting another show into the can?

My glance kept drifting back to the mirror. Nothing. Eighteen years together, *Leonore's mother*, and I didn't know her from Eve. Didn't know myself either. That cosy nesting in Jekyll and Hyde pigeon-holes. Superficial. Meaningless. I say I say I say, who was that man fiddling with Marion Leeds last night? I do not wish to know that, Mr. Lugosi, kindly leave the screen. Still, there had been *something*. It wasn't just reading *Playboy*, or playing with electric cooker demonstrators, or buggering off to Dalston to see *The Vampire Bat*. Something had occurred: I had actually felt something. And here I was driving Leonore back to her mother, the one thing I had promised myself not to do.

'There's no need to go so fast. We all know you can drive.'

I slowed down. Yes sir, at once, sir. I was literally falling apart, going to pieces. Night trains and Leonore and league tables, what did they have in common? Maybe if I concentrated hard enough, the pieces would glue together, even if they didn't belong to the same jig-saw. Yes sir, madam, more slowly. I steered the car up the drive. My house. *Not* my house. I got out, opened the door for Linda, unlocked the boot, offered to take Leonore's case inside. Her Christmas presents were stowed away in it. I'd meant to tell Linda about that.

'We can manage now,' she said.

I kissed Leonore.

'You're not staying, Daddy? You're going back?'

'That's right. Never mind, love. Never mind.'

She had known all along. No doubt blamed herself. All her fault that Daddy wasn't allowed inside the house. I saw the anxiety in her eyes, felt the Dreaded Eight O'clock Blues coming on: the sackcloth and ashes of connubial bliss.

'I'll call you tomorrow, love,' I told her with desperate joviality. 'Come round and pick you up the day after, allright?'

'Oh, but Daddy...'

'Come along, darling. There's a draught if I keep the front door open. Auntie Elspeth has a cold.'

'No, but, Daddy, who's going to cook your Christmas dinner?'

'Mustn't worry about that, love.'

Linda had placed Leonore's case in the doorway. She came back very slowly, took hold of Leonore's hand.

'I'm sure your father has made suitable arrangements for his Christmas dinner....'

'He's got nobody to cook his Christmas dinner, I ought to know,' Leonore said stubbornly. 'Can't he come in, Mummy?'

'Please get back into your car, George,' Linda commanded.

'Yes,' I said.

'Ask Marion,' Leonore cried, inspired. 'That's a good idea, isn't it? You ask Marion, Daddy. She likes you. She'll cook you a nice Christmas dinner.'

'Yes,' Linda said, smiling 'cheese'. 'You ask Marion.'

She was half-guiding, half-dragging the child into the house.

'Merry Christmas,' I called out insanely, hot air billowing from my mouth. I thought: What a fantastic scene to shoot. Just can't beat real life for drama, can you?

'Merry Christmas, Daddy.'

Then the door was shut in my face. I could hear Leonore greeting sister Elspeth, and then—yells of delight—her cat. I turned and walked along the drive, and into the road, and round another corner, to the bus stop. Hadn't brought my overcoat. Started hopping about to keep warm, singing Tatiana's Letter Song from *Eugene Onegin* at the top of my voice, a vast orchestra backing me. Had planned to use a bit of that aria in my last abandoned production. Not a soul in the street. Then I remembered they didn't run buses on Christmas Day.

That's how I came to spend Christmas Day walking all the way from Kew to Hampstead. Coatless. Eight miles. Singing Puccini, Verdi, Gounod, and as much of Beethoven's Seventh Symphony as I could remember. A cleansing experience, I'm sure that Crane, my golf-playing agent, would have approved.

Some Christmas cards had been dropped through the letter box. One from Joe and Marion, one from Ellis Trawley, one from Crane (forwarded from Kew), one from Leonore and Mrs. MacWhirter. Dick never bothered with Christmas cards.

I looked out of the window. Old Rover was back, and so was the poor sod behind the wheel. Business as usual. Getting treble rates, no doubt. I opened a bottle of Scotch.

Merry Christmas, Daddy.

Television director found dead under Christmas Tree in Hampstead flat. The Scott Fitzgerald of the sixties. A truly tragic end.

Our Broadcasting Correspondent writes: Mr. George Kane came into prominence as a director of television plays in the late fifties, when ...

Now she'll feel sorry. Weep her heart out.

Last night, Mrs. Linda Kane, 41, was receiving medical attention in her home in Kew. 'He seemed quite normal and cheerful this morning when he took myself and my daughter out for a drive,' she told our reporter.

Doorbell! Fantasy over. Lurched into the hall. Life insurance paid up to date. *Death of a Salesman* (Columbia, 1952). Lady Whitestone on the threshold, proffering cold white Turkey on a plastic plate. Regarded me more in sorrow than in anger: find the family dipso. I was wearing a grubby purple bathrobe, Ray Milland in *The Lost Weekend* (Paramount, 1945), thanked Lady Whitestone profusely. Bit of a headache, nothing serious. As soon as she was safely back upstairs, I carried the cold turkey down to Old Rover, who evinced no surprise at my seasonal attentions.

'Thank you, sir,' he said. 'Very kind of you.'

I watched him from my bedroom window, tucking in, enjoying it.

Marion came round on Boxing Day, with a kitten in a wicker basket and a baking tin.

'Sorry I couldn't make it yesterday,' she said, brushing my cheek with her lips. 'You need a shave, darling. Joe might have got suspicious. I couldn't get a ginger kitten, this one is quite nice. Black.'

We toyed with the kitten, unsuccessfully trying to determine its sex. Marion poured milk into a saucer, spread breadcrumbs on the baking tin to construct a lavatory. Her movements were endearingly childlike. The kitten used the baking tin almost at once.

'How super,' Marion cried. 'Such a tiny thing, and already house-trained.'

I shaved, squirted deodorant under my armpits, glanced out of the bathroom window. Old Rover, bloody fool, had taken the afternoon off. We shed our clothes, got into bed, made complicated teenage love : Bonanza.

Here was the woman for whose sexual requirements Dracula was the perfect pleasure instrument. His vampirical games appealed to some deeply-rooted passivity in her nature; his methodical delays incurred aphrodisiac rapture; whatever new role he chose to assign to her she performed with matchless insight; the more convoluted his demands, the more capably she responded.

'Oh George, how marvellous,' she sighed after her fourth (clitoral, and partially self-induced) orgasm. 'I'm normal after all.'

Then insisted on a ten-minute catnap.

'Joe may come round to pick me up. Don't want my face to look all squashy when he arrives.'

'I like Joe,' I said thoughtfully.

'He's a lovely man, darling. He really is—straight, know what I mean? They just don't come any straighter than Joe.'

'You're not going to *tell* him?'

'I *never* tell him.'

Pause.

'Why should I hurt him, darling? Besides, he always forgives me. He's super that way.'

'You mean you *are* going to tell him?'

'Light me a cigarette, darling. Then I'll get dressed and make my face up.'

High time to hit back.

'Listen, Marion, I ought to tell you, there's something wrong with me...'

'Darling, if four times an afternoon is wrong, who needs right?'

'What I mean to say, Marion, I'm not capable of deep relationships, that's why I'm in this mess. I touch people and run away...'

'Darling, you have only one unfortunate tendency, you like to over-dramatise your own problems.'

'Yegods, Marion, *you* can talk...'

'You're such a worrier, darling. Like Joe. What a worrypot *he* is! Even worries that sometimes he hasn't got anything to worry about.'

'You're on the whatsit, I suppose?'

'Joe's going a bit odd actually. Did you know he's taken up astrology?'

'Marion, do you take the pill?'

'Tried three different brands, darling. They just don't suit my metabolism.'

I expostulated, became incoherent.

'Darling, what an old worrypot you are. I wasn't born yesterday, love, I know what I'm about.'

'Yes but...'

'Not one of your little scrubbers, you know.'

'*What* little scrubbers?'

'Oh, George, Dick told me. You lay everything in sight. *I* don't mind... sexy old thing.'

'You don't use a cap either?'

'Safe periods, darling. Like the R.C.s.'

'Yes, but .'.'.'

'Safe as houses, my love.'

'Famous last words.'

'Leave it all to me, darling.'

Later Joe came round with Barry and a pile of old *Variety*'s. To help me get through the Christmas holidays. Barry, cantankerous, wanted to be taken home to play with his new presents. Joe was in a cheerful mood. His new guru, the astrologer Lucas Maturin, had prophesied literary recognition for the coming year.

'You can't mean you really believe that rubbish,' I told him.

'What are you?'

'Gemini.'

Shrieks of delighted recognition from both Marion and Joe.

'Wouldn't you just know it,' Joe said. 'If you can give me the exact time of birth, George, I'll work out your horoscope.'

'It's bloody rubbish,' I reiterated. 'What are you, then?'

'Virgo,' Joe said. 'Marion is Aries. So there you are. Infallible.'

To keep Barry quiet, Marion raided my ice-box and fried bacon and eggs. I ate ravenously. Joe talked at length about writing a letter to *The Times* concerning literary critics who didn't read the books they reviewed. Marion talked about her nutty director, wondered whether her new serial would be reviewed.

'Criticism has become the executive arm of public relations,' Joe told her.

I mopped up my plate with toast. Marion, with Barry squirming on her lap, said:

'We've certainly got the publicity boys behind this one. Going to be photographed for a *TV Times* cover.'

Joe squeezed banana into Barry's mouth.

'Then you'll get reviewed. Television critics take dictation from the P.R. boys.'

Nice cosy evening, I thought.

'The photographer's already been on to me,' Marion said. 'Meant to tell you, George. Old mate of yours. Arnold Roger. Or something.'

After they had gone, I retired to bed, read two *Variety*'s from cover to cover. Dan Wymans' latest epic, I registered with some satisfaction, had grossed a slow $4,500 in Seattle. Fell asleep. Woke up from a nightmare (about a coach or tram depot) with indigestion, jumped out of bed, searched for paper and pencil, sat down to compose a list. George the Creep checking up on George the Gambler. Painstakingly I wrote:

MARION	LINDA
Jewish.	Non-Jewish.
Dark, straight, swarthy.	Auburn, curly, pale.
Enthusiastic, devoted.	Plaintive, detached.
Actress, ambitious.	Non-actress, bone-idle.
Non-political, uncritical.	Political, critical.
Uninformed.	Informed.
Predominantly clitoral.	? (what an admission!)
Fast.	Slow.
A mum of sorts.	A mum.
Promiscuous.	Promiscuous of late.
About to meet Roger Arnold.	Knows Roger Arnold.

The last three items gave me cause for concern. Dick had always claimed that choice of mate was compulsive. The Repetition Syndrome, he called it. I opened another bottle of Scotch. Had she really come four times? Fooled Joe, hadn't she? Why those guffaws when I said 'Gemini'? Turned on the radio. Madrigals. Linda loved madrigals. We must remember the Queen's Proctor, Mr. Kane. Melud, the balance of my mind was temporarily disturbed. Leonore, my own darling, it must be hard for you to understand why pushing my Willie into Marion's Thing should make me a better Daddy. If Melud pleases, must we listen to any more of this filth? We will now ask Mr. Roger Arnold to take the stand . . .

Shortly after noon the next day, the telephone rang. Sister Elspeth.

'Hello,' I said.

It would not be possible for me to collect Leonore this afternoon. The child had an upset stomach. Was expected to be better tomorrow.

Dialling tone.

I drank more Scotch, watched TV. Marion's black kitten made a mess on the sitting-room carpet. Soccer or Tom and Jerry? Leonore loved Tom and Jerry. I chose Tom and Jerry, making amends for screwing Marion.

Neither Elspeth nor Linda called the following day. I read *Variety*, drank Scotch, did the pools for the following Saturday, and the Saturday after that. In an effort to sober up I finished off a pint of milk. Dozed.

It was already dark when I decided to act. Couldn't procrastinate any longer. Picked up the receiver. The number! I couldn't remember my Kew number! George Kane, you miserable castrato, you can't have forgotten your own number! Had to look myself up in the telephone directory. There I was. Kane, George. Felt a profound sense of relief, dialled.

Sister Elspeth answered.

'Hello,' I said.

'Oh, you.'

'Yes, me.'

They *both* had upset stomachs, Linda as well. Now *listen*, I said. Both in bed, ring again tomorrow. Oh no, I'm coming round *now* to pick up the child. That was the deal. Don't bother, said sister Elspeth, voice chilled by nine hundred years of loathing for the male.

Dialling tone.

I put down the receiver, aquiver with apoplexy. Thank you, Mr. Tetheridge. I ordered a self-drive hired car, put on some clothes. Why hadn't Marion called? Probably being photographed nude by Roger Arnold. The last bloody straw.

I called Tetheridge. Not there. Called his home. Gone skiing. Davos. Fed Marion's kitten, went out to pick up the hired car, drove to Kew on an empty stomach. Up the dark drive, crunch of gravel, wind through the trees. Sibelius, Andersen. Almost like the country, Daddy.

Linda took her time coming to the door. She was wearing a red dressing-gown, new to me. White lapels and a white belt. Father bloody Christmas. In drag. Leonore trailed behind her, fully dressed.

I strode past Linda, reached for the child.

'I didn't say you could come in . . .'

'Feeling better, darling?'

'Only an upset tummy, Daddy.'

'You're not coming in, I said.'

'I *am* in. Where's her bloody bag?'

Linda planted herself before me, arms melodramatically outstretched. Striped red and white frontier post.

'The child leaves this house when I say so.'

Leonore was pressing Lucy to her chest. For mutual protection.

'Got you that pussy, love, all black.'

'Get out of this house.'

'Don't talk rubbish.'

Then Linda started thumping me, arms flailing. Thwacking my head. Kicking my shins. I stood and swayed. *White Zombie*. As she rained blows down on me, I felt no pain, indeed some obscure pleasure. Caught a glimpse of Leonore's blue eyes, big and incredulous at first, then narrowing with fear.

'How dare you!' Linda kept screaming, as she punched me in the face. 'How dare you!'

'It's a game,' I shouted at Leonore, protecting my teeth with my elbows. 'Mummy and I are playing games.'

The cat had jumped out of Leonore's arms, scurrying away between my legs.

'Lucy,' Leonore cried, 'Lucy, don't run out.'

Linda suddenly stopped banging and kicking me. Exhausted, she turned and ran out of the hall. I heard a door slam, then the sounds of noisy lamentation.

'Linda?' This was sister Elspeth's voice calling from upstairs. 'Has he gone yet?'

I gathered Leonore up in my arms. At first rigid, she quickly curled herself into a feathery ball, I rushed her upstairs.

'Flying baby,' I yelled. A game we'd played when she

was two years old. 'My flying baby. The oldest flying baby in the world.'

Up in the nursery, her case lay on the floor, open, unpacked. Some Christmas presents were strewn about her bed. I put Leonore down, tossed some items of clothing into the case, locked it, grasped the child's hand, pulled her out of the room, abandoning toys in our flight. I struggled down the stairs, case in one hand, grabbing Leonore's fist with the other. The hall echoed with Linda's sobs.

'All a game, love, a silly old game. Flying baby.'

Then we were safely out of the house, and Leonore was beside me in the car, clasping a rescued doll to her chest. I started the engine and drove off, filled the ensuing silence by cataloguing the multiple attractions of Marion's kitten.

'You needn't have hit Mummy like that,' she said flatly.

'Me? I didn't hit her, love. She hit me.'

'You hit her back, though.'

'No. I didn't.'

'Yes, you did.'

'Can't understand what got into your Mummy.'

'It was awful.'

'Wasn't serious, love. *We've* had fights, haven't we? You fight with your mates at school, don't you? You told me.'

'It wasn't pretend.'

' 'Course it was pretend. You don't think your Mummy and I would have a proper fight, do you? We *love* each other.'

'You don't.'

'People can have a fight and still be fond of each other. Let me tell you a...'

'Going to have nightmares about it.'

'No, you're not. And I tell you why not, darling. Because we're talking about it, see? Things you talk about never give you nightmares.'

'Who says?' she asked.

'Won't happen again, promise.'

My voice sounded like a death-rattle.

'Once is quite enough.'

Who dat speaking? Linda?

'Tell me about your presents. Tell me what you got for Christmas, love.'

I was driving very fast now, sweating like a pig. I could smell myself.

'We ate some fish,' she said. 'Must have been off.'

'You're better now.'

Tried to clear my throat.

'Tasted allright,' she said flatly. 'Must have been off, though.'

'What sort of fish was it?'

You like fish, don't you, the kind man in the electrical appliances shop asked the boy. What fish do you like?

What fish? What was English for *Schellfisch*? No idea. Haddock was an esoteric word I had not yet learned.

Schellfisch, I said. Which, I learned one minute later, was English for fish inside shells.

Shellfish?, the man echoed, horror-struck. You eat shellfish at home? In your own house, your people eat shellfish? Pork too? Ham you eat? Game? Hare? Venison?

No never. (Never heard of venison. What kind of animal was that?)

Never eat venison, you say? But you eat shellfish! You just said so. I ask you for your favourite fish and you say shellfish. Lobster, eh? Crab?

No, not crab. Hated crab. *Schellfisch*.

That's what I said you said. Shellfish, you said. The boy's been brought up on *traife* food. Shellfish he eats!

The boy trembled.

'Poor Lucy,' Leonore said. 'You frightened her, Daddy. She ran out.'

Along dark streets. Barnes. Putney. Down on the accelerator. Why so little traffic? Can she smell my sweat? That dream last night. All coming back now. A coach station? Pavements thronged with beggars, people in rags, hounded unfortunates, eyes blazing greed and fear. Rubbish piled high in the gutter; shit everywhere; not a taxi in sight. That's it, needed a taxi to get me to the station. (*Station?*) Depots of the night. Tram Depots? Beggars, smelling of mice, were storming driverless coaches. From crowded windows, they pelted a ragged old woman with rubbish, old cabbage leaves, shredded and slimy. Where were the drivers? Suddenly the coach station was empty. Just me and this red-faced woman, beside herself with rage. At me she raged! At me, the only one who hadn't pelted her. I only wanted a taxi ...

'Don't drive so fast, Daddy. That was a red light.'

Leonore was cowering in her seat, holding her Christmas dolly to her chest. You're not leaving your father behind, you're not. Not in a coach station. Or a tram depot. Or on a station platform. Won't permit it, not leaving him behind. Understand?

I turned to look at her for only a fraction of a second, Melud. First I heard her cry, then the dull crunch of metal, then the splintering of glass, and only then, Melud, the scream of my brakes.

You're not leaving your father behind.

A tiny scar near her left temple might not heal completely. Otherwise merely a case of slight concussion and shock. *Men in White* (M.G.M. 1935). Nothing that a couple of days in bed shan't put right. Yes, we've taken the liberty of telephoning your home, Mr. Kane. Your wife has already driven the child back. Yes, to Kew, of course to Kew. Must be a relief to you, Mr. Kane, to know that she's allright ...

In these regrettable circumstances, Tetheridge mourned on the telephone, it would be pointless to proceed with the Custody Hearing. The Other Side would run a four-horse carriage through our case. The child was back in Kew, convalescing. Possession was nine tenths of the law.

After his return from Davos, he had worked out a detailed Interim Agreement with the Other Side. This, the Court would later be asked to approve. The child would remain in Mrs. Kane's care and control. Mr. Kane would be granted reasonable access, provided he agreed to Mrs. Kane's maintenance proposals. Mr. Kane would relinquish all rights to the Marital Home. Mrs. Kane would wind up the company, retaining profits, but staying her demand for the borrowed £8,000. All legal costs to be met by Mr. Kane.

As to the divorce proceedings, Mrs. Kane would shortly be seeking leave to amend her petition.

We might have done worse, Tetheridge concluded.

I gave Mrs. MacWhirter two weeks' salary in lieu of notice. She cried and departed, dragged down by carrier-bags full of leftover vegetables. Red-faced old woman with cabbage leaves. Odd. I decided to leave the garden flat, then realised I had nowhere to go.

I called Crane, my agent. My circumstances, I reported, had dramatically altered. I could go out to work again. His secretary took my message. Crane, my agent, would call me back. He didn't. I packed up the remainder of Leonore's things. Joe volunteered to take them round to Kew in his Renault. Marion collected her kitten, gave it to Barry as a present. I received a police summons for dangerous driving, also a claim for damages from the Car Hire firm. Ellis Trawley came round to tell me that he had gone into analysis. He tried, but failed, to remember his analyst's name. Joe sent his doctor to examine me. The doctor prescribed Librium. I wrote a long, sentimental letter to Leonore. Read it through, attempted to squeeze a genuine tear onto the paper, tore up the letter.

I'd tried to kill her.

Shortly before midnight on New Year's Eve, I got out of bed to answer the front door. Marion and Barry stood on the threshold, separated by two bulging suitcases and a wicker-basket, containing the black kitten.

I let them in. We helped Barry to dismantle the Christmas tree, left a thick layer of brittle pine needles on Lady Whitestone's carpet. After singing Old Lang Syne, Marion put Barry to bed in Leonore's old room, then went into the kitchen to make a pot of tea and peanut butter sandwiches. She ate the sandwiches, drank the tea, got undressed, came to bed. I took her in my arms, she said she loved me. We fell asleep almost at once.

'Darling,' were her first words next morning, 'now you have a brand new family. Isn't it marvellous how things work out?'

Four

MARION had omitted to pull down the blinds the night before. We liked going to bed spontaneously (before she had time to wipe off lipstick or mascara), wanted our sex to be 'unmarried'. I woke up, gazing out at a rectangle of grey sky and skeletal chestnut trees. Bleak Bergman fade-in. I could tell they were chestnuts. Only tree I know. When Leonore and I go for our walks, she tutors me on botany. Her exasperation over my ignorance pleasures me.

Beside me Marion sighed. Didn't have an early call. Nutty Director was starting rehearsals after lunch in defer-ence to this week's guest star—Dame Joan Ormonde, eighty. I'd told her—faulty serve, sorry Dick—that she could have a sleep-out, I'd do the chores.

I registered bare branches, cracked window frames. Winter. Which meant : Huddling in front of electric fires; drinking scalding tea, dreading to go out; shivering at the thought of my professional paralysis; yearning for Marion to come home, so that we might once more leap spontaneously into bed and make unmarried love, and I could forget winter, and stop reproaching myself for let-ting them take Leonore back to Kew.

Marion's hand was softly slithering across my naked chest, plucking grey hairs. Barry scampered into the bed-room, pyjamas trailing. Marion groaned and turned over.

I got up, dressed Barry, then prepared the lad's break-fast. No harm in this, whatever Dick might think. Didn't Marion do the shopping on the way back from rehearsals? Also sometimes cleaned the flat, didn't she? Besides, she paid half the rent. I was anxious not to repeat the mistakes of my marriage, but you had to be *fair*.

And Barry was a nice kid, solemn, intelligent, not as emotionally demanding as Leonore. Had taken a liking to me, never mentioned Joe, called me Uncle George.

I walked him to school, came back, shaved, sorted through the mail. Tetheridge wanted money. Flake needed vouchers. A note from the Home Counties Horse alleged that when she had been good enough to admit Leonore to her establishment, I had agreed to pay a year's school fees in advance. Would I kindly send a cheque for £158 17s. 8d. by return of post.

Tossed the letters into the rubbish bin, went into the bedroom, threw off my clothes, dived back into bed, where Marion lay, a furry *croissant*, wrapped up, warm. Diligently wooed her breasts, manipulated her clitoris. She shuddered sweetly, briefly. Came. Grateful for this acknowledgement of my presence, I mounted (no complaints about knees and elbows here), was sucked into her body, rode leisurely to climax. After which I re-wound, ran the entire film through again. *The Great Lover* (Paramount, 1949). Watched her sleeping, contented face. Crows' feet around mascara-smeared eyes. Lipstick fragments flecking bottom lip. Slut. Adorable.

Hardly over-communicative about her soiled past, Marion had fed me enough scraps of data to enable me to devise a Rough Treatment : *Starlet*.

Raised in North London Jewish orthodoxy. Seduced by neighbour's son plus two abortions before she was nineteen. Off to try for an acting career, evading threatened twenty-first birthday party. Ostracised by family. Father, rag-trade dervish, had died four years ago. Mother, bridge-playing, Bar-Mitzvah-attending Tory, had not talked to her since.

Montage. Experiences common to over-ambitious, under-trained actresses of her era. Sharing bleak flats in Kensington with disapproving la-di-dah models. Work-

172

ing behind bars of dire afternoon clubs. Auditioning hopelessly for totally unsuitable parts. Drinking gin before lunch. Decorating parties for visiting American stars, anxious to perpetuate potency legends. Propping up Battersea intellectuals' tentative orgies. Going off to Juan-les-Pins with status-seeking producers. Taking excessive but never fatal doses of seconal. Sleeping with modish photographers, who printed up naive pornography (starring Marion) for the delectation of friends.

Occasionally, she got herself cast in small parts on television. A pragmatic way of life which inevitably culminated in despondency, but meanwhile trained her to be giving to predators, brutal to softies.

Joe, most determined of the Softies, did his best to serve her and to understand. Turned her into a wife and mother, provided a respectable base for the pursuit of her professional ambitions. Aware of Marion's emotional versatility (encompassing lesbian, nympho, actress, suburbanite, exhibitionist in her range of fantasies), he asked her to spell out her sexual needs in the manner of a Fortnum and Mason assistant helping Madam to choose from available delicacies.

Joe's approach inhibited Marion. She started shopping for orgasms elsewhere.

'I mean,' she concluded one confession, 'if a man can't discover things like that for himself, what's the point of rabbiting on about it? It's not the sort of thing you can put into words.'

'You had a shot at it with me,' I reminded her.

'That's different. You're just as sneaky as me.'

'Were you unfaithful to Joe right from the start?'

'Only marginally, darling, only marginally.'

Chose not to pursue the matter. I had plenty of work on hand keeping my head above water in our own devious power-games. She'd told me once too often that in many little ways I reminded her of Joe. Remembering Dick's warnings about maintaining the correct tensions, I pretended to her that we would stay together only for as long as desire lasted. Untruthfully I hinted that, besides keeping her happy, I indulged with the occasional girl on the side. Return of Dracula.

'That's me,' I'd boast. 'Not going to pretend otherwise. Never going to change. Don't even want to.'

Game-player to her fingertips, Marion absorbed such attacks, pretending to believe every lie, making due allowances for her lover's colossal sexual appetite. Agreeing that our relationship was compounded of temporary convenience and sexual greed (the reiterated 'I love yous' just one of many devices to keep the juices flowing), she provided me with the perfect partner.

Technical obstacles came to the aid of our Grand Design. Though Old Rover had vanished overnight, we rarely went out together, spent most of our time together in bed. As we waited for the long-threatened amendment to Linda's divorce petition to materialise, we took good care to avoid old stamping grounds, where her friends, or Linda's, might spot us. Inevitably Marion socialised a bit on her own. After all, she had a career to pursue, whereas I only had to wait for the postman to deliver cheques for commercials I hadn't shot. This didn't worry me unduly. Mr. Hyde had made his emotional arrangements. So had Dr. Jekyll. Fancied myself in another role too—that of hardy Lone Ranger, crossing and recrossing the rugged, enemy-infested terrain that stretched between Kew and Hampstead: polarities of an old-timer's winter lovelife.

In return for financial security, Linda permitted me the privilege of seeing Leonore three times a week. Melud, called upon to approve the terms of our pact, pronounced them eminently satisfactory, congratulated Linda and myself upon the wisdom of our legal advisers. Thank you, my lord, we mumbled and bowed. Linda, befurred, hair gleaming a metallic red, freckles covered by a layer of white face powder, stood up so proudly upright that I was tempted to pin a medal on her chest.

Another Melud had meanwhile pronounced me unfit to drive, revoked my licence for two years. Taxis or mini-cabs were mirages of luxury. On access days I set off for Kew at eleven o'clock in the morning. Walked down winding roads to Swiss Cottage. Took a number 2 (or a 2a or even 2b) bus to Baker Street. Waited for the 27 bus. Rode to Kew, 50-minute drive. A twenty-minute route march finally brought me within sight of the Great Gates of Kiev, the iron railings of Leonore's old school.

At twelve-thirty-five, she came running out of the playground; we lunched at a gloomy little Italian café nearby, where I ordered one portion of everything, then divided the food on two plates. Me, Award-winning director. After taking her back to school, had to kill two and three quarter hours until it was time to report back to the school gates. Usually spent them in the Italian café, drinking pots of tea and reading newspapers. Sometimes I visited a public library two miles away, or dozed in an Odeon among sweet-rustling old-age pensioners. When it wasn't raining, I walked a mile to the local football ground, watching a Metropolitan League side training its reserves.

Collecting Leonore punctually at four fifteen, we marched off to join the queue of afternoon shoppers waiting for the 27 bus. Journeyed to Baker Street. Thence by a 2 (or a 2a or even 2b) bus to Swiss Cottage. Finally the culminating uphill stagger to Lady Whitestone's residence. Made Leonore's tea, played Monopoly, watched television. Before we could get warm, it was time to leave. Onwards: To Swiss Cottage, to Baker Street, to Kew in the rush-hour, to Linda's mansion. 'Bye, Daddy. Then back again, alone: Kew, Baker Street, Swiss Cottage, home. Exhaustion.

Saturdays were easier; called for Leonore at midday, had her with me all afternoon, delivered her back at seven o'clock precisely, as requested.

On none of these expeditions did I ever catch sight of Linda. Nor did Leonore express surprise that I never ventured beyond the garden gates. Sometimes, after hastily kissing me good-night, she whispered, 'Wait, Daddy,' then ran up the drive and into the house, front door silently opening and closing, as if moved by magic. While I waited in the dark, I could observe my Jaguar, resprayed a gleaming Royal blue. After a couple of minutes she was back, breathless, pressing into my hand some object rescued from my off-limits study : stapling machine, pencil sharpener, empty can of film.

Chain-smoking my way through those long wintry bus journeys, Lone Ranger persuaded himself that all was mighty fine. Leonore did not complain. I had not abandoned her. She had not abandoned me.

For a while I tried to conceal from her that Barry and Marion were living with me. Organised complicated in-out schedules for my mistress and her son. Credited Marion's presents to Joe or Ellis Trawley. Hastily stuffed bottles of perfume and Barry's daubings into drawers and suitcases. Interpreted telephone messages for Marion as calls for Lady Whitestone.

One afternoon, Leonore found washed nylon tights hanging in the bathroom. I had to go into a quick reverse : Super news! Joe, Marion and Barry had *all* moved into the flat to keep Daddy company. The Network hadn't called me Old Reliable for nothing. I deceived Leonore as diligently as once I'd deceived Linda. Persuaded myself that this winter was the happiest time of my life.

'Pinter,' Joe confided one evening, 'I'll tell you about old Harold.'

Between us, we'd just managed to soothe Barry off to sleep, now sat drinking Scotch, waiting for Marion to come home from rehearsal. She was working hard, playing a compassionate Vicar's wife in her twice-weekly serial, which had shot up into the Top Twenty and looked set to go on forever.

Joe visited us at least twice a week. Liked to keep in close touch with Barry, lectured me on the responsibilities of fatherhood. His method of dealing with the break-up of his marriage was to pretend that it hadn't happened. He and Marion continued to treat each other with affectionate civility. Nor could I fault Joe's attitude to me. Guarded emotional neutrality, wrapped in chummy professionalism.

Pinter: a safe subject. Joe looked greener, more troll-like than ever.

A film-rewrite, for which his agent was competing, had been assigned elsewhere. According to Ellis, Pinter was doing it.

'Let me tell you how that man works,' Joe went on without bitterness. 'Goes to bed with a full bladder.'

I looked at my watch. Marion should have been home an hour ago.

'Now then, before long, he nods off, Harold nods off, see? But two or three hours later, because of this full bladder, he wakes up, needs to spring a leak . . . you follow?'

'Needs to spring a leak . . .'

'Right. Now most people in that situation would get up and go to the bathroom. Not Harold Pinter. Wills himself back to sleep. That's his secret. He's got to go, but instead, back to sleep he goes. With this full bladder.'

Tonight Joe had brought along some toy balloons for Barry, and the electric under-blanket from his own bed. I had protested vigorously. Knew he loved his electric blanket. Never mind, Joe reassured me, Marion was working hard, needed that blanket. He could always get himself another one

'So off he goes to sleep again. Right? With this full bladder. And starts to dream. No, wait, George, I'm coming to the point. Finally he *has* to wake up, pressure on his bladder has become crucial. So here's the pay-off, George. When Harold comes back from the bathroom, instead of going back to bed, what he does, he's off to his study, see? With what he's been dreaming still pristine fresh in his mind. Get it? Switches on his tape-recorder. Speaks this dream into the machine, exactly as it happened, dialogue, pauses, the lot. Next morning, secretary comes round, types what's on the tape. That's it. All Harold does, he sits down, edits the typescript. Radio play, television adaptation, film rights, Broadway, West End, Prize Italia, Oscar.'

'That's your theory, is it?'

'Take Ionesco. Uses the same system. The full bladder school of creative writing. Beckett as well. Maybe even Kafka...'

Why was Marion so late? The way she kept demolishing that nutty serial director: suspicious. Barry had left some blown-up balloons scattered about the room. Joe picked one up, a yellow one, started bouncing it about.

'You don't look well, George,' he said, flicking the balloon into Lady Whitestone's open cocktail cabinet. 'It's all that rushing about by public transport you do. Tearing yourself apart. For what?'

'You come and see Barry.'

'I know, George, but a man's got to *work*.'

'It's allright for you, Joe...'

'I have my problems, too, believe you me...'

'How can I work if I haven't got a job?'

'I seem to have lost my wife...'

'All you need, Joe, you need a desk...'

'I'm not complaining, mind you. My fault. As she's no doubt told you, I don't satisfy her...'

'A desk and a blank sheet of paper and a pencil, that's all you need...'

'You apparently have the knack. Well, nothing I can do about that. I'm a realist.'

'I need a whole organisation behind me, Joe. Crew, technicians, money, a script ...'

'That's why I go on working, George. You're only half a father if you don't work. They notice it, kids I mean. Don't like fathers who're not working. Makes them feel guilty. Think it's their fault ...'

'I almost killed her,' I said, and immediately wished I hadn't.

Joe looked suitably embarrassed.

At that moment Marion let herself in, affecting the usual breathless entrance. What a day. Stroked my head in passing, kissed Joe's cheek, collapsed into a chair. Rehearsals. Costume fittings. Hairdressers. Shopping. Been rushing about like a blue-arsed fly.

'Gezonk,' she concluded, stretched her legs. I loved her. She irritated me.

'Joe's brought the electric blanket round,' I said.

'I'll switch it on for you, darling.'

She propelled herself out of her chair. Busy.

'A pot of tea, cold goodies, and bed, darling.'

Leading with *Activity*, I confirmed. If I allowed her to get away with that, there would be endless stories about the incompetence of hairdressers and the laziness of actors who just sat there doing crossword puzzles, refusing to contribute their fair share of energy to rehearsals. If I let her win that round by showing sympathy, she would follow up with *Prompts for Jealousy*. Nutty director wanted private rehearsal sessions to get her genteel vicarage accent right. This would leave me no alternative but to trump her with *Complaints of Illness*, a card she herself played to squash me whenever I opened with *Confessions of Emotional Atrophy*.

'I'll be off then,' Joe sighed, extracting a neatly wrapped package from his breast-pocket. Bottle of *Femme* for Marion.

'Darling, how sweet of you.'

Kissed him fondly. How could they do it? So courte-

179

ous, so civilised, while Linda and I went on tearing at each other in frenzied fantasies of retribution.

Marion linked her arm in Joe's, showed him to the door. I waved vaguely, picked up Marion's *Evening Standard*. Alarming thought: she was behaving towards Joe exactly as she had behaved towards me, while still living with him. *Illness* was the only card left to play.

I rose, mimed a sore throat. Might be 'flu, I groaned, doing some head-clutching and reeling. Astutely she absorbed my attack.

'I've switched on the blanket,' she said, embracing my waist as we stumbled into the bedroom. 'Tea and two aspirins, my darling, that's what you want.'

'Might be gastric 'flu,' I muttered, started to tear my clothes off. Quite a feat to modulate smoothly from *Complaints of Illness* to *Erotic Domination*. Still, it could be done. Jane Russell in *The Outlaw* (Howard Hughes–RKO 1950).

'I'll nurse you back to health, my darling,' she soothed. 'Don't you worry.'

'Perhaps I'd better sleep in the sitting-room.' An inspired card, which even Dick would not have been ashamed to play. 'Don't want to be sick all over you, do I?'

'My darling, I've held many a heaving head over a lavatory pan in my time.'

Mercifully, the telephone rang at that moment, enabling me to retreat into the sitting-room to regroup forces.

Dick.

Would I do him a favour? Send him some back numbers of *The Field*. Urgently. Matter of life and death. I promised to help, then volunteered a brief summary of my current situation with Leonore.

'In other words,' he said, 'you've lost her.'

I explained about Marion. Things had changed. I had changed. I was happy.

'As far as I can make out,' he said, 'your bloody career's

down the drain. You've lost the kid. Got yourself a new castrator. And two bloody divorce actions on your hands.'

'Started your play?' I asked in self-defence.

'Don't bother to send those copies of *The Field*. Just get them, I'm coming over to sort you out.'

He'd hung up. Receiver felt clammy. Games. That's all my relationships were: games. Which reminded me. Sickly Dr. Jekyll would now have to metamorphose into rapacious Mr. Hyde.

Clumped into the bedroom, invoking the incredible mastery of Rouben Mamoulian.

'Darling, I *thought* I felt funny,' Marion greeted ever-ready Mr. Hyde. 'Started the curse.'

Can't win 'em all.

'What shall we talk about, Daddy?'

'Anything you like. Sleeping-trains.'

'Why do you always want to talk about them?'

'You tell me.'

'Mummy? I mean Daddy? Auntie Elspeth says it won't ever go away.'

'What won't?'

'That scar. On my forehead.'

'Hardly shows, does it? Got your curls hanging over it, love.'

'Do you like the colour of my hair, Daddy?'

'Very much.'

'Mummy says I take after her in looks.'

'You do. In looks.'

'Auntie Elspeth says it was all your fault. The scar. I mean the accident.'

'I didn't do it on purpose, love.'

'She says something else about you, Auntie Elspeth I mean.'

'What else does she say?'

'Oh, Daddy, look at all those lovely pineapples. Aren't they huge? And only three shillings each.'

Stay buoyant. Don't mope. Children notice everything. Not a bloody thing escapes their attention. Put your arm around her. Cuddle her. No, wait for her to take *your* arm. She likes that, reaching up for you, hanging on to you, trying to look grown-up. She's your daughter. She loves you. Don't watch for *signs* all the time. She'd love you even if you didn't knock yourself out to see her. Stay buoyant.

Sometimes, on Saturdays, I rang the changes, cut down on bus-journeys, didn't drag her back all the way to Hampstead, foraged into the West End. To feed the pigeons in Trafalgar Square. Or visit the toyshops. Or something. Anything.

The morning had come up a crisp blue, promising mild warmth. We had gone by train from Kew Bridge to Waterloo. After the pigeons: Chinese lunch, special treat. She liked all those little dishes on hot plates, the inscrutable waiter, the piped Muzak; spilled sweet and sour pork onto the starched white table square. Will the waiter mind, Daddy? Will we have to pay for washing the tablecloth? Not to worry, darling, not to worry.

I nibbled. Never could eat much when we were together. Always this hard dumpling rattling about in my stomach. Anxiety neurosis. With a grown-up woman it was different; you could melt away into her softness. Release. Oblivion. Sleep. With a girl not yet nine, how could you melt away? Your presence was required. In the train, she'd had a giggling fit. Pummelled me, using my body as a punching bag. Sparring partner.

In the same carriage, sitting opposite us: attractive young brunette in a zipped-up rabbitcoat, reading the *Daily Mirror*. I shielded my face, as mittened blows rained down on me. Everything inside me was rigid, frozen. Couldn't breathe. The girl in the carriage never looked up. Old geyser with a horrible kid. Not Her Kind. Don't *try* so hard . . .

After lunch we visited a cartoon cinema. Cats and dogs trying to kill each other. Came out into the cold, strolled along the stalls and barrows of Berwick Street market. Leonore loved busy markets. She wore a hooded, pleated blue anorak, black corduroy trousers, blue mittens. The furry boots I'd bought at Harrods that time; the memory warmed my stomach a little, the dumpling began to dissolve.

Nostalgia already? For that bleak period of high crisis? At least we'd been alone, just the two of us. Honeymoon. At Dick's we'd even slept together in the same bed. Those were the days, my friend. She'd been perfectly happy, no getting away from that. Now the boots were pinching her toes. And Mummy had told her that if Daddy had any sense, he would have bought a larger size.

It was getting dark. Dusk shrouded stalls and barrows. Old women in head scarves weighed apples with frost-bitten hands. Redfaced men in blue overcoats, butts glowing in their fists, shouted blurred invitations, bellowing the same insistent phrases into our faces, over and over again. Only Leonore didn't feel the cold.

We went up to the pineapple barrow. I bought the biggest pineapple the man could find. Tossed and turned it in a brown paper bag. To take home to Mummy.

'Aren't they cheap? Perhaps they're all rotten inside.'

'What else does Aunty Elspeth say?'

'I bags to carry the pineapple, Daddy.'

'What else does she say about me?'

'Oh nothing . . : says you're a Jew.'

'Half-truth.'

'We're not Jews, are we?'

'I am. You're not. What does it matter?'

No doubt Linda would want her confirmed. I felt ashamed.

'Auntie Elspeth says the Jews killed Jesus Christ.'

'If they did, it's hardly my fault, is it?'

Yegods, I sounded like Linda. Could we walk a little faster, please? A bit further down, I knew a stall which sold lovely sparkly jewellery. They hadn't killed him. The Romans had done it. And what's more, Jesus himself was a Jew.

'He wasn't, was he?'

'Of course he was. Don't they teach you anything at school?'

'I'll tell Auntie Elspeth, shall I?'

'Yes, you tell Auntie Elspeth.'

'I don't think she knows about that.'

We sorted about among the costume jewellery. She wanted to buy me a pair of cufflinks. No darling, don't want cufflinks. Oh, please, Daddy, please. Daddy doesn't need cufflinks. Lend me the money, Daddy. I'll take it out of my piggy-bank.

'How much pocket-money does Mummy give you now?'

'One and six a week. That makes half a crown with your shilling.'

'From now on I'll give you one and six as well.'

'Oh *thanks*, Daddy.'

'Don't you waste your money on rotten old cufflinks for me.'

'Allright then.'

A bad mistake that, raising her pocket-money. Appeasement. I'd be getting it in the neck for that.

One by one, the lights were being switched on in the shopwindows beyond the barrows. Squares of warmth and activity. Hold my hand, love. Let's have a run, play knights. *Charge!* Escape that acrid-sweet smell of fruit. Why did the name Anderson keep running through my head? Lindsay? No, the other one. Andersen. Fairytales. Little Matchgirl. Snow Queen. Encased in ice. Don't give in to self-pity. Why? Because she can tell. You be proud of your Daddy, my love, he's a highly respected figure, won an important award, once. Thought to be extremely dependable. By whom? Not by old Jack Martinsell for a start. Abandoned.

What had I ever done for which she could respect me? Over a hundred forgotten television slots. Down the drain, tapes wiped. All she could remember was that Family Biscuit commercial. Which I hadn't shot. Whoring actors whooping it up round an overlit table. Teatime. Directed by a foreign genius. Your Daddy wouldn't be seen dead making such crap, my darling. Why had we come to this bloody market anyway? To keep buoyant. Buoyant! I can't go on like this, my love, dumpling rattling about in my empty insides. Dying. Must get away. Take her up on a magic carpet, a cold night train; sleeping-train, she called it. Going South? No, not South. Done that before. In an easterly direction, over weedcovered rails, into stations with locked iron barriers. If you could crash those barriers you got your chance to start all over again. Soccer on gravelly grounds. With Leonore. Violet jerseys. Goal.

'Mummy, I mean Daddy?'

'Yes?'

'Mummy says . . .'

'I'm freezing to death, darling. Let's make tracks for home, shall we?'

'Mummy says we may be moving again soon.'

'Does she?'

'To Beaconsfield she says.'

'Where?'

'I think that's the name of the place. *Beaconsfield*. A lovely little cottage with a garden and flowers. It's proper country. We can keep lots of pets there, Mummy says.'

'You don't want to change schools again, do you?'

'Don't mind.'

We stumbled on. Silence. Ice-bound.

'Daddy, will you be cross?' She had stopped in her tracks. 'If I say something, will you be cross?'

'What? How do I know before you say it?'

'I love you, Daddy.'

I looked down at her face, past her eyes. The hood of her anorak was down, the wind blowing her curls about. What kind of game was this?

'I love you better than Mummy. Honestly.'

She clasped my waist, brought my face down to hers, kissed me on the mouth, long and wet and hard. We stood in the gloom, tightly enlaced, buffeted by a grey, shuffling crowd.

'What do you want to say a thing like that for?'

'I knew you'd be cross.'

The brown paper bag with the pineapple slumped down, landed between our feet. I bent down to retrieve it.

'Nice pineapple for Mummy,' I said. 'She likes pineapples.'

Didn't want her to go on. Betraying Linda. Again. Creature from the Black Lagoon will get you for this. As sure as God made little apples.

'Come on,' I said sharply. 'Let's get a move on.'

'I love Mummy as well, but not as much as you.'

'We all love each other. All knights: *Charge*!'

'Poor Daddy. I only told you because you look such a misery.'

I will take you on that night train, your sleeping-train. Which runs straight into a tram depot. Was I dreaming again? I avoided her eyes. Get her to that tube station. Quickly.

We arrived in Kew earlier than usual. There had been less travelling to get through. Just a couple of tubes. The house was dark. No eyes of light. I waited at the garden gate. She came running back.

'There's no one in, Daddy.'

'We're probably early. Mummy won't be long.'

Pitchdark. I put my arm around her. She struggled out of my reach, climbed the gate, started swinging on it.

'Do you remember Mrs. MacWhirter?' I heard her call out. 'Nice old soul, wasn't she?'

Funny tone of voice. Leonore too? Nostalgia? For those days, my friend?

'Do Joe and Marion sleep in her room now?' she asked. 'Mrs. MacWhirter's room?'

'What? Yes. I told you . . .'

'It's a bit tiny for them both, isn't it? Mrs. MacWhirter used to complain, said it was too small for all her things. How do Joe and Marion manage in a single bed?'

She went on swinging in the dark, her back turned to me. The gate creaked. I stood under a tree, straining my eyes. Couldn't think of anything to say. Rat gnawed away at the dumpling in my stomach.

After a long wait, heard the sound of a car approaching and slowing down. Leonore, her face illuminated by headlamp glare, jumped down to open the gate, the Royal blue Jaguar glided through. Linda was at the wheel, her sister sat next to her, looking straight ahead. Two identical noses high up in the air, sniffing.

' 'Bye then, Daddy.'

She ran after the car. Brakes. Doors opening and closing. Key turning in lock. Voices in the dark, far away, fading.

'We've been waiting for half an hour, Mummy, where on earth have you been?'

'Daddy knows he should bring you back at the proper time.'

'I've got a pineapple for you, Mummy. Present from Daddy.'

Front-door slammed. Voices dying. Murderous ruminations. Middle-period Fritz Lang.

By the time I got back to Hampstead, a thousand resentments were bubbling away inside my head. Marion was on the phone, in bed. Buttery warm, her body doused with *Femme*. I kissed her. She went right on talking. I made myself a cheese sandwich in the kitchen, drank a glass of beer. Pleasant dreams, Harold Pinter.

I got undressed. She was still on the bloody telephone, prattling away to Joe, calling him by his pet name ('Joe-kins', if you'll credit it), discussing a plan to share the services of Mrs. Chapple, the cleaning-woman who'd worked for them at their maisonette. She had since remained attached to Joe. Marion claimed we needed Mrs. Chapple. She said it twice, three times, then started again from scratch, said it a fourth time. Joe was agreeing to everything, of course. I got into bed. She took her time wishing Joe good-night.

'He's finished your horoscope,' she informed me. 'Isn't he nice? He really is a good man.'

'Lovely.'

'Snuggle up then.'

Snuggle up? Tomorrow I'd have to call Tetheridge about that mooted move to Beaconsfield. Didn't want to snuggle up. Wanted a furtive bang with that *Mirror*-reading girl in the train from Kew.

Was it for this that I had sacrificed all? Deserted Linda, abandoned my worldly goods and chattels? *Snuggle up?*

Clear your mind, George, be methodical in your madness. Do something. Make a list ...

To get stuck into a variety of anonymous birds, that's why I'd done it. To have Leonore close to me. To watch soccer on Saturday afternoons. And not *one* of these plans had materialised. Pathetic routine of domestic cuddles. Didn't want it. Home-baked, anti-erotic.

Marion, playing games, offered me a lighted cigarette. Tasted of *Femme*. Resentments kept boiling away. Why should I have to rely on Leonore to fetch bits and pieces out of my study? Wasn't part of the deal. Tetheridge needed a stick of dynamite placed under his arse. Abandoned! My books, my files, my cans of film clips, my press cuttings! Most of all I wanted *Quigley's International*

Motion Picture Almanac of 1956, bound in black-and-orange. *That's* what I wanted. Running down a list of feature releases, 1944–55, might be as soothing as contemplating football tables. Had meant to go to that foreign paper shop in Old Compton Street, buy the latest *France Football*. Who was heading the first division in Czechoslovakia? Where was Fortuna Hansdorf? In the heat of that love skene with Leonore, I'd forgotten all about it.

'Darling, do talk to me.'

Talk to me! Snuggle up! Marion was no more aware than Linda of Mr. Hyde's secret needs. Mr. Hyde wanted no chatty snuggling. Mr. Hyde was cold and secretive, always snatching at some elusive scrap of colour from his past, dreaming of hungry, fruitless journeys through the dark. The more warmth Dr. Jekyll found in Marion's furry embrace, the more pressing became Mr. Hyde's demands.

I want *France Football*! I want *Quigley's International Motion Picture Almanac of 1956*! I want my bloody freedom! Alone on cold night trains with *France Football*, girl in a rabbitcoat unzipping my flies, violet jerseys in the sunshine. Jean.

'Darling, you're so restless. Can I get you anything?'

'*Quigley's International Motion Picture Almanac*, 1956 edition. And the latest *France Football*.'

'Stretch your legs, darling. Let all your aches flow into the bed.'

'Marion, for Christ's sake, don't give me bloody baby-talk. I'm not Barry.'

'Don't be cross with me, darling, but when you're feeling like this, you should ring Leonore and tell her you can't manage ...'

'I'm feeling fine.'

'She'd understand.'

'You spend every free moment with Barry, I want to do the same with *my* kid. Why shouldn't I?'

All wrong, that plaintive voice. If I make love to her now : fiasco.

'Sometimes I think you only go to all this trouble to get even with Linda. And all you do is *help* her. By taking Leonore off her hands.'

'I see Leonore because I want to.'

'Then don't complain so much.'

'Who's complaining?'

Like some old married couple. I raised myself up on my elbows, brushing away her soothing hand. Deal with a complaint the moment it comes up, Dick had advised, never postpone it, or it will curdle into resentment.

'Listen, Marion,' I said. 'When you met me, I didn't know who I was. Well, now I know. *I am what I do.* Right? Not a TV director. Not a husband. Just a father. That's all I am. A father.'

Sententious rubbish, sentimental and false : Kirk Douglas sounding off in C.S. to save some lousy fiftyish 'progressive' script. Set it to music, you might even ascend to the plateau of Oscar Hammerstein II.

Why?

Because Marion was right. I *was* seeing Leonore to get even with Linda. But not in the way she thought. Even now I craved her approval. Bloody pineapples I tried to smuggle through to her. Too shit-scared to go into my own house and fetch a copy of *Quigley's International Motion Picture Almanac of 1956*! Even now, after nineteen years, I was trying to woo her. That's why I had let her steal my savings, confiscate my house, take away my child. Hadn't even bothered to counter-petition for divorce on the clear-cut grounds of screwing car-hire managers. And I'd give her more. Still more. Anything she asked for I'd hand her on a plate. For a smile. A glimmer of humour. A forgiving word. Admiration. Knowing all the while that I would never get any of them from this mild-mannered, intelligent, musical woman with her freckles and metallic red curls, partner for life, mother of my child, who charged my entire system with a monstrous, amorphous dread.

I did as asked. Snuggled into Marion. Hot soothing fur. Warm hole. Dick, why do I never learn?

The consequences came promptly.

'Darling,' she said, 'I saw that old chum of yours this afternoon.'

'What old chum?'

'Roger Arnold. Who took those super pictures of me.'

Arctic waters. Sibelius. Mezzo-forte strings ebbing away into nothingness.

'You see, what happened, he rang me up. Has this super scheme . . .'

'I thought,' I said, 'you spent the afternoon with Barry.'

'Roger's branching out. Always wanted to produce films, he says. He's going to make this experimental movie. A co-operative venture. Has some marvellous way-out ideas . . .'

'That talentless phoney? Producing a film? Couldn't produce his way out of a . . .'

'Darling, he wants me to be in it.'

'Isn't that serial keeping you busy enough?'

'He's only going to shoot me at week-ends. Got this super pad in Hammersmith . . .'

'You've been to his *place*? To Roger Arnold's *place*?'

'That's what I'm trying to tell you.'

'I don't believe it. I just don't believe it.'

'Darling, don't turn away from me. Please don't turn away. This could be my big chance, darling. To do something really worthwhile. Roger's got some financial backing. And Paramount are interested.'

'And no doubt *he's* interested in screwing the arse off you.'

'Darling! It's nothing like that. Anyway, he's queer, isn't he?'

'Is he? You tell me.'

191

'You know Roger better than I do. Told me you've known each other for ages.'

'I haven't set eyes on that grasshopping opportunist for over fifteen years. And it hasn't escaped my notice that every randy so-called producer who comes sniffing round your private parts is dished up to me as being queer.'

Show of jealousy. She was winning hands down. I was starting an erection. She'd been absent-mindedly touching me up.

'Would you like to talk about it, my darling? This thing you have about Roger. Might be something buried away in your sub-conscious.

'Spare me the paperback Freud, Marion. And let go my cock.'

'I think I *do* understand how you feel.'

She couldn't even begin to understand. That talentless sycophant was dogging my footsteps like some character in the *Tales of Hoffman*. The one who popped up in a green spotlight at the end of each act. Turning up as a photographer to glorify Dick. Now flaunting himself to Marion as a movie producer. Out to destroy me.

'Turn round, kiss my nipples.'

'Can't get round me by talking like one of Dick's novels, Marion . . .'

'I *can* get round you, my darling. I'll get you excited, and then . . .'

'Not so hard then. What are you trying to do? Castrate me?'

'You're jumping to pretty farfetched conclusions anyway. Roger just likes my work.'

'Shut up and concentrate on the job in hand, Marion. If you must.'

'I must.'

Yegods, what a bizarre compound of warmth and deviousness! Promiscuous and unprincipled. I really would have to reform her. Hold it. Hadn't I started off with Linda, trying to reform *her*? Was there no way of escaping one's compulsions?'

'I can feel the warmth going right through my body, my love.'

One of her nipples was in my mouth. The other she squeezed between thumb and forefinger, exciting herself.

'Go into me, my sweet, go into me.'

Deluding myself that I was punishing her, I wasted no energy trying to make her come first. Pleasured myself, conjuring up images of rabbitcoated girls in trains, and electric cooker demonstrators. Before long I was done, flat on my back, reaching for a cigarette.

Roger bloody Arnold coming between me and Marion as he had once tried to come between me and Linda.

Fantastic! Marion was humming, wiping her legs with Kleenex. The punishment fix had failed to take. It wasn't Marion who had withdrawn into an ice-cube. The familiar aspic of ice contained *me*.

Turning into Linda? Not a bad idea, come to think of it. Superior horror movie. Synopsis: Husband s-l-o-w-l-y metamorphoses into his wife: a suspected werewolverine. Setting: Eerie castle in Provence. Climax: Wife confronted in her bedroom by homicidal double. Vincent Price in drag. Two Vincent Prices in drag. Roger Corman might produce it. Or Roger Arnold, blast his soul. Talk it over with Dick. He might consent to do a treatment for me. The ice was melting. Was I girding my loins to start work again?

Or wait—event better, more bizarre: Heroine (Mia Farrow) s-l-o-w-l-y turns into the child she loves. Who happens to be a vampire. Regression to the age of nine. Fangs. Climax on edge of a cliff. Below: the moonspattered sea. Hero (John Cassavetes) confronted by Fanged Creature. His own child? (Could be played by a dwarf.) Would I remember it all in the morning? Would it seem as potent in the light of day as it did in the dead of night?

I'm coming back, Jack Martinsell! Clear the decks! Return of Dependable George Kane.

They came on a bad day.

Dick was attended by a new girl-friend, predictably flat-chested and submissive. Antje. A rug of straight, blonde hair fell down to her shoulders; melancholy fringe concealed forehead and eyebrows. Dutch, a student of architecture. Only spoke when spoken to.

Assigned to Mrs. MacWhirter's old room, Dick moved the furniture, while Antje hung the walls with Toulouse-Lautrec posters. Then they began to sort about among an alarming clutter of suitcases.

I had planned to impress Dick with my new freedom, my fantastic erotic power over Marion, my *sang-froid* in solving accumulated problems, but with Marion away at the studios, taping her show, I had to look after Barry. Also it was one of Leonore's access days. And I had previously agreed to let her bring a friend to tea. Barry and the friend, a chubby large-nosed girl with a lisp called Eva, loathed each other on sight, spent most of the afternoon locked in combat on the floor, Leonore occasionally coming to Eva's aid with Lady Whitestone's bijou toasting fork. When I wasn't trying to separate the contestants, I was groaning over a hot stove, cooking fishcakes and mashed potatoes and peas.

Dick chose to ignore the chaos; evidently meant to bide his time, deliver judgement when we were alone. For the moment, he concentrated on projecting energy. Bullied Antje, monopolised the telephone, proclaimed that he was, once more, A New Man.

Since my last visit to Cannes he had taken stock of his life and found it wanting. Janine had been a Big Mistake. Wasted his powers by requiring him to sort out her personality defects. Janine, the neurotic, had to go. What did I think of Antje? Though I found her almost indistinguishable from her predecessors, I grudged a few words of cautious admiration. Shouting for cigarettes, Dick launched into an analysis of Antje's virtues, paced about the kitchen. I mashed potatoes.

'She's got a quality of real responsiveness. Even you must see that, George. Haven't you noticed how she responds to me?'

'She carries out your orders,' I agreed bleakly.

'It works,' Dick said, flicking ash into a milkjug. 'It really works this time.'

He had been perfecting his system of creating tensions and counter-tensions, by which women could be happily dominated, while the male ego remained intact. What did I mean, Rule of Terror? Had I ever seen a happier woman than Antje?

Sieved peas, conceded I had never seen a happier woman than Antje.

Furthermore, I learned, Antje had read his play and thought highly of it. Antje had genuine inspirational gifts. Naturally, to keep her happy, it was essential to let her think herself stupid. That way she would keep on trying.

'What play?' I asked, prising frozen fishcakes from their cardboard wrappings.

'Didn't I tell you? I've finally written the play.'

The one he had gone South to write. He'd come to London to arrange for its production. Had asked Jeremy Shirlwell round to the flat to discuss managements. He had written his last thriller. The whole thing was finally scraped out of my system. Did I know any good directors?

Fishcakes spattered hot fat in all directions. I told Dick to get stuffed.

'Sorry, thought you had retired.'

He was looking for a *young* director with box-office appeal. Joe was bringing round Dan Wymans. What did I think of Wymans?

'He directs movies,' I told him, 'and he's fifty if he's a day.'

I ladled food out on three plates. Dick helped himself to one of the fishcakes. Trying to resist this manœuvre, I dropped one of the plates, smashed it.

'Coffee,' Dick shouted. Antje appeared instantly.

'Get a move on,' Dick told her, 'I'm dying for a cup of coffee.'

I balanced the plates on a tray, carried it into the sitting-room. The kids were sprawled on the floor, wrestling, pulling hair, squealing.

'Sexy little sods,' Dick commented, kicked Barry's arse.

I switched the TV on, served the fishcakes. Eva demanded tomato ketchup. I stumbled back into the kitchen to fetch it. Dick followed, gave Antje a cursory embrace.

'Time you had a bath,' he told her. 'You stink.'

Antje smiled blissfully. I found the ketchup. Antje, lost in Dick's embrace, let her milk boil over.

'Christ,' I said.

'What's up?' Dick asked, affronted. 'If you're short of milk, I'll send her out for more.'

Antje poured the rest of my milk into a saucepan.

'How does Leonore strike you?' I asked, wiped the hotplate with a damp cloth, burned my fingers.

'Pain in the neck, but that's how you like your women, isn't it?'

Leaving them to continue their love-making. I returned to the sitting-room. Any minute now what was left of my milk would boil over. Dick would feel he had scored a point.

Pain in the neck?

The kids were munching peacefully, watching the commercials.

'You haven't opened your letter, Daddy.' Leonore held up a buff envelope. 'May I open it?'

I was stalking about, picking fishcake off the carpet.

'It says On Her Majesty's Service. Lovely red writing inside. Is it from the Queen?'

Income-tax demand for five thousand, three hundred and sixty-six pounds, fourteen shillings and elevenpence. Final Reminder. Found some clean envelopes lurking between two telephone directories, selected one, slipped the demand inside, addressed the envelope to Conrad Veidt, UFA, Berlin, Germany.

'May I lick it, Uncle George?' Barry asked.

'I bags to lick it,' Leonore demanded.

Let all three of them have a good wet lick. So easy to keep kids happy when you know how.

The flat began to fill up with Dick's guests. High time to take Leonore and Eva back to Kew. Linda would be on the warpath. I was kept busy answering the door.

Joe arrived first; had Ellis Trawley in tow, looking pale and noble. Joe wore a clean white shirt, frayed at the collar. Dan Wymans came dressed in flowery silks, his hair arranged in a fringe, waving a fistful of first-night tickets. An American Underground group were performing in a basement in Baker Street: The motherfuckers. The children, hearing Dan's announcement, gurgled with rapture.

Joe brought a bottle of Scotch, asked for a corkscrew. Dan Wymans assured Dick that he loved his stories, would give his eye-teeth to direct one. I fetched glasses from the kitchen, started handing out drinks. The doorbell rang. I admitted Jeremy Shirlwell.

'Toujours Borehamwood?' Shirlwell asked wittily, peered over my shoulder to sort out my guests in order of importance, automatically assumed a kneeling position in Dick's vicinity. Barry and Eva had started fighting again. I asked Leonore to call her mother: she might be home late. While she dialled, I went into the bedroom, hastily stuffed Marion's pill factory into a suitcase. Then I called the children in, got a game of Monopoly going

When I came back, Ellis Trawley was declining Dick's invitation to attend the Underground performance.

Whatshisname, who had seen the group in Los Angeles, had told him all about it. The sheerest filth, culminating in a simulated act of fellatio. Great versatility was required of actors these days, he mused.

'Besides, who wants to go to the theatre to see *that*?' Dan Wymans interpolated shrilly. 'You get enough of that at home, don't you, my lovely?'

Joe sneaked a furtive glance at his watch.

'Marion shouldn't be long,' I reassured him.

'Quite allright,' he said curtly, avoiding my eyes.

Dick had started to narrate his play to Dan, who punctuated the story with exclamations of astonishment. I could hear the kids battling away in the hall, went to pacify them. Didn't want to play boring old Monopoly. Went to answer the doorbell again. Jack Martinsell, white-haired, short-legged. I blinked. He hugged me gravely. I smelt hair-oil.

'Dick called me,' he winked. 'Boy, it's great to have the old team in harness again.'

He stomped off into the sitting-room, yelling kingsize greetings at Dick. Leonore had flung her arms around me, kissed me wetly, lips parted.

'That's how they do it on the telly,' she informed Eva, who was straddling Barry, jumping up and down on his stomach.

I fled back into the crowd. Jack Martinsell was stroking back his hair, shifting his weight from one foot to the other, laughing out loud at nothing in particular. Dick instructed Antje to bring him a drink, then continued to explain his play to Dan.

'Didn't know it was a party,' Jack exclaimed, coming up close to breathe executive-lunch garlic into my face, kneading my shoulders. 'Gee, you look great. Why haven't you *called* me?'

Turned to answer the telephone. Tetheridge.

'I've been trying to get you all day,' he said bad-temperedly. 'Why is your telephone always engaged?'

I placed my hand over one ear, requested silence.

Nobody heard me, except Dick, who immediately raised his voice.

'Got the amendment at last,' Tetheridge said.

'What amendment?'

'The amendment to your wife's divorce petition . . .'

Pressed my left hand harder to my left ear. Out of the corner of one eye I saw Marion making an effusive entrance. Joe rose from the sofa, tactfully retreated into a corner to evade the roundelay of affectionate embraces. Marion was kissing everybody, even Antje. Dan Wymans cradled her cheeks between his palms, kissed her lips langorously. Dick fondled her bottom. In the hall, Barry was bawling for his mother. The noise in the flat was deafening.

'Can't hear you,' I told Tetheridge.

'Cruelty,' Tetheridge shouted.

'Darlings, you must all be starving,' Marion recited. 'Dick, you look so lovely and brown. Super . . .'

'Don't understand . . .'

'There are some thirty-seven items. I see no point in reading them out to you now . . .'

'What do you mean "items"?'

'The petition mentions a certain amount of physical cruelty, but most of the items seem to lie in the area of mental cruelty . . .'

'You mean she hasn't included *her* in the amendment?'

'*Her?*'

'Marion Leeds. Your friend Joe's . . .'

'I should be very careful what you say to me, Mr. Kane. As I had occasion to remind you before now . . .'

'Coming to the motherfuckers, doll?'

Dan Wymans was embracing Marion. (*The Sheik*, Rudolph Valentino, 1925.)

'Can't wait, darling.'

'We shall need to discuss your Answer to these charges,' Tetheridge advised, taciturnity in his voice.

'I'm telling you, man, in the last act, they're not only at it like knives, they get the audience to join 'em.'

Tetheridge was reading selected cruelty allegations. The three kids came roaring back into the room. Leonore clung to my elbow, swinging her legs. I signalled to Marion, who chose not to notice.

'The majority of items,' Tetheridge continued, 'stress acts of infidelity and habitual associations of an adulterous nature . . .'

'For God's sake, Marion . . .'

'Darling, why hasn't your Daddy taken you home yet?'

'What? . . . I can't hear you, Mr. Tetheridge . . .'.

'. . . causing your wife profound distress . . .'

Marion had succeeded in loosening Leonore's grip on me, turned to Joe, who loitered alone by the window.

'Darling, do make yourself useful. Put Barry to bed. I'll prepare some goodies.'

Joe jumped to it, dragging his son out by the scruff of his neck.

'Cruelty, of course, can be very difficult to prove . . .'

'Dick, baby,' Jack Martinsell bawled. 'So when are you starting to write for us again? *Carte blanche*, baby, always got *carte blanche* with the Network . . .'

'. . . I admit she hasn't a very strong case, Mr. Kane, but defending would mean washing a certain amount of dirty linen in public . . .'

'I don't give a bugger about that.'

'Moreover, do bear in mind that if you defended successfully, you'd still be married at the end of the day.'

'Can I help you, Mrs. Kane?' Antje asked Marion respectfully.

'Darling, did you hear what she called me? Oh, do get off that *bloody* phone . . .'

'Marion, I'm trying to . . . hold on a sec, Mr. Tetheridge . . .'

'Then there's the question of costs, Mr. Kane. If you

decide to defend, total costs might well run up to five figures.'

'You've just *got* to take those girls home, George . . .'

'Of course, if you gave Mrs. Kane satisfactory adultery grounds, I dare say she'd be advised by Counsel to stay her cruelty petition. If I correctly interpret her tactics . . .'

'Dick, baby, right now we've got this really great series on the drawing-boards. Now I know what you're going to say, baby, but hold it. We only call it a series to keep foreign sales happy. It's a goddam anthology, I give you my word. World's Great Fairy Tales. The old magic brought up to date . . . bet your sweet bippy we'll do it with taste, Dick . . .'

'That would still leave your wife's initial adultery petition to be taken into account . . .'

'Aren't I supposed to sue *her* for adultery?'

'We want *real writers* for this show, Dick . . .'

'And another thing. This projected move to Beaconsfield . . .'

'Daddy, are you talking to the man about Mummy?'

'Marion, I beg you, *get Leonore out of here* . . . No, Mr. Tetheridge, I . . .'

'Got to see about the eats, darling.'

'Since the marital home is now in your wife's name, she can of course sell it, and move any time she so desires. She could *not*, of course, reduce the amount of access specified by court order . . .'

'How the hell am I supposed to get out to Beaconsfield three times a week?' My voice was a hysterical rasp. 'I've had my driving-licence cancelled . . .'

'With all respect, Mr. Kane, that's hardly your wife's problem, is it?'

'Surely that's already been done on the box. Grimm? Andersen? That Frenchman, whatshisname, you know . . .'

'You're wrong, Ellis. Grimm's virgin territory! We

checked. Can't you see it, Dick? *Cinderella* with all the submerged Freudian undertones brought out and developed! *Little Red Riding Hood* retold with real imagination. We see it as a valid contribution to the race problem . . .'

I finally put the receiver down, took a deep breath, cleared my throat.

'What do you know,' I announced to the room. 'Linda's sueing me for cruelty.'

'Doesn't that grab you, Dick baby? The wolf we visualise as this basically sympathetic buck nigger. Gambling boss. The Firm. As for Little Red Riding Hood, she's come down from the sticks, simple, good-natured Yorkshire girl with big tits, doesn't know her ass from her elbows. Drifts into stripping, see? Very trusting and vulnerable. We'll get whatshername for the part . . .'

'Don't tell me,' Ellis interrupted. 'Marvellous actress. We worked at the Vic together, whenwasit, er . . .'

'No, not that one, Ellis. The other one, you know, whatshisname's girl-friend.'

'She's still married to whatsit, surely. . . ?'

Marion was flitting round the room, dispensing embraces and snackettes. Joe, having read Barry to sleep, had provided the girls with soapy water and a plastic bubble blower. Now he was trying to open a couple of bottles of wine, which Antje had produced from one of her suitcases. Joe managed to cork the second bottle.

Dick was outraged.

'Jesus,' he screamed at Joe, who looked green and crestfallen. 'Clumsy bloody sod. That's château-bottled wine you've corked. Joe, you're falling apart. What the hell's the matter with you?'

'He didn't do it on purpose, Dick,' Marion pleaded, laying a protective hand on her husband's shoulder.

'You're just destroying him, aren't you, Marion?' Dick

bellowed at her. 'You've castrated a fine writer. That's château-bottled wine.'

'Take it easy, Dick,' Joe said quietly. 'Don't play your bloody games with Marion.'

He turned to push up a window, let out some accumulated smoke. The children clambered onto the window-sill and blew coloured bubbles into the night.

I sat on the floor hiding behind *What's On*. A title among the local cinema listings caught my eye.

'Darling, do please take those little girls home,' Marion begged from far away. 'They'll catch their deaths of cold.'

I got up from the floor, poured myself a large Scotch, gulped it down. On the sofa, Ellis Trawley was trying to engage Antje in polite conversation. I heard Dick pull the chain in the lavatory. The familiar sound of famous names being denigrated drifted over from a corner to which Dan Wymans (probably sensing imminent domestic catastrophe) had withdrawn with Jack Martinsell and Jeremy Shirlwell.

I commanded the girls to put on their overcoats. Dick came back, asked me curtly where I thought I was going.

'The kids ...'

'Always those fucking kids. Relax, can't you?'

'Should have taken them home ages ago.'

'Oh, screw that. We're going to the motherfuckers.'

I signalled desperately: Don't-use-language-like-that-in-front-of-the-children. Leonore will tell Linda. Injure My Case.

Too late. Leonore and Eva were rolling about on the floor, probably pissing themselves. Marion was swinging round the room, refilling glasses.

'You haven't even got a flaming car,' Dick expostulated. 'Joe's got a car. He'll take the kids home. Won't you, Joe?'

'Don't ask him.'

'Don't mind, can't stand first nights,' Joe said tersely,

marching out into the hall to search for his overcoat.

'Why should I let him do my dirty work?' I hissed at Dick.

'Because he likes it, that's why.'

'Bloody humiliating for him.'

'Joe's problem. He could have refused.'

I gathered up the kids from the floor, kissed Leonore.

'Tell Mummy I'm sorry you've been kept out late,' I instructed her. 'Enjoy yourself, did you?'

'Yes, lovely.'

Flat tone of her voice gave me a moment's anxiety.

Marion accompanied Joe and the children as far as the front door. Dick announced he wanted to change, ordered clean socks and under-pants. Dan Wymans tweaked my arm.

'No idea you and Marion were having it away,' he confided. 'Got it made there, my lovely. Plate expert of all time. Fuck me.'

Turning away, I found myself eyeball to eyeball with Jack Martinsell. His glance absconded over my shoulder for help. Too late.

'Boy, it's good to see you,' he whined.

'So how are things back at the ranch?'

'Hear you're doing some very fine commercials, baby. Very fine.'

'Has Crane been in touch with you?'

'Crane? Let me see. We were due to lunch last week. Had to cancel. Jesus, George, we're *that* busy . . . how *is* old Crane?'

I was staring at his hand lying flat against my sleeve. You can always tell an American executive by the way he deploys his hands. Non-American executives *curl* their fingers. American executive fingers remain stiff. All the time. When American executives use their hands, all four fingers stay rigid and parallel. Maybe non-American executives curl their fingers because they're ashamed' of showing dirty fingernails. In London my own fingernails are usually filthy. American executives always have clean fingernails. Maybe that's why they can afford to keep their fingers rigid. And parallel.

'We've just *got* to get together,' Jack groaned, sweating. 'When are you coming back to work, baby?'

'When you ask me, you rotten bastard. The original smiler with a knife, that's you.'

'Darling,' Marion said, groping for Jack's arm. 'He's having you on. He doesn't mean it.'

Jack flashed small yellow teeth at Marion.

'Sure he doesn't mean it. Just one crazy son of a bitch, that's all. Right, baby?'

'I'm a vampire,' I said. 'And cruel to boot.'

'A laugh a minute, that's you, baby.' He turned to Marion, brushing sweat into his white mane. 'That's why we love him.'

'He respects you so much,' Marion affirmed.

'Sure he respects me. And I respect him. And if he wasn't such a crazy son of a bitch, you know, more *reliable*, I'd let him write his own ticket.'

'Reliable?' I yelled, 'I'm the most reliable bloody director you ever had.'

'Chee-sus,' Jack said, stalking off on flat feet. 'Chee-sus X. Christ.'

I looked down at my hand; still clutching *What's On*. Turned tail, sat down on the sofa to study it. What was that title again? My father, whose face I couldn't remember, had once slapped my face. Just once. I had refused to go shopping for my mother. Scared of those little thugs who hung about the tram depot in their black-and-brown uniforms. Didn't want them to see me shlepping my mother's shopping net. So my faceless father slapped my face. Only once I refused, and he slapped me. Hard. Tomorrow, I decided, I'm going to write Jack a lengthy letter of apology. Yegods, I *wanted* to work. *Mark of the Vampire*. That was the title. Turned a page. Showing in Brixton.

'*Mark of the Vampire* is on,' I heard myself say, voice cutting through overlapping dialogue. 'I'm off. Brixton.'

'*Mark of the Vampire*?' Ellis echoed. 'Isn't that with old whatsit? Er ...'

'Lionel Barrymore,' I prompted.

'No. Er ...'

'Yes. Lionel Barrymore. M.G.M. 1935. Lionel Atwill. Bela Lugosi.'

'That's it. Old Bela. Tragic story. Such a charming man, too.'

'*You knew him?*'

I was catapulted up from the sofa.

'Bela? Oh yes, knew him well. When he was over here. Touring in you-know. Er. Whatsit. Whenwasit?'

'*You knew Bela Lugosi?*'

I was across the room in a flash, flinging my arms around Ellis Trawley's drooping shoulders.

'*You-actually-knew-Bela-Lugosi?*' I screamed at him.

Total silence had descended on the room. Dick was back, shoeless. Shirlwell, still on his knees, was smirking up at him, seeking my loss of sanity confirmed.

'Ellis,' I commanded. 'We're going to Brixton. Now. By taxi. My treat.'

'Well, I'm not sure ...'

'Don't let me go on my own, Ellis. We'll buy cream buns on the way.'

'Darling,' Marion lamented. 'I thought we were all ...'

'Very good idea,' Dick cut her short. 'Haven't got enough tickets to go round, anyway.'

I was pushing a reluctant Ellis Trawley out into the hall.

'Call me,' Jack Martinsell implored somewhere behind me. '*Call* me. You and me and Dick. The old team. The old one-two, baby.'

Halfway through *Mark of the Vampire*, self-awareness

returned. Maybe I was sobering up. Suddenly I wanted to see no more of *Mark of the Vampire*. What, in God's name, was I doing in a Brixton cinema on a cold winter night, watching a thirty-four-year-old horror film in the company of an elderly queer?

'Where are you going?' Ellis hissed in alarm, as I pushed my way past protesting knees.

'Ice creams,' I yelled back.

Ice creams, my foot. I was heading straight for the exit. Pushed iron bars, lurched out into the night, boarded the first bus going Northwards. Clambered upstairs, paid my fare, dozed.

When the conductor called out 'Elephant', I woke up with a shudder, clattered downstairs, jumped off. Raised the collar of my jacket, started to walk against a rough wind.

Give that tram depot a miss, too many Nazi louts. That conductor must have been out of his Jamaican mind. Wasn't the Elephant and Castle at all. Couldn't have changed that much in thirty years. All those concrete office blocks towering above me. Subways. Barriers. Giant hoardings. Huge electric signs. Vast shopfronts. A bloody piazza.

Hurried down an inviting subterranean passage. Walked a hundred miles. When I emerged on street-level again, found myself twenty yards from where I had descended. Couldn't see the Trocadero anywhere. Had they razed it? Vandals! Not a single cinema in sight. Where were the fleapits of yesteryear? What had happened to my youth? Should have stayed in Brixton. With Ellis Trawley. Bela Lugosi. Sonny Tufts.

The trouble was the *clutter*. Too many people needing to be loved. God in heaven, why had I listened to Dick? Should never have let Joe drive Leonore back to Kew. Chickening out. Why contribute to the making of a Saint? I had tried to talk to Joe, have it out with him.

Relieve my conscience? Where was the lovely old Ideal? Pulled that down, too?

I don't hold you responsible, he'd told me. Marion always comes back. Just one word of warning, though: Don't put all your emotional eggs in one basket, know what I mean? Should never have permitted him to take Leonore home. If he crashed, that would be no accident. Let us not mince matters, Melud. The respondent, who denies all charges of cruelty, who wishes us to believe that he loves his daughter, was apparently content to delegate care and control of this child to the estranged husband of his current mistress. If Melud pleases, one doesn't know where to begin; one couldn't justify such behaviour however hard one tried...

Dick, my friend, why have you too, forsaken me? Had I really told Jack Martinsell what I thought of him? That was the last straw, the end of the line. Iron barrier retreated into long-shot. Reverse zoom. Tiny figures huddled in the dark, white faces staring, arms groping, hands stretched out. Feeding pigeons...

Letting myself into the flat, I noticed that the lights were still on in the sitting-room. Also heard voices in Mrs. MacWhirter's old room. Dick was delivering a sermon of sorts. Cowed interjections from Antje.

Don't go in there, I told myself. Keep out.

I opened the sitting-room door. Marion was squatting Turkish fashion on the sofa, flanked by two men. She was bright-eyed, gushing, glass in one hand, cigarette in the other. Probably stoned out of her mind, reverting to old habits. Must start reforming her. I looked at the two men. One of them was Joe, instantly distracted by my arrival, glancing at his watch, stumbling to his feet, sucking the inside of his cheek. The other man: silver-haired, conservatively-dressed. Something pedantic about him. Rimless glasses. When he first greeted me, smiling, I thought I detected elocution-training in his voice. Covering up a foreign accent? It wasn't until I'd asked Joe about Leonore, and he had reassured me that all was well, Linda wasn't angry, that I registered the identity of the silver-haired man on the sofa with Marion.

Roger Arnold.

'I'm a sick man,' I told Dick next morning. 'Need a doctor. Going to ask Ellis Trawley for the name of his analyst.'

He sat back in my best chair, wearing my bathrobe, rattling several empty cigarette packets before snapping his fingers for mine. I lay sprawled on my sofa, perspiring, clutching a glass of Alka Seltzer. I'd slept on the sitting-room floor. My clothes clung to me, painfully chafed in private areas. I needed a bath, remembered last night, the strange quartet sawing away at polite conversation.

I'd found Roger Arnold charming. No green spotlight, no trauma-revealing confrontation. How extraordinary to find ourselves in the same line of business. After all these years. So to speak. As it were. His taught voice flowed on mellifluously. Yes, he was going to produce a film. For his sins. An old ambition. He looked prosperous. And predatory. Success-hound to his fingertips In the half-light, gold fillings glinted, Marion's eyes gleamed betrayal. We gossiped fluently for the best part of an hour. Then, without warning, I lifted Roger Arnold to his feet and dragged him out into the hall. Unheeding Joe and Marion's protests, I opened the front door, tossed him down the stone steps into the garden. There he lay for a while, muttering bemused astonishment.

I remember Marion flitting past me in the dark to see if Roger Arnold had sustained an injury. Joe stayed in the sitting-room looking green, sucking his cheek, pretending it hadn't happened. After helping Roger Arnold to his feet, Marion spent a further half-hour with him, chatting in the front seat of his Mercedes. I knew it was a full half-hour: timed them. Joe slunk off, politely waving to Marion and Roger as he passed the Mercedes.

When Marion finally came back, she headed straight for our bedroom, slammed the door, locked it. Silence. I finished off my Scotch, switched on swinging Radio One, eventually fell into a fitful sleep, punctuated by the usual nightmares about tram depots.

In the morning, the curtains had been pulled back, the bleak sun threw von Sternberg patterns onto the carpet, Marion had made off for the studios. Dick, I noted, had prevailed on Antje to walk Barry to school.

'I'm going to talk to you on one condition,' he said. 'For once try to be really serious.'

I nodded, eagerly roused myself to commence the ritual of self-abnegation.

'What you've got to understand, Dick, these last few months have been sheer bloody hell for me. Worked my guts out to ...'

'... that you try to be really serious, I said ...'

'It's true ...'

'Don't agree. Not the real situation at all.'

The real situation. Dick's basement, his bookshelves, poor Brenda. Nights at the Villa Rameau, the terrace bathed in moonlight, sore-throated conferences about my need to jettison Linda. All over now? Let me go, Linda, please let me go. Blow the final whistle. I deny you the right to feel yourself wounded by me. The real situation.

'The real situation is that you've been bone-idle and totally irresponsible, nursing your bloody neuroses. Let's get that straight for a start. You've never been more inactive in your whole life.'

'Yegods, Dick, I tossed Roger Arnold down the bloody stairs last night. If that isn't being active ...'

'You're always tossing Roger Arnold down the stairs. Compulsive infantile patterns ...'

'I haven't done it for nearly twenty years, Dick ...'

'. . . like popping off to see horror films with queers. The fact is you don't feel any better for having tossed Roger Arnold down the stairs, do you?'

'Worse.'

'Exactly. You're dodging the real issue.'

'Allright. I'm dodging the real issue. I'm inactive. Where do we go from there?'

'We?'

'Where do *I* go from here, then?'

'For a start, George, you're going to chop everything. As Arthur Miller says in one of his plays, I forget which, "*The first step to wisdom is to stop.*" '

'Jesus, isn't that just what I *have* done? On *your* advice!'

'Didn't go far enough.'

'Not far enough? Dick, I've chopped Linda, lost my house, my money, my car . . . I tear myself into small pieces to see Leonore . . . You know how much I owe the Inland Revenue?'

'Not interested.'

'Your trouble, Dick, you've got no sense of responsibility. The burdens of love . . .'

'Same old rubbish. Bloody German Jew, doesn't mean a thing. Tell me, what do you regard as your role in life?'

'Role? Father. That's my role, Dick. Father.'

'Very pat. In actual fact, of course, you're nothing of the sort. You're a son. I mean look at us now.'

Didn't understand the first thing about me: Sense of paternal responsibility, need to slice your life up into segments like an apple, each segment requiring specific tasks, duties . . .

Tried to put this into words for Dick. He cut me short.

'You've only got one duty. To stay intact. To be yourself. To function as George Kane. It's not much, I'll be the first to admit, but it's all you have. So for a start, stop splitting yourself into picturesque little bits and pieces. You haven't chopped anything. You've simply replaced Linda, got yourself a new Mum.'

'I'd hardly describe Marion as a . . .'

'Wasn't thinking of Marion.'

'Leonore?'

'Didn't even have to spell it out, did I?'

Awful. Not true. Got up, begged Dick for one of my own cigarettes. Hand trembled. Not true at all.

'You simply don't understand, Dick. I *love* her. Linda is trying to alienate her from me. I *need* to be with her.'

'Do you? I wonder. Existentially, Leonore drives you up the wall. You don't even enjoy her company. For that matter, she doesn't enjoy yours. You let her see what an effort it is. Same old compulsion, George, same old mistake.'

'She needs me, Dick.'

'Like a hole in the head. You and Linda use that poor kid to lam into each other, and Leonore knows it.'

'You haven't got children, Dick. You don't appreciate my technical difficulties . . .'

'So what you're going to do now, George, you're really going to chop it. For a start you're going to ring up Linda, and you're going to tell her you're terribly sorry, but you can't see Leonore for at least a fortnight.'

'I couldn't possibly . . .'

'Make that a month. One whole calendar month. Think of it, George. She's going to be saddled with that kid for a whole month! One in the eye for old Linda, eh?'

'Can't do it, Dick. Can't be done.'

I argued, but in the end I called Linda. Told her I had work to do. (Watching me, Dick nodded approvingly.) Needed to be out of town for a month. The lies, as always, came trippingly off my tongue.

'I see,' my wife said.

Dialling tone.

'Simple, isn't it? Leonore will miss you. Might even

start growing fond of you. You feel better already, don't you?'

'No.'

'Do you feel better? Yes or No? I'm not going on with this, unless . . .'

'Allright. Better, yes. Better. Now may I drag myself to bed, and . . .'

'Why? We've hardly begun . . .'

He called for Antje. He was having a ball. Called her an Antwerp harbour whore, ordered breakfast. Two fried eggs. Bacon. Toast. Butter. Rose's Lime Marmalade.

'There isn't any Lime Marmalade,' I interpolated.

'Then get some,' he told her. 'You'll find money in my trouser pocket. Rose's Lime Marmalade. Got it?'

I watched her drift out of the room, wafted on a magic carpet of bliss.

'Sorry about that,' Dick said, 'but occasionally I have to attend to my own problems. Spot of Ejaculatio Praecox last night. If I didn't exert some authority this morning, she'd be trampling all over me.'

Saw an opening to hit back.

'No trouble of my own in that department,' I told him.

'Really? Then why does Marion wipe the floor with you?'

'You must be joking.'

'Runs the bloody show, doesn't she? Let's you think you do, but meanwhile she stays intact, prick and all.'

So Marion was to be the next target. Well, he hadn't a ghost's chance there. I quoted chapter and verse. Sexual prowess. Erotic bliss. Record number of orgasms. No reversal of roles this time. None.

'Then why can't she even bother to make you a decent breakfast?'

'I don't eat breakfast.'

'Irrelevant. If, once in a while, you gave her a chance to *behave* like a woman, Marion might actually end up as one.'

'You just won't take account of the technicalities, Dick. Marion's working like a blue-arsed . . .'

'. . . and you're not. Precisely. So she wears the pants, and knows it, let's you have it right in the groin. Whammo.'

'Rubbish . . .'

'You really are pathetic, George. Here you are, one of the best directors in the business. Or so you keep telling me. And you let a scrubby little small-part actress move in, run your life, castrate you. And you're not even married to her. Remember, George, *one* cock is all you have . . .'

'You're getting this whole thing out of perspective, Dick. Marion is emotionally dependent on me . . .'

'Is that why she plays her squalid little games? Right here, *in your own flat?*'

Roger Arnold again. The big producer. In a green spotlight. Dick was hitting below the belt.

'Chop it,' he said, 'throw her out.'

'What?'

'Throw her out,' he repeated, leaning forward, making a grab for the cigarettes. 'Then we'll see how emotionally dependent she is.'

'She's got nowhere to go,' I protested. 'She's left Joe. On *my* account. Where is she going to live?'

'She'll think of something. Won't sleep on Hampstead Heath, that's for sure. So chop it.'

'What about Barry?'

'Sodding kids again! He goes as well. Out. Not yours, is he? Christ, George, do you have to play nannykins to every snottynosed infant in London to prove your manhood? Ring her up. Now. Tell her to collect her things and *go* . . .'

'She won't know why . . .'

'Then she'll have something to brood about, won't she? Let her want *you* for a change. Create some bloody tension . . .'

'Who's going to pick Barry up from school?'

'Let Joe do it. He's the father, isn't he? Go on, ring him up, tell him you're sending Marion back to him. By registered post.'

'Why should I want to hurt Joe?'

'Hurt him? He loves Marion. You'll be giving him a new lease of life.'

'Joe's in bad shape, Dick. I've tried to have it out with him . . .'

'No, you haven't. You avoid poor old Joe like the plague. Sheer cowardice on your part. You've screwed his wife, you're stealing his son . . .'

'Not true.'

'Get on the phone. Tell him to collect the kid from school and take him home.'

A son? Maybe Dick was right. What was he making me do that I hadn't secretly desired these past few weeks?

I called Joe. Easier than falling off a greased log. Then I called Marion, having her coffee break in the studio canteen. Offered her my prepared speech, scripted by Dick.

'You're joking, darling,' she said. 'You must be.'

Told her I was dead serious. Pack up your things and *go*, I said. Sounded like a declaration of love.

'Can't we talk it over tonight, darling? I'll cook you a nice meal and . . .'

'I'll be out,' I told her. 'You'll find your things packed in a couple of suitcases.'

George the Gambler back in total control. The scent of Badedas and burning bridges in my nostrils. Chips rattling in my pocket. *Rien ne va plus.*

'But you love me,' she lamented. 'You can't just tell me to go. Just like that.'

'Doing it.'

'Where am I supposed to go?'

'Think.'

215

'How can I think? I'm in a state of shock. And Barry . . .'

'Joe is taking care of Barry.'

'But I love you, George. I do love you.'

'See? It works,' Dick muttered. I was holding the receiver away from my ear, so that he could listen in.

'You should have thought of that when you started playing your squalid games with Roger Arnold.'

'But I didn't do anything, darling. We weren't even alone . . .'

'What about that half-hour in his car?'

'For Christ's sake, don't *discuss* it,' Dick hissed. 'She's got the message. Chop it.'

'It's so unfair,' she cried. 'I only brought Roger back to the flat because I thought he might help you.'

'Help *me*?'

'Don't weaken,' Dick prompted.

'Who's that with you?'

Silence. Then:

'Do you seriously expect me to rehearse after *this*?'

Put down the receiver, knew I loved her.

'You're better than I thought,' Dick approved. 'See what you can do when you really try?'

Antje came in with a fully laden breakfast tray. Dick sent her out of the room for the salt, tucked into his fried eggs. I got up, averted my eyes in order not to be sick, zig-zagged about the room, Bunuel's *El*. Sat down on a cushion on the floor, picked up *What's On*, Fritz Lang's crazed Dr. Mabuse. Disorientated. Antje came back with a packet of salt, knelt down by Dick's side. He fed her with bits of dripping buttered toast. I retched.

'Feel better?'

'Suicidal. Wish you'd try your bloody scripts out on someone else.'

'One thing you can be absolutely sure of: *She's* feeling worse.'

216

Was there one chance in a hundred that Dick knew what he was about?

We lunched at the Mirabelle; Dick's treat. He didn't bring Antje. Hadn't done anything to deserve the Mirabelle. Also, being the only woman in the flat, she must not be deprived of the enjoyment of cleaning it. What action would make Antje deserving of the Mirabelle? That, Dick replied, was Antje's problem.

Dick ordered cigars, chose a Romeo y Julieta with care. I declined, told him I was looking forward to an afternoon in bed. With the telephone off the hook.

'There's one more call you have to make,' he said. 'You're going to organise a sleeping partner for yourself. I'm not having you mope about. You depress me when you're randy.'

Didn't know anybody. Lost touch.

'Investigate your fantasies, George. Must be somebody around you'd like to bang.'

I muttered. Something about a girl from the Electricity Board.

'Call her.'

Didn't even know her name. Besides, lightning never struck twice in the same place. One syndrome I had taped.

'Allright,' he said. 'Who else?'

Unaccountably, haughty boutique-owning Cara strayed into my mind. By now I was feeling so bruised, I spoke my thoughts out loud.

'Call her,' he said, drawing fulsomely on his cigar. 'Sounds fun.'

'Friend of Marion's,' I demurred, suddenly knew why I had thought of Cara in the first place.

Back at the flat, I plundered Marion's packed suit-cases, found her little red address-book. Dick commanded Antje to repack the cases. Cara was called to the telephone by an assistant. Yes, *of course* she remembered me. Joe and Marion's friend. With the little girl.

'Correct.'

(Found myself playing Dan Wymans, ancient swinger.)

There was this little party I was tossing for my old pal Dick Bligh. Just over from the South of France. Yeah, Richard Bligh, the writer.

She most certainly had heard of him. Admired his books greatly. Was he as groovy as his books?

'Tell her I'll give her a joint,' Dick prompted.

A load of laughs, I promised. My pad. She hesitated, flirtatiously.

'Ask her if she takes grass or juice,' Dick hissed.

I elaborated, painting the non-existent party in psychedelic colours; even threatened LSD. Was enjoying myself again : irresistible challenge of another betrayal. Maybe I loved Marion because in her destructive urges I saw a mirror of my own habitual conduct. She had probably moved heaven and earth to drag Roger Arnold to the flat, thereby hoping to provoke a situation. When narcissists clashed, something had to give.

No sooner finished conning Cara, than Tetheridge called, solemnly communicating panic. He had just heard from The Other Side. Linda was threatening to refuse me further access to Leonore, if it meant contaminating the child's psyche through contact with Marion Leeds.

'Must say,' Tetheridge added, 'I don't pretend to understand the implications of ...'

Not to worry, I said. He could reassure The Other Side. No further contact.

Tetheridge wouldn't let it go at that.

'I do feel I must warn you again on this score ...'

'What score?'

'If we are to counter-petition on grounds of Mrs. Kane's adultery, Mr. Kane, you realise you will have to submit a statement of your own adulteries, if any, asking the Court to exercise discretion...'

'I know all that...'

'Quite so. But if it can be established that you enjoined adulterous relations with persons not included in your discretion statement...'

'I'm living like a monk, Mr. Tetheridge.'

'I appreciate that Joe and Marion Leeds are close friends of yours...'

'Like a monk, Mr. Tetheridge.'

Even after Tetheridge got off the line, Dick did not allow me to go to bed. It was absolutely essential, he counselled, that we were *out* when Marion came to collect her suitcases. If I made myself available for a Scene, all our good work would be down the drain. Besides, he wanted to tour the better bookshops to ascertain that his latest book was given due display. Shirlwell, he suspected, was slacking.

Spent two hours shlepping round West End bookshops. Could hardly keep my eyes open. Was accused of being a middle-aged drag. After all he had done for me, too. Antje bought two coffee table volumes. Dick scrutinised photographic cut-outs of himself: pensive face, and naked to the waist.

When we got back, Marion's suitcases were gone. Hopefully, I searched for a little note of love, found nothing.

'What do you expect?' Dick asked. 'She's returning service. Don't expect her to surrender without a fight, do you? You're doing fine.'

Cara arrived at the appointed hour, unsurprised that the party was a non-event. Darker, more Junoesquely alluring than I remembered her. White leather suit. The gaping V below her neck promised forbidden action. The old 'H' Certificate.

Dick played bronzed author, Cara projected swinging

chick (not a day over thirty, I guessed), Antje cast herself as procuress. I was kept busy dispensing drinks, running the record-player, stemming the mounting tide of my own concupiscence. Maybe Cara was rosy on both sides. Never know your luck.

When conversation (high life on the Côte d'Azur, modes in current fiction, all swimming in a glue of sexual innuendo) began to flag, I turned up the volume of the record-player. Antje helpfully scattered cushions on the floor, doused the lights. This, God help me, was one scene I could direct. Modulated from modern jazz to seduction selections. Stroked the back of Cara's neck. Ah nice, she said. Dick produced pot. What about the acid, Cara wanted to know. Were we worried about the fuzz? The telephone rang.

'Don't answer it,' Dick said, chipping and chopping away at his pot, then rolling a couple of thick, messy cigarettes. The telephone stopped ringing. The pot was passed round. Decent old dyke that she was, Cara played along, talking gibberish about turning on and dropping out. We filled our lungs, pretended to get high.

Gradually our postures became horizontal. Dick encouraged Antje to take off her dress. She lay back on the cushions in rather depressing-looking winter underwear, began to sing along with Frank Sinatra, whose lived-in voice began to sound increasingly sharp and musical. Cara dutifully mumbled 'Groovy, baby'. Taking advantage of her pretensions, I unbuttoned her leather jacket. She lay heavily against me, eyes closed, breathing hard. As I struggled with her bra fastenings, one profound thought penetrated the general haze : Certain moments with strangers would always be more exciting than the best moments with the woman one loved.

Couldn't manage to remove the bra from the back, attended to the front, scooped out two large, lifeless breasts from nylon cups. Nipples weren't bad : Small and pink; hard after assiduous attentions.

'Good?' I asked.

'Good,' she agreed, without excessive enthusiasm, and replaced the breasts into their containers. Firm, ringed, managing hands.

Dick rose. Antje stopped singing; meekly followed him out into Mrs. MacWhirter's room. Alone with me, Cara instantly discarded her turned-on swinger role.

'Uh-uh,' she clucked, Doris Day reminding Rock Hudson of her quintessential virginity.

I began to operate on the zip of her white leather skirt, generalised loathing escalating to active dislike. She was lovely, I told her, what a superb body. She confessed, stylised regret in her voice, that she just did *not* sleep around. A party was a party, but there had to be *limits*.

Assured her that if I'd thought she slept around I wouldn't have touched her. Couldn't stand promiscuous women. Her fastidiousness had been obvious to me from the start. Which is why I found her so maddeningly attractive. (Didn't want her, didn't even want to tease.)

'Just lie back, darling. Relax. Nothing spectacular is expected.'

Imagine that I'm Marion, I almost added, refreshing my tumescence. She patted my hand in friendly fashion. Going to turn on sentiment, I thought with dread. I was right.

'That night at Joe's,' she sighed. 'I hoped you'd talk to me.'

'You didn't show it. Too busy seducing my poor accountant.'

'Oh him. Not my type. Strictly from Cubesville.'

She dismantled Doris Day, rapidly tried to assemble Julie Christie. I went on talking rubbish, relieved her of her skirt. She protested, then—in self-defence—kissed me ably, objectively, squeezing her thighs together. With all that tongue-lashing and lip-licking going on, I eventually managed to get my hand between them.

'Don't do that,' she said. 'Shan't let you.'

She was wearing tights, of course. Struggles. Kisses. Protests. Gained more leverage, pulled down the bloody tights. Frank Sinatra droned on interminably. Fingers made contact with dry pubic hair, a mildly aroused clitoris. Her eyes remained shut. I applied myself.

'Bloody hell,' she groaned, clenched her fingers into a fist. 'Obstinate bastard, aren't you?'

By now I had my own eyes closed. Sweat dripped from my brow. I fantasied her as Marion. Then I fantasied myself as Marion. With my free hand, I unclenched one of her fists.

'That's better,' I said, continued mechanically.

She pretended to come, then curled herself up into an embryo, large white back turned to me. Selfish dyke that she was, she couldn't even be bothered to return favours.

'Wow,' she exhaled.

I let her rest for a minute, then laid her on her back, pushed down my trousers, fucked her. Done in one minute flat.

'Allright?' she asked, deep purple remorse in her voice.

'Yes. Allright for you?'

'Groovy.'

'Makes a change, doesn't it?'

'What do you mean?'

Forget it, I thought. Why taunt the poor bitch? Got off her. Had my revenge. On Marion. On Dick. On life in general. She said something about splitting, gathered up her clothes in a bundle. Brushing hair back with a managing hand, she went off to find the bathroom.

I smoked a cigarette. Dracula was dead.

'I hope we haven't made a baby,' she giggled, coming back, pottering. Was I to be spared nothing? 'It's allright. Only finished the curse yesterday.'

On this romantic cadence we brought the party to a close.

'Thanks for coming,' I said, letting her out.

'Richard is charming, isn't he?' she replied.

'Anytime,' I told her.

Slammed the door behind her.

'How was it?' Dick asked.

I sat up and blinked. He'd walked into the bedroom, switched on all the lights. Sat down on the edge of my bed. To smoke a last cigarette, he said.

'Fan*tas*tic.'

'Good,' he said. 'Glad to hear you've got some sexual vitality left in you. Even when it's only trotted out for a scaly old dyke . . .'

'That was no . . .'

'Come off it. I know your syndrome. You love teasing Lesbians. It's so safe.'

I glanced at the plumped-up pillow next to my own, then at the framed photograph of Leonore on my bedside table.

'I do believe I've destroyed five lives today,' I mused. 'Not bad going.'

'Don't kid yourself, George,' he said. 'You've destroyed nobody. Just been yourself. For once.'

'So what now?'

'So now you'll be of some use to me. Get a good night's kip. You're starting work tomorrow. We're going to make a movie.'

Five

A DIRECTOR just doesn't work like that.

You had to get the story right, needed planning conferences with designers and technicians, an extensive period of Active Preparation.

Dick wasn't having any of that. When I got out of bed next morning, he had already started. Antje had adorned the sitting-room walls with sheets of cardboard (pulled out of my laundered shirts). Dick, walking from sheet to sheet, was making notes with a black fibre marker: the script I was to be privileged to direct.

He appeared taken aback by my lack of instant enthusiasm.

'You want to work, don't you?'

Yes, I wanted to work, had already grasped that not he but Roger Arnold had sparked off that desire. The hinge from paralysis to action would always be envy.

I mimed interest, told him my idea: a really original horror film. About this vampire child, who . . .

'Forget horror,' he cut in, scribbling away on his pinned-up cardboards. 'Forget sodding children. I'm doing you a favour. From now on, you're working on the pleasure principle. Going to direct something that interests you for a change.'

He began to outline his own ideas, which seemed to have jelled overnight: a feature-length documentary about Real People, observed in their own Life Situation. No Plot. No tatty story-line. No 'construction'. No semblance of artifice. Just a series of apparently unconnected, more or less improvised scenes, revealing the daily lives of an occasionally interweaving group. Shot without comment. Ferocious naturalism.

Message understood. Intrusion on privacy, fast film stock, hit-and-run camera work, overlaid sound tracks. Good old John Grierson, laced with Jean-Luc Godard and *Man Alive*.

Yes, I mused, that swings for me.

Couldn't fail. We'd observe people whose private lives triggered off our own imaginations. Nothing would be invented. We'd simply record. *Shape* a little, maybe, in the cutting room.

With a shock compounded of fear and pleasure I registered Dick's intention : unfettered artistic cannibalism. Our stars were to be our friends, acting out the minutiae of their existence for the eye of our camera. Revealing, Dick added somewhat superfluously, the reality of their situations.

He was pacing about the room, rehearsing the hieroglyphics on his cardboards, adding to them as inspiration fired him.

For a start, there was Ellis Trawley, a name that wouldn't harm the film's commercial chances. We would give audiences the *real* Ellis Trawley : lonely, ageing, deprived of human contact, failing to communicate because of his flawed memory, visiting irritated old chums, trudging to his analyst, talking directly into camera about The Last Days of Bela Lugosi.

Intercut this, Dick went on, with the daily battles of Jack Martinsell. Wouldn't he just love parading himself and his drama emporium for public consumption? The great TV executive, stocky, courageous, visibly exhausted, wheeling and dealing, pretending to a quest for quality, while keeping one eye on the ratings. Coming home to his third wife, photogenic dolly presiding over his final castration.

Exhibit No. 3 : Joe Leeds. Looking after his little boy in his wife-deserted home, glossing over a broken marriage, composing horoscopes for friends. The ex-critic, soured by the lack of impact of his novels, haranguing other critics (in close-up) for their surrender to the pressures of public relations...

'Not Joe,' I protested. 'We can't do it to poor old Joe...'

'Why not?' Dick asked innocently. 'He'll do it like a shot.'

'Look, I've abused Joe's hospitality. I've scrounged his food, got pissed on his Scotch, warmed my arse on his electric blanket, screwed his wife. I can't now hold him up to public ridicule as well...'

'How he comes out is up to him. Besides that's your relationship, George. He gives. You take. That's the way you both want it. Why go against the grain?'

Before I could voice further objections, Dick was extending his cast list. Cara would be roped in, of course. Running her trendy boutique, keeping in the swim. Unfulfilled swinger of thirty, scattering her Lesbian libido in a round of permissive socialising. For good measure, why not include that landlady of mine? Lady Whatsit, playing Bridge with other old ghouls every afternoon, letting off parts of her house to make ends meet. And Linda! Brooding in her big Kew mansion, wrapped in consoling fantasies of punishment and revenge. How did that grab me?

I drew the line. Ellis and Cara: yes. Jack Martinsell: a pleasure. Joe: possibly. But not Linda. Linda was out. Tetheridge would never stand for it. Nor would I.

'Pity. Linda would have fitted into the framework beautifully, poor old cow.'

We compromised. I reluctantly agreed to Joe, Dick promised to abandon all further thoughts of Linda. (I thanked my Maker that he hadn't thought of Leonore.)

That our film would be called *The Cripples* had to remain our secret. For the benefit of our victims, we'd use some ego-boosting working title, like 'Eyes' or 'Strangers'. Touch of your John Cassavetes.

The Machiavellian notion of using Jack Martinsell was described by Dick as his masterstroke. Jack had hinted that if only Dick would help him get his Fairy Tales off the drawing-board, he could script one of those one-shot sensitive personal documentaries produced by the Network to appease the ITA. Dick now proposed to write Jack a Kleinian *Sleeping Beauty*. In return, Jack would get the Network to underwrite our movie. It wouldn't cost much. Our actors would work for peanuts and self-advertisement. We needed a crew for a tight four-week schedule and masses of film-stock. Here was the pay-off: After we'd shown Jack the finished product, he'd want to lie down and die. We'd negotiate with a distributor to buy the rights from an embarrassed Network. On the strength of Dick's name.

'We're in business,' he concluded.

'Now I see why I'm to be deprived of my daughter for a month,' I said grimly.

He wasn't listening, transported on manic flights of creative fancy. Struck by a Moment of Truth whilst watching the motherfuckers. Commitment. New Man. He was through providing masturbation fantasies for the sexually underprivileged. Writing conventional plays was out, too. Obsolete. The play he had struggled to perfect for twenty years was for the cultural garbage can. He'd written about the decline of the English Upper Class. That's why he'd needed copies of *The Field*. To check his facts. Didn't know the first thing about the English Upper Class, cared even less. Witnessing that act of simulated fellatio had finally liberated him from all arty abstractions.

'From now on, I'm simply, a tape-recorder,' he declared. 'Recording what interests me. I *am* interested in those Hampstead cripples. And so are you, George. After all, you're one of them.'

Did he mean to tell me that he'd turned my life upside down, cut me off from my child, chucked out my girl-friend, merely to facilitate the production of some movie?

'Healthy self-interest,' Dick said. 'Can't think of a more honest reason for doing anything. Can you?'

The dapper, nimble-footed Jewish traveller, grinning as if he had just bought himself a First Division football club, spieled his patter: a line of accessories for which Cara had no use. She did not wish to order, neither did she want to humiliate the poor little man by denigrating his wares. Two dollybirds, hunting novelties, claimed service. In the changing-room, Cara's blonde model-friend smoked impatiently, waiting for Cara to close the boutique and take her out to dinner. Frowning at her fried-egg watch, Cara pulled a feathery cloak from its hanger, displayed it for the dollybirds.

Uninterrupted three-minute take.

We had our main camera set up on a tiny raised gallery, keeping the whole scene in cool long-shot. Meanwhile Benny, the second, more imaginative, camera operator, was picking out details with a hand-held camera: Cara's eyes darting anxious glances in the direction of the changing-room; the traveller's grin widening as he registered failure; one dollybird peeking at a price-tag, miming non-concern. By mistake (but we'd print it) Benny zoomed to Crane's tongue licking his moustache.

Leaning on his umbrella, probably fantasying that he was Producer, Crane, my agent, had come to watch the last day's shooting, threw an occasional conspirator's wink at me to show artistic appreciation.

I was Golden Boy again. Making a living. Shooting a Richard Bligh script. Under contract to the Network.

He nodded sagely as Dick explained the subtle under-currents implicit in the scene. The sound man groaned. He had picked up Dick's whispers. The Jewish traveller,

231

accomplished amateur actor having the time of his life parodying himself, stopped in mid-spiel.

I yelled 'Cut', for Crane's benefit threw a temperament. Dick joined fingertips, prayed to be forgiven. On the set he accepted my authority without question. Script or no script—and for the most part it was no script—he knew he was condemned to remain on the sidelines while we improvised. But now he came over to argue, and to impress Crane.

'I just don't see it anymore,' he complained. 'Yesterday we had this mass of detail. Now it's all gone. Take Cara's repressed anti-semitism...'

Even after a month of shooting, Dick still couldn't grasp that though amateurs might perform as ably as professional actors, especially when playing themselves, they could never *repeat* a desired nuance. If you didn't get it into the can first time, you'd have to try for something totally different.

'Just one more time, Mr. Jason,' I called down to the traveller. 'Try and remember the "older type client" bit this time, O.K.?'

'Got you, Mr. Kane.'

Curled thumb and forefinger to make a circle, cleared his throat, actually shot his cuffs.

Out of the corner of one eye, I caught blonde model-friend hoisting up her tights under her dress, snapped my fingers at Benny. He had already smelled opportunity, hiding behind Crane's back, camera purring.

'We'll go for the long take again, O.K., kids?'

It was the last shot. I was almost sorry. I had been bloody good. Would have known it, even if Jack Martinsell had not heaped fulsome paternal praise on me after seeing the second week's rushes: Joe's sequence. The best of the lot.

Joe had given us everything we wanted, written most of his own dialogue, laid his head right on the chopping block. We'd shot him pottering about his maisonette,

making notes for his novel, brewing tea for Barry. We'd
filmed him gambling alone at the Playboy Club, sitting
in his bath composing horoscopes. We kept the camera
running as he ran, dripping, from the bath to take a call
from Marion. They were planning an amicable divorce.
Marion, who had volunteered to produce fake adulterous grounds, sounded worried about unfavourable publicity. Might harm her image of the immaculate serial
heroine.

'Don't worry, love,' Joe told her, while we zoomed in
on his slipping glasses. 'If it doesn't come to them in a
handout, they won't print it.'

Watching this scene, Jack Martinsell's enthusiasm was
such that he agreed to let us run a thousand pounds over
budget. Wise old bird, he also went back on his promise
to let himself be included in the film's coverage.

'You bastards,' he riled. 'You conned me. Good luck to
you, but you're not murdering me like you've murdered
poor old Joe.'

In some haste, we substituted Dan Wymans for Jack:
Dan Director swinging at the White Elephant, Dan
Sycophant buttering up Sam Spiegel at a West End
Première, Dan Lover casting bit parts in his flat, Dan
Daddy letting his kid ride the swings and roundabouts
on Hampstead Heath. (In that sequence, I need hardly
add, I surpassed myself.)

I was relishing every moment. Directing my own betrayals, evading reality in the act of reproducing it on
film, I was releasing energies I had almost allowed to
atrophy. I celebrated my renewal. I had risen from the
smoking chaos of my life unharmed. The vain pursuit
of Leonore's undivided attachment, the quixotic battles
to renovate Marion's personality; both had left me intact, after all.

After the inactive months, catatonically crouched in
front of a television set with Leonore, I suddenly found
time to go to my tailor, have myself measured for a couple

of suits, time to get new glasses, time to have two cavities
filled at the dentist, time to study Fred Flake's incompre-
hensible tax returns, and to delay disaster by returning
them for further work, time to press the hand of my respectable P.A. in the back of a taxi and guide it hopefully to the zip of my pants, time to have myself pummelled at a new health club, to which Dan Wymans
had introduced me, time to grow and groom a Wyman-
esque Chinese war-lord moustache. My concession to
middle-age, I told Dick, though the truth was that I
needed tangible evidence of my renewal. Goethe had it
all wrong. The eternally *adolescent* leads us onwards.
(As if he didn't know, the devious old goat, still having
it away with the odd fan in his seventies. Jesus.)

I even found time to write out detailed answers to
Linda's thirty-seven charges of cruelty. No, Melud, the
lists of girls which Linda had trapped in her safaris
through my personal effects (causing her 'profound and
lasting distress'), did not refer to my mistresses, but to
actresses I hoped to employ. No, the Durex in my back-
trouser pocket did not establish that I was constantly
searching for amorous encounters. If Melud pleases, the
French letter referred to in the Petitioner's complaint
had come my way as a jokey birthday present from my
camera crew.

I also found time to see Leonore.

Picked her up from school, took her for walks in Kew
Gardens, lied to Dick about non-existent technical conferences that did not require his presence. Enjoyed deceiving him.

Seeing Leonore in secret added to the pleasure. Yet I
kept searching for signs that she was slipping out of my
reach. Did not kiss me goodbye with that old voluptu-
ousness. Walking under already budding trees, she with-
drew into withering silences. I sensed reproach in her
stance as I kneeled in front of her to zip up her anorak.

Insecurity inspired challenge. I asked her to remind Mummy that I needed that viewfinder for which I had asked repeatedly, and which still stood on the mantelpiece in my study. And the *International Almanac for 1956*, please..

'What do you want those old things for?' she asked, 'you're not working in the telly studios now.'

And again I detected the exact inflections of Linda's ice-cube voice.

She also reported complaints from Mummy that I was not giving her enough money. Continuing to wage her war on all available fronts, Linda used the child to convey messages of complaint. I used her to carry back replies.

We were having tea in the little Italian restaurant near her school.

'What about the money you owe Mummy?' Leonore asked me.

The day before, I had received letter No. 87 from Tetheridge. Unless I was willing to pay at once for certain necessary renovations—a sum of £980 was mentioned—Mrs. Kane would have to sell her house, buy a smaller, more convenient one in Beaconsfield.

'I've got no money, love,' I told her. 'Look what I'm living on. Frozen chicken pies and Ribena.'

'Mummy says you spend all your money on having selfish fun. That's what she says.'

'You believe her?'

'How am I supposed to know?'

'You're not supposed to know.'

'Well, then ...'

I paid the bill.

'I know what,' I enthused, 'let's look in on the dinosaurs on the way home.

'Not those flipping dinosaurs *again*,' she grumbled.

But I did see her. Kept in touch. And Dick never knew.

We wrapped up the final shot. The crew slumped collectively, looked thirsty.

'Wonderful,' Crane commented, shouldered his umbrella, departed.

'I feel bloody good about this picture,' I said. 'I have a bloody good feeling.'

Cara, who had co-operated like a trouper—the substance of Dick's 'undercurrents' had been withheld from her, of course—invited everyone to a booze-up at her pad. Working with her, I gradually warmed to her pretensions and self-deceptions. She no longer attracted me.

Conferring with my sound man, I noticed that Cara's blonde modelfriend had breasts. Told Dick to be a good lad, fetch a taxi. He hesitated, grinned to show he was humouring me. Temperamental director. Then he did as he was told.

I soaked in Badedas, the telephone rang. Antje (my housekeeper, Mr. Tetheridge, and engaged to be married to my best friend) answered.

'Whoever it is,' Otto Preminger directed from the bath-tub, 'I'm not in.' And treated himself to a superfluous shampoo. Modelfriend's breasts came to mind. Dick came in. Antje followed, asking for permission to clip his toenails.

'Marion?'

'Don't call back. Let her stew a bit longer.'

'Until I've cut the picture, you mean.'

'She sounds very troubled,' Antje contributed, wiping the steamed-up mirror clear with a pair of old tights.

'Can't you see there's a naked man in the bath.' Dick remonstrated.

'He's got bubbles all round him,' Antje said.

'That's not the point.'

Poor old Dick. Middle-aged, bourgeois, insecure. And a premature ejaculator to boot.

'I am calling her back,' I said. Shooting was over, I was tired of playing games, I wanted Marion. Or model-friend.

Antje was snipping away at Dick's toenails.

'Maybe she needs something,' she said, 'she did really sound very troubled indeed.'

'Marion has managed without George for thirty-five years. He's not her keeper. Or her son. But then George likes to turn all his women into mums.'

'You can talk,' I said. 'You turn yours into kids.'

'Comes from being forty. My kids obey me.'

He ordered Antje to leave. She left. I asked Dick for the scissors. Holding a hand-mirror in one hand, I started to clip my Chinese war-lord moustache.

While shooting *The Cripples*, we'd never discussed Marion. The subject had cropped up once, professionally. We had been filming at Lady Whitestone's. It had yielded little. After seeing the rushes, Dick wanted to scrub the lot. We should have used Linda. And if not Linda, then Marion. Yes, *Marion*. What kind of a director was I, anyway, always allowing my Oedipus complex to interfere with my work?

Not that there was the remotest chance of using Marion, even if I'd wanted to. She had got herself a new agent, a Mod youth who organised Marion's professional life as a sideline to running a couple of millionaire pop groups. Hoping to cash in on the popularity of her TV soap opera, the youth arranged for her to attend garden parties, starve for Oxfam, open recordshops. Her remaining energies she lavished on her performance as a junkie in Roger Arnold's way-out movie, which he had conned the ubiquitous Hammond Fraser to direct for him.

Joe had proudly divulged these scraps of information while we worked on his sequence. Marion herself filled in the gaps. She had moved in with an elder sister (words that set off shrill alarms in my mind's early warning system) in Maida Vale. She and Joe were sharing Barry, who was 'lovely and undisturbed'. Just like darling Leonore. Her divorce, when the time was right, would be amicable and uncomplicated.

She often called me late at night, reporting with disturbing objectivity that she was working like a blue-arsed fly, enquiring about the progress of my film, sending regards to Leonore.

'It's so lovely to talk to you,' she would coo, 'I do appreciate that you need this period completely to yourself. You've been through such a nasty time, darling.'

Never an admission of regret that we were no longer living together; never a syllable of reproach that I had tossed her out on her ear. She usually signed off with a disarming gush of professional detail. Her new agent was super. Hammond, peacocking about in his pink corduroys and Beethoven teeshirt, was having tantrums and worrying the life out of poor old Roger. Mentioning the forbidden name rounded off her pose of emotional nonchalance. I retaliated by trying to sound overworked but buoyant.

After those midnight calls, I would lie back, missing her badly, take seconal to empty my mind of jealousy and desire. Marion's reaction to her own expulsion was identical with Joe's response to her desertion: no acknowledgement, no dissection. They were eerily alike, *Made For Each Other* (Carole Lombard, James Stewart). They would undoubtedly end up *Together Again* (Charles Boyer, Irene Dunne).

Was she biding her time until Dick returned to Cannes, and could no longer control my actions?

I bitterly resented this interpretation of my conduct. It was undoubtedly true.

I got out of the bath, towelled myself down, wanted to

call Marion, fantasied cunnilingus with Blonde Model-friend, put on a new suit. We taxied to Cara's pad. I'd treat myself to a celebration. *Remember the Night* (Loretta Young). I had actually got a movie in the can! Me, George Kane, forgotten man, having *The Last Laugh* (Emil Jannings) on Roger Arnold. Think about Marion tomorrow, put things right with Leonore the day after that. *Next Time We Live* (Margaret Sullavan).

Elation held for some time after we arrived, found the room packed with Cara's friends, members of my crew, some of The Cripples in person. I sipped Scotch, lit a cigarette, rested my arse on a ludicrous pink satin love-seat, waited for the circus of congratulations to converge.

Glancing around, I saw the content of my movie fully substantiated. Cripples, all of them, walking with the aid of invisible crutches, over-projecting non-existent confidence. All except George, The Gambler, who knew what it was all about.

Then suddenly, without warning, elation drained away, replaced instantly by a sense of disorientation, total and annihilating. Anti-climax and exhaustion after a concentrated period of work? No, something infinitely worse: The Blacks.

What was I doing here?

My eyes cut haphazardly between a variety of objects, Cara's domestic comforters: Life-size Panda with red ribbon tied around its neck, mahogany shelf, festooned with dusty Edwardian dolls, fish-shaped bottle-opener with gleaming mother-of-pearl scales, creeping Ivy leaves garlanding book-spines.

I could hear Dan Wymans' harsh cackle obligato rising above the natterchatter. Close to my ears (probably sitting on the reverse end of Cara's trendy loveseat) Ellis Trawley's leaning tenor served echoes of the Night of the

Brixton Vampires. Cara was frugging with two members of the camera crew. Dick sprawled on Antje's lap.

Ought to be somewhere else.

My presence was urgently required. Glinting daggers lurked behind the love-seat. Keep away from that tramyard, George Kahn, we know your secret. Plagued by damp itch between buttocks. Pre-Raphaelite portrait of Leonore's face, blue mittens, auburn hair curling over scarred brow, projecting innocence. Early Bunuel. Legs milling about. Velvet Underground screaming in stereo. Fish-shaped bottle openers. Love you, Marion. Love you. *Love.*

If Melud pleases, the Court may find the Respondent's conduct subsequent to this brainstorm difficult to comprehend, but I put it to the Court that we must make the attempt:

At the exact moment that his mind registered the panic of genuine involvement, his eyes focused with satyrical intent on a pair of legs jerking by.

Melud, the day after my son died, overcome by love and compassion for my wife, I secured carnal knowledge of three different women ...

If the Court pleases, I shall continue to describe the Respondent's behaviour. His eyes panned up from the afore-mentioned jerking legs, found them to belong to Modelfriend, nameless still and therefore, Melud, doubly potent in unleashing the Respondent's lust.

We had selected her from several acquaintances whom Cara had caused to audition for the part: modish chick, not too young, with a butch *jolie-laide* face, framed by blonde hair, cropped down to punished collaborator minimum. Hard breasts bouncing self-importantly inside flame-red minishift, fringed and bangled, slashed to waist-level. Wore neither shoes nor stockings. No longer dancing, but chatting up my P.A. Pillar of the permissive society. Cara again, as Cara was Marion again, as Marion was Linda again. All of them failed Jeans.

'When it takes you,' she proclaimed to my earnest P.A. 'who needs some draggy necking-session on a goddamned sofa, for Christ's sake? You say, O.K., I dig the chemistry, don't bug me with preliminaries, man, screw that coffee and brandy bit, help me out of my pants and let's groove...'

Sheer poetry. What's more, ostensibly she might be addressing my P.A., but she was *playing* to Dracula, crouched on that love-seat right below her, ready to pounce. Nameless? Another dyke? Hateful? All the better to torture me with.

Melud, it has been claimed that the choice of mate is compulsive...

I was on my feet, ready for action, efficiently displacing my nonplussed P.A., meeting provocation with aggression.

'Come off it,' I attacked, blowing the whistle for the ritual game to begin. 'That guff you were giving Pat just now. All bark and no bite. Let someone offer you a quick uncomplicated poke, and you'll wet your pants with fright. What are you—some kind of would-be swinger?'

Battle was joined. The Blacks had vanished, leaving a sediment of feeble rationalisation. Life with Marion had geared me to enjoy continuous gratification. For weeks I had denied myself. Normal male instincts were surfacing.

Surfacing, Melud? I was being swept along on a torrent of mindless erotomania. Dracula, long thought destroyed by the good burgomaster's silver stake, had risen from the grave.

Sublimely engrossed, I thrust cropped Modelfriend into Cara's corridor, illuminated by one naked orange bulb. There, maintaining my verbal onslaught, calling her sham and virgin, I pressed her up tight against bogus bullfighting posters. Modulating from calculated insult to praise of her physical equipment, I thrust a knee between her legs, impelled once more to re-enact the Cara scene, rummaging for a piece of breast, a chunk of buttock, fangs ready for the bite, while what I really wanted was to curl up with Marion, a parcel of flesh tied up with pink ribbons of love. Faithful, Melud, to the end of time.

As it turned out, cropped Modelfriend remained unmoved. Had not played to me at all, but to my P.A., who (as I'd discovered to my own cost) had two infants at school, and loved her stupid husband, who sold insurance and built model ships in bottles.

At a critical moment in our doomed negotiations, Dick and Dan Wymans passed by, returning from Cara's kitchen. I hesitated, thereby placing the final seal on my dismissal. Even more disastrous than my actual failure was the fact that cropped Modelfriend repelled me *with kindness*. Didn't slap my face, or twist my arm. Soothing, motherly, daughterly. Took my hand, begged me to be good. Flattered that a man of my distinction should respond to her so *physically*. She too was often rocked by similar sensations, God knew, temptations that just could not be resisted. Why, once, she illustrated, dining with this man, this old lover, she had met this other man, a complete stranger and kaplonk. This man, this stranger, without uttering a *word*, had taken her hand, led her into this little restaurant manager's office, locked this door, and right there and then, laid her across this desk ...

So she really and truly did *understand* these things. It was her bag, too, but the right chemistry had to be there or it was strictly from Dragsville. A man of my maturity couldn't help but dig that.

I dug allright. Which did not prevent me from calling cropped Modelfriend a loudmouthed, frigid, lesbian twat, whom I wouldn't touch with a ten-foot pole, even if she *was* the last fucking woman on earth.

With those fine sentiments off my chest, I stomped back to join the party, in time to hear Cara laughingly describe me to Dick as a seedy little lecher with the *corniest* bag of middle-aged tricks...

And Dick, dear old pal, his back turned to me, oblivious of Antje's desperate eye-signals, contributed the information that you could always tell when Old George was getting ready to pounce because he started picking his nose. Roars of laughter. As Dirty Old Men went, Dick went on, encouraged by Cara's shrieks and Ellis Trawley's guffaws, George had the peculiar distinction of having been one from the age of twenty. Please God, I thought, bring Marion back and I'll never ever play Dracula again. Is it a deal, God? Everybody got a Second Chance in life. (Who'd said that? Confucius? John Osborne? Cary Grant?) I'd got mine, bloody nearly muffed it. Infantile games of destruction.

As I attempted a dignified exit, cropped Modelfriend was at it again.

'When those female hormones start playing me up,' she was telling my poor old P.A., 'I don't give a bugger where the hell I am ... a room full of people ... Christ, I was having dinner with this man, this old lover. ...'

Good night, sweet Prince of Darkness. And flights of baby vampires sing thee to thy rest ...

God is *not* dead.

I got home, found Marion in my bed, wearing her shorty night-dress, reaching out for me with a pudgy hand, holding a lighted cigarette, smelling of *Femme*. She had let herself into the flat with her unsurrendered key. Joe had told her that our last shot was in the can. Could we now resume?

I flung off my clothes, dived into the warmed bed, tried to weep, couldn't make it, exchanged instead the ageless imperatives of lovers reunited.

After the loving was done, she sat up, began fumbling lengthily in her handbag, at last found what she was searching for, an oblong slip of yellow paper. She handed it to me. With a kiss on my brow.

'Well, there it is, my darling,' she said. 'It's all super.'

She snuggled her face into my armpit. I read what was printed on the slip of yellow paper.

'Oh, darling, I'm so happy,' she sighed. 'Aren't you?'

I read what was printed on the slip of yellow paper.

'The first time I went, they gave me a pink slip. Didn't know they could make mistakes, but it seems they do, darling.'

I read what was printed on the slip of yellow paper.

'And don't you start worrying about Joe,' she said. 'I'll give him the glad tidings when the time is right.'

I read what was printed on the slip of yellow paper.

'Darling,' she whispered, 'if anyone should know, I should, but do they really inject rabbits with your wee-wee to find out?'

They were twins, identical girls, monstrously gifted; only ten months old, but already yakking away as they horsed around, unattended, at the base of a fruit-laden chestnut tree. While the twins fired spiky chestnut shells at one another, we adults lay supine in our deck-chairs, legs dangling, feet scything high meadow grass. Someone had neglected the lawn. Patches of buttercups. Daisies. Marion and Linda wore bikinis. Their faces, upturned to trap the sunshine, were greased with oil.

Kew—my dream was quite emphatic on this point—now belonged to Marion. Acting the glossy hostess, something snooty about her. The guests were cardboard cut-outs on a child's model stage. Linda, her body shiny and tanned, lazily fanned herself with a copy of the *Observer*, unconcerned by the twins, the change of ownership of the house, my relationship with Marion.

I was naked, taking photographs.

While Marion kept up her chilly hostess act, click, Linda was leaning forward, smiling as she tried to sort out the twins, who had crawled into our midst. I watched, click, naked and aghast, waiting for them to call me Daddy.

Then Leonore sauntered on, click, very serious and grown-up, hair tied at the back in a clasp. First she kissed Marion, then, click, Linda, her Mum. One big happy family: post-impressionist idyll.

And then, as Linda chatted on about making marmalade, click, something strange was happening to her face. It was gradually taking on Marion's colouring—hair turning black, lipstick changing to Marion's particular shade of rich purple, patches of soft down appearing on her cheeks. I thought: Why doesn't Marion notice? Why doesn't she do something? Why so cool? Can't she see poor Linda's plight?

But Marion, lying back in her bikini, eyes closed, stayed silent. Clouds cruised across the sun. Something, click, was now happening to her face, too. *Turning into Lon Chaney jr. as Lawrence Talbot, the Wolfman?* No, over her skin, click, crawled a slimy film of *ice*, transforming her face into an opaque mask: the face in the ice-cube. Click. Linda laughed. Super party-trick!

I woke up, and for about fifteen seconds had no idea who or where I was, eventually reached the correct conclusion by a process of elimination.

'What's the matter, darling?'

'Nightmare...'

Used the pillow to wipe sweat off my forehead.

'The one where I turn into Linda...?'

I reached out to stroke her swelling body.

'Shouldn't have those talks with Tetheridge late at night,' Marion said. 'That's what brings them on.'

Oh yes. Remembered now. Conference with The Other Side. Linda had refused to stay her cruelty petition. I would have to defend it. And even if I admitted all thirty-seven items of cruelty, I would still have to deal with her separate adultery charges. Linda had instructed her solicitors to serve writs on all seventeen women listed in her petition without further delay. The joke was that if I defended successfully, we would end up still married to each other.

'It appears,' Tetheridge had ventured glumly (and Counsel had concurred), 'that your wife doesn't really want a divorce, Mr. Kane. She wants a fight.'

'What is it, darling?'

Running the palm of my hand over the convex curve of Marion's stomach, I lulled my brain with a new intuitive certainty. Linda was insane. Zelda. Painstakingly devoted to my destruction. The destruction of Leonore's father.

Somehow Leonore had to be protected . . .

'Talk to me . . .'

'My next project. Flash. Film about the life of Scott Fitzgerald. Must see Dick. Soon as I've cut this picture. Get him going on a treatment.'

I sounded suspiciously calm. Maybe it wasn't Linda who was crazy. Maybe I was the nutter.

'Super!' Marion had propped herself up on her elbows. 'I'd love to play Zelda.'

'What are you saying, Marion?'

Poor Leonore. Had to be protected from all this madness.

Went back to sleep for a while, sought refuge in my ice-cube dream.

Dick and Antje had returned to Cannes sooner than planned. Irene Raeburn was ill, Charlie had succumbed to melancholy. Dick flew South to sort him out. I retreated to a dingy Soho cutting-room, began cutting *The Cripples*, spinning out the work for as long as possible. I was back on salary with the Network.

Technical problems, of whose non-existence Dick had briefly convinced me, were sprouting like neglected weeds. I could no longer bring Leonore home. Marion and Barry were back in the flat. Working hard, I had no time to remove evidence of their presence. If Leonore discovered the truth, and communicated it to Linda, access would be withdrawn forthwith. Unthinkable to make Leonore member of a conspiracy.

Marion had stopped working. The Roger Arnold film, like my own, was being edited. Her part in the TV serial had been written out with indecent haste. The Mod Youth, burdened with her confidence, flipped his cool. This was the 20th century, for Christ's sake! Had she never heard of the pill, a woman of her age, or about legalised abortion? Such unprofessional conduct was beyond his powers of comprehension. They parted company.

As for Joe, Marion had finally found the 'right time' during a *diner à trois*. Visibly shaken, Joe quickly recovered his poise, offered congratulations and obstetric advice, asked us to make a note of the baby's exact hour of birth, so that he could work out a horoscope.

Fortunately, he was working hard: sixth rewrite on a doomed thriller about diamond smuggling. He applied himself to his task, relieved at being able to postpone his blocked novel. Aware of his sense of rejection, I tried placating him with tokens of friendship.

Marion thought he might have a girl-friend tucked away somewhere, I doubted it. He visited the Playboy Club, gambling heavily, losing. I knew, because I went with him.

One morning he came to the cutting-rooms. To help me edit his own sequence, he said. He made some useful, extremely self-damaging suggestions. Struck dumb with shame, I invited him to lunch at the Caprice. In desolate silence, we finished off two expensive bottles of Beychevelle.

Marion, meanwhile, was nesting. We rarely went out, spent our evenings watching television, Marion knitting baby bedjackets. Living with her in such intimacy, I rediscovered her qualities. Her disposition was sunny. She saw no evil. Pregnancy had stilled her quest for experiments. For bouts of sickness, there were pills; for domestic problems, the panacea of good intentions. Everything would come right in the end. Inventing technical adjustments, she saw to it that we made love regularly and pleasurably.

One night, after praising my skill in overcoming the obstacles of her condition, she observed:

'I hope you don't mind me saying this, darling, but actually when we first got together you weren't all that good. I had to pretend a bit. Just as with Joe. But now you're quite marvellous, because you love me.'

I accepted the compliment graciously. Recent experiences with Marion's friend, and Marion's friend's friend, had left my ego bruised. Marion would never guess how appalling I could still be, given half a chance.

Leonore, meanwhile, had to be protected . . .

Every other day, I hurried off to Kew to take her to lunch, leaving my one-armed assistant in charge. I'd return to the cutting-room for a couple of hours of work, then taxi back to school to collect her for tea.

Sometimes, in desperation, I brought her back to the cutting-room with me. She'd sit in a corner, visibly bored and detached, reading a comic, or drawing with feltpens I provided, briefly blinking up at me with an expression of mild reproach.

One afternoon—my assistant was away with a cold— I said: 'Come and have a look at this, love.'

She came across, smirking reluctance. I put my arm around her shoulder, she leant forward tortoise-like to peer at the flickering images on the movieola.

I had been cutting the Dan Wymans sequence. Dan, engagingly self-conscious, was pushing his lout on the swings, fur collar covering his chin, unlit cigarette stuck to his lips. Jump-cut to Ellis, waiting for a train in the Hampstead tube, leaning against an Academy Cinema poster, reminiscing about Bela Lugosi's Last Tour.

'All of them gone,' he was saying in close-shot. 'Bela, Boris, er . . .'

Finger-snapping. Camera stayed relentlessly on his pained face as he tried to recall Peter Lorre's name.

For some days I had been considering using a subliminal insert here: Lady Whitestone shuffling a pack of cards. Seemed right somehow.

'What about it?' Leonore asked me, with latterly-perfected scepticism. Her Fishing-for-Compliments voice.

I didn't reply, too stunned by what the running film had just revealed. That in my quest for her approval, I was seeing the movie through Leonore's eyes was nothing new. What those eyes now registered, however, was not a film by me at all. It was a film *about* me. Someone other than George Kane must have directed this picture, because *all the characters in it were me . . .*

Confusion. Had tried for a documentary about friends and acquaintances, ended up with Confessions of George Kane, his life and loves. Eerie. Horror film after all.

'Don't you like it?' I asked Leonore hoarsely. 'Isn't it fun?'

'What's fun about it?'

'If you don't like it, *say* so . . .'

'Well, it's nothing special, is it? Just your friends doing boring things. Like Mummy's home movies when we go on holiday.'

Home Movies?

'This is a very fine film, Leonore,' I raged at her. 'You tell your Mother. Your Daddy's made a very distinguished motion-picture. Probably a work of art.'

Leonore shrugged her shoulders, tried to squeeze back into her corner to read her comic. I held on to her sleeve.

'Now wait a minute. I'm not standing for any more of your sulks. I show you my work and you just sit there, shrugging and sulking. Not good enough. If there's something the matter with this movie, you come right out with it.'

She shrugged again.

'Nothing to do with your movie,' she said.

'What then?'

'Don't have any fun. The way we used to . . .'

Stuffed her hands inside her skirt band, gazed at the floor, kicked at a loose curl of celluloid.

'O.K.,' I told her. 'O.K. So I've had to cut this picture. My job, isn't it? Your Dad has to make a living once in a while. Right?'

She sighed.

'Don't go on about it then, Dad. Stop rowing.'

I swallowed. Parched throat.

'Tell you what we'll do, love. Next Wednesday, we'll go to the flix. *Alfred the Great, Oliver!* Anything you like. You pick the movie.'

She just stood there, toes stabbing away at frames of film.

'Oh dear,' she said. 'Never mind.'

'What's all this oh dear never mind then?'

'Well, Betty Smith is coming to tea on Wednesday . . .

'Wednesday is one of *my* days. Mummy ought to know better than to . . .'

'Not *her* fault. Betty's Mummy only lets her come out on Wednesdays. But it's allright, Daddy.' Big sigh. 'I'll cancel it. I'll come out with you instead. Allright?'

Turned to withdraw into her corner. I almost hit the roof. Yegods, thinks she's doing me a favour, seeing me! Milady dispensing bounty! I pretended to examine one of the lengths of film strung along the length of wall, celluloid stockings hanging up to dry. Looking for excuses not to go out with me, that's what she was up to. Didn't love me.

Images of trains and violet jerseys assaulted my mind. The train roared out of my head, whistling through the cold night. I held her in my arms in the corridor, protecting her. Couldn't do without her. Might learn to live without Marion, as I had learned to live without Linda. Not with this sulking little red-headed girl, not with her. Could never play games, take risks, gamble. The one betrayal-proof relationship of my life.

She didn't love me.

My fault, obviously. I'd been the provider of her bread, her circuses. Now she sensed a division of my loyalties. Had I give too much of myself to Marion? To Dick? To that hapless mess of autobiographical celluloid?

I *had* betrayed her, often thinking of her with pain, even with dread—dread of my inadequacy, of all the inconvenience she was causing me. She had noticed. Caught out. I had become careless. Lost her.

I unclipped one of the lengths of film, stared at the frames, eyes blind. Just remember this, George, don't placate her. Never works. Whatever else you do, do *not* now placate her.

She was immersed in the thrills of her comic, oblivious of my panic. Hoping the afternoon would end soon, so that she could go home to mother.

'How about a stroll round the market, eh? You used to like that ...'

'Don't mind.'

I took her hand, we ran down an alley, began ambling along the stalls of Berwick Street market. Pushed her arm through mine, the way it had been that dusky winter afternoon, long ago. Just the two of us. Sentimental jerk, I reproached myself, you'll pay for this.

It was spring now. No enveloping dusk to make us huddle close for warmth. No Andersen fairy tale atmosphere. No magic. Just a sunny afternoon, like any other.

'Why don't we ever see Marion and Barry now?' she

was asking plaintively. 'Don't you like them anymore?'

That unforgotten descending scale: drip-drip-drip from the ice-cube.

Ignore it. Squeezed her arm tight against my ribs, stopped to buy a pound of apples, walked on to find that cheap jewellery stall. Anxiously watched her mittenless fingers sort through a carton of bracelets.

She looked up at me, rubbing an apple on her blouse. 'Have a bite, Dad.'

I took a crunchy bite of yellow apple, a real hard bite. She had actually offered me a bite of apple. Her own apple. Peace-offering. I could attack.

'Did you mention to Mummy that I want my view-finder?' I asked her sternly. 'And Quigley's *International Motion Picture Almanac of 1956*?'

'Lots of times,' she replied, munching contentedly.

'And?'

Shrug. I lurched on. She followed.

'I'll ask her myself tonight,' I told her.

'No, don't,' she said, quickening her pace. 'Please don't.'

'Why not?'

'Max won't like it . . .'

'Max?'

'Mummy's friend, you know, he's got this car-hire firm . . .'

'Oh . . . ?'

'Don't want you two having another blazing row. You and Mummy.'

'We never . . . What did you say about . . .'

'Like the other time, *you* know . . .'

'No, I don't know. Your mother and I never have rows. We may choose not to live together . . .'

She stopped, took another bite of apple, spoke with a full mouth:

'I *saw* what you did, Daddy. You beat Mummy up.'

I stared at her. She didn't flinch.

'I beat Mummy up? How can you say such a thing, love? I've never laid a hand on your mother!'

'Go on. I *saw* you. That night at the house. You had a row, then you beat her up. Mummy often mentions it.'

'Look,' I said, 'you've got this all wrong, love.'

Stood motionless, hands deep in my pockets. She was blinking up at me, finishing off her apple, right down to the core.

'Never ever beaten your Mummy up, darling. Would never do such a thing. . . .'

'I *saw* you, Daddy.' Stubbornly, patiently. 'Saw you.'

From a nearby recordshop came the blare of anonymous pop. We stood staring at each other. Hopeless to persuade her; she was convinced. Burnished sunglow. I grabbed her right arm, then both arms, clumsily tried to embrace her, tugged at her sleeve. Stammering.

'Just isn't true, love. Wasn't the way you think. Wouldn't ever want to hurt you, either of you . . .'

She threw the browned applecore into the gutter. I took her warm face in my hands, kissed her. She seemed to like that. I clung to her little body. She struggled free, began to walk away. I followed. Keep it going. Somehow.

'Does Mummy really tell you . . . no, never mind . . .'

'Auntie Elspeth asked me where we went when you took me out for tea, and I said you never took me home these days . . .'

'Well, there's a reason for that, my darling, you see . . .'

'. . . and then Auntie Elspeth said "Don't you dare call that place Home. *This* is your home", and . . .'

'Never mind . . .'

'. . . and I told her, I told Auntie Elspeth. I said, I've got two homes, I can call Daddy's place Home if I like. And then Uncle Max, I mean Max, he said . . .'

'. . . don't want to hear . . .'

This time, when we stopped, it was Leonore who wanted to kiss. Felt dampness. Made her cry. Discovered that the smears on our cheeks were not caused by her tears at all. Wanted her to taste the damp. Let her know that' Dad was Man enough to break down, weep. On a sunny afternoon in Berwick Street.

'Never you mind, my little love, never you mind.'

I thought: I *can* stay behind that iron barrier at the far end of Platform Two. Hold on to those bars, let her go. On that night train. Alone. If it saves her life and costs mine, let her go. Must let her go. Could never afford to lose her.

When I let myself into the flat, Barry was asleep, Marion had taken a pill. She dozed, with all the lights on, over a copy of *Nova*. I switched off the bedside lamp.

A bad time. Return to The Black Lagoon. The front door had opened, moved by invisible hands, Leonore had slipped inside, turning in the doorway to blow me a kiss. Heard her clattering upstairs, placed a foot in the doorway. Voice behind the door asked icily what I thought I.was doing. The Black Lagoon. Barred.

'I want my viewfinder,' I told Voice. 'And my 1956 *International Motion Picture Almanac.*'

'I haven't time to look for them now,' said Voice.

'I've asked for them repeatedly, Linda. My property.'

'Then you'd better write the appropriate letter to your solicitors, hadn't you?'

'Look, Linda, it's a simple, concrete thing I'm asking. I would like to have my viewfinder and my 1956 . . .'

'And I've told you I haven't time to look for them now.'

'They're on the mantelpiece. My study. All you have to do . . .'

'If you're going to make a scene, I'll call Elspeth . . .'

'Screw Elspeth. You lousy bitch, I have every right to ask for these things. And don't think I don't know you're living with Max . . .'

'What a charmer you are.'

Door thrown into my face. I'd momentarily withdrawn my foot. Shouldn't have mentioned Max. Given away Leonore's secret, abused her confidence. Lurched round the corner to the nearest pub, gulped down a large Scotch, found an early edition of the *Evening Standard* on the saloon bar counter, opened up the sports pages, pored over pools forecasts and league tables, asked the barmaid if she knew the number of a minicab firm. She handed me a card. Went into a public call box, dialled, ordered a cab, thinking, what if Max answers? Drank another Scotch, waited. Half-an-hour, the man had said. Not Max. Picked up the paper again. Heard the rattle of a train, grimy, soot-covered and steam-driven, blowing an old-fashioned whistle. Saw myself swaying in the vibrating corridor, gripping a brass handle, letting down the window, cold night wind blowing, blinding me.

Marion mumbled away in a drugged voice. Dick had called from Cannes. Very urgent. Was it about Irene Raeburn? She grunted, fell asleep. I tiptoed into the sitting-room, picked up the phone, dialled the thirteen digits, surprised myself by remembering them.

Dick answered after the first buzz. Had he been sitting by the telephone waiting for my call?

'How's Irene?' I asked.

'Probably cancer,' he said. 'Very sad. But never you mind about that. I'm dealing with Charlie. How quickly can you get *The Cripples* over here?'

'Network wouldn't wear *The Cripples*. It's called *N.W.3.* now.'

'How quickly can you rush a rough-cut over?'

Sounded manic. Had probably been sorting out Charlie's real situation. *Film Festival*, he shouted down the line. He'd been wining and dining an important member of the selection committee all week. If we played our cards right, we might wangle to get our film invited to the Critics' Section. Or something. Wasn't listening very carefully. They were looking at new stuff all next week, and . . .

A fine print wouldn't be ready for at least a fortnight, I told him. Some tracks still had to be dubbed in . . .

'Don't give me all that technical codswallop.' Sounded affronted. 'You've always been an opportunist, George. Try to act like one for a change. Get that film over here in the best possible condition, I don't care how . . .'

'Need the Network's O.K., Dick. If Jack . . .'

'Leave Jack to me. Grab those cans of film, get on the Night Ferry. . . .'

Chinese gong sounding in my ears. Boy stood on the burning deck. No, burning bridge. Flames licking along wooden boards. *Bridge over the River Kwai* (David Lean, 1957). Biggest bridge of all. My throat was dry. The thrill of it. Action!

'Now you listen to me, Dick,' I said very calmly. Old clip from *Creaking Doors*. 'Just you listen, and don't interrupt. I'll lay this on, but only if you'll do something for me.'

'What?'

I spoke rapidly but precisely. Told him to get a letter to Jack into the very next mail, telling him that there was a fifty-fifty chance our film would be selected for a representative showing at the Festival. Feather in the Network's cap. Wasn't a hope in hell of pulling it off, though, unless I, the director, went there, *in person*, to show the unfinished movie, make a sales pitch to the Committee.

'Got that, Dick? Now here's the most important point of all. You tell Jack that I must have £500 expenses to do the job properly. I'll repay most of it when I get back, but it's got to be five hundred smackers. *In travellers cheques*. Otherwise no deal. He won't take that from me. From you he'll take it and like it. If Jack comes through, I'll be over with the film next week. Right?'

Dick fumed a bit. Typical of me to confuse a perfectly

simple technical problem with my neurosis. However, he'd write the bloody letter, if I insisted. I put down the receiver, touched my face. Wet. Dick hadn't caught on. Didn't guess a thing. When it came to playing for high stakes with George the Gambler, he was a babe in the woods.

I collapsed into a chair, lit a cigarette. My last counter *en plein*. Killed off Dracula. Now the Creep was for the chopper. Didn't even want to make a list.

For your sake, my darling.

Ecstasy.

Directed by Gustav Machaty, 1933.

NOT yet May, but already the sand under your feet was baked. Striding over unshaded portions of the beach, you had to curl your toes to avoid getting blisters.

I lay on a yellow foam-rubber mattress, sipping the ritual Pernod, half-listening to the lazy lapslap of sea smacking over sand, the fluting of an *ambre solaire* tenor from Marion's crackling transistor.

Protective plaster stuck over her nose, purple straw hat shading her oiled forehead, Marion lay slumped in a deck-chair, white towel modestly flung across her plump midriff. From time to time, a spray of sand hit my legs: Barry, brandishing a shovel, was burying Leonore alive. (Hadn't I dreamt this scene, with minor variations, only a few nights ago?)

Charlie Raeburn had recommended one of the cheaper beaches to the west of Cannes. Here, he'd advised, you could save at least four francs per person on mattresses and umbrellas. And the food was just as good as at the Carlton or the Martinez. At a fraction of the cost.

Charlie, like Dick, was absent. The day before our arrival, an ambulance had rushed Irene off to a hospital in Grasse. Emergency operation. His own dilapidated Consul had broken down under years of neglect—Charlie considered French garaging fees excessive—and Dick had to drive him up and down the winding mountain roads in his Buick. Sparing no effort to keep his tame selection committee member friendly, Dick wasn't always available for this chore.

'Charlie, wouldn't it be worth your while to hire a taxi while you've got all this going on?' Dick had asked him in our presence. 'God knows I don't mind chauffeuring you about. Morning, noon and night, if necessary. It's your own convenience I'm thinking about.'

'I happen to know what local taxis are charging these days,' Charlie replied. 'I'm not having them exploit my predicament. Question of principle.'

He had aged about five years since my last visit. Dread of losing Irene had carved deep lines across his forehead. His skin, pallid and puffy, hung in tiny folds over his cheek bones. Abjectly lost, he could do nothing but pace about in Dick's salon, biting his nails, waiting for Dick to find time to drive him to his wife's bedside.

Was *this* love?

Leonore and Barry had now reversed positions in their grisly Edgar Allan Poe game. Leonore was energetically shovelling damp sand over the boy's prostrate body. Only his pale intelligent face (shaded, masking the sun) poked up. He caught my eye, grinned sourly. Resembles Joe, I thought with a start. Poor Joe. Must try and make it up to him somehow . . .

Sipped my Pernod. Been looking forward to playing roulette. Now, because of this mood of premature mourning, I knew that if I suggested going to the Casino, they'd think me heartless. I waved at Leonore, blew a kiss. She didn't notice, digging away, burying her friend.

Getting them all to Cannes had required the mobilisation of all my wits and guiles. Jack's vanity, as expected, had been tickled by thoughts of festival glory; I got my travellers cheques.

Linda's response had been similarly predictable. Permission to take Leonore to visit Dick during Leonore's Easter holidays? Over her dead body. Did I imagine I could engineer another furtive attempt to abduct her child to the continent?

Dialling tone.

Got hold of Tetheridge, applied pressure. Lawyers met in expensive conclave, worked out the usual 'amicable arrangement'. Before a Commissioner of Oaths, I swore on the Bible that I would fly Leonore back to London before her planned birthday party. This would cut my trip down to a mere week. I also signed an agreement, allowing Linda to take Leonore on an Atlantic cruise during the summer holidays. ('To salvage the child's health, adversely affected by my husband's actions.') I deposited three hundred pounds with Tetheridge. Or rather Marion deposited it. She also bought our tickets.

'Darling,' she said, 'I've just got Roger's cheque. It's the least thing I can do. It's marvellous of you to take us along.'

Suspecting that Linda might turn up to see Leonore off, I made Marion and Barry take an afternoon flight. Leonore and I followed by night sleeper.

'Remember complaining that we never see anything of Barry and Marion these days?' I asked her as we moved out of the Gare de Lyon.

'Well?'

'Wouldn't be at all surprised if Dick's invited them too,' I told her.

Leonore's response: it would have been more fun to take another sleeping-train from Paris to Cannes. Day trains were boring old things. I offered to play Twenty Questions.

Marion reached out, gripped my foot. Sandy.

'Isn't everything just perfect, my darling?' she asked sleepily.

Perfect. My forehead tingled: the beginnings of a tan. Back on square one. This time, by God, I'd make no mistake.

I heard a car door being slammed, looked up to see Dick sauntering down the steps that led to the beach. Antje was trailing behind him, carrying a load of rolled towels. From the way she hung her head I could tell that something was seriously amiss.

'It's all off,' Dick announced, handing me a piece of blue paper. My first thought: Linda hasn't followed us.

'That bastard,' Antje mused, disconsolately squatting down on the hot sand. 'And after all Dick did for him.'

I shaded my eyes to read the telegram.

REGRET CHAIRMAN RULES NW3 UNAVAILABLE REPEAT UNAVAILABLE FOR FESTIVAL EXPOSURE BEFORE NETWORK TRANSMISSION TVWISE STOP EYEBROWHIGH IN TROUBLE RE EXPENSES STOP COME HOME BOYS LOVE JACK

Dick had wandered off to the shaded beach-bar. I rose, brushed sand off my arse, followed. To console him with a large Pernod. And to pretend I cared.

During the late afternoon, puffy wisps of vapour began to appear on the horizon, blown by a moist wind across the mountains in the West. Long before sunset, the clusters of cloud had flattened out. A fine spring rain drizzled down from an overcast sky.

The atmosphere in the salon of the Villa Rameau resembled a wake. We froze. With its marble floors and indoor fountains, the house had been built for a tropical climate. The moment the sun disappeared, one reached for thick sweaters. Neither Marion nor I had thought of bringing any.

At first confused, then driven desperate by the absence of television, Barry and Leonore had been sent to bed with an armful of comics that Marion had providentially bought at London Airport. She and Antje now huddled in a corner of the gaunt room, chatting about breast feeding and nappy services.

Dick remonstrated with me. Prattle about babies could conceivably ruin his relationship with Antje.

'Bloody Marion,' he thundered. 'She's got *you* under

264

-her thumb. Now she needs to disrupt *my* sexlife.'

Followed up by castigating me *sotto voce* for permitting Marion's pregnancy. Had I learned nothing? Did I have to turn every tart I screwed into a Mum? Was I determined to be dragged once more into sexless, tensionless domesticity? I should have bloody well insisted on an abortion. Never mind what Marion *wanted*. She ought to want to please her man; otherwise the relationship was doomed from the start. Anyhow, how could I be certain the brat was mine? Could be Roger Arnold's. Had I thought of that? I had not. Well then, start thinking about it, George. Show some activity.

He ordered Antje to make herself useful, divert poor Charlie with a game of chess. Antje and Charlie started a listless tournament, neither of them wishing to play, both too terrified of arousing Dick's wrath to argue.

Charlie tried projecting calm, but every time a chair scraped, he jumped. He was expecting a call from the hospital. Irene had been operated on that afternoon. The doctors had promised to call. He had written down his own number and Dick's number. They did not expect Irene to regain consciousness before morning, but they had promised to telephone anyway.

While Charlie scurried upstairs to make sure that his own telephone was in working order, Dick warned us to prepare ourselves for the worst. Meanwhile, he argued, what Charlie really needed was a good night's sleep. He would have taken his own receiver off the hook, if he weren't himself expecting a critical telephone call. The friendly selection committee member had promised to communicate the committee's final decision in the course of the evening.

Though Jack's cable had made this decision irrelevant, Dick decided to hold an interim inquest. The role of chief witness fell to me.

Somebody had screwed us up. Would I cast my mind back, remember what I had done to offend the Network's Chairman? I shouldn't have asked for all that money. What did I want it for, anyway? Was he charging us rent?

I sought refuge behind a copy of the *Indicateur Européen Cook*. Dick used it as a doorstop. I now employed it to calm my nerves. Time-tables soothed almost as efficaciously as football results.

'I've just decided what we're going to do,' Dick announced. 'We've never received that sodding cable. Right? If they select the film, we'll show it anyway, argue afterwards.'

I went on turning pages of the Railway Guide. *Venezia—Trieste—Villa Opicina—Ljubljana*. The Direct-Orient Express. No little black beds. Turn to page 412 for summer services..

'Present the bastards with a *fait accompli*. If the Network wants a bloody scandal, we'll give it to them. I'll call a flaming press conference...'

... *Genova PP—Milano—Chiasso—Lugano*. Little black beds.

'... I'll get the *Express* stringer on the phone. Make Jack Martinsell wish he'd never been born...'

... *Goslar—Bad Harzburg—Wolfenbüttel—Braunschweig—Osnabrück—Bendabrück—Uelzen* ...

I looked up quickly, searched for Marion's eyes across the room. Had she noticed anything? Knitting more bedjackets. Charlie and Antje had resumed their game of chess. Back to the *Indicateur*. There had to be a connection. If one took the night express from Marseilles and changed... Where? Basle?... see page 98 ...

My heart was thumping away, hurting my ribs, blotting out Dick's voice. Marion looked up, blew me a kiss. Violet jerseys with white facings. On a gravelly pitch....

'... real situation is that poor old Jack can't bear rejection. That's why he needs to concoct this cock-and-bull story about the Chairman. Hedge his bet in case the picture is turned down...'

Hamm—Gütersloh—Bielefeld—Lohne—Bad Oeyn-hausen. No little black beds. Had to have little black beds.

Pacing up and down, smoking, Dick dropped his glass. Clank and clatter. An onyx knight, just captured from Antje, fell from Charlie's trembling hand.

'Better call the hospital in case . . .'

'Charlie, you're beginning to get on my tits. If they have news, they'll call you. Right? Get on with your game.'

Charlie sat down again.

Cloppenburg—Oldenburg—Varel . . . get off the Nord Express at 4.42 . . . no, much too early. She might still be fast asleep . . . wake up in darkness . . .

'I was in such a state,' Charlie said, 'I might have given them the wrong number. I must telephone . . . excuse me.'

He rose, stumbled across the room. Marion kept her eyes cast down, concentrating on her knitting. Dick hesitated, could not quite bring himself to tell Charlie he wanted the line kept clear.

Where was I? *Cloppenburg—Oldenburg* . . . lost my place.

Seconds before Charlie's hand reached the telephone, it rang. Charlie picked up the receiver, turned his back on us. Dick stood close behind him, right arm placed firmly around Charlie's sloping shoulder, left hand picking up the extension.

'Hel . . . hello . . .' Charlie stuttered.

'Hello,' Dick shouted, lips nowhere near the mouthpiece.

'Dead . . . I mean the line . . .'

Dick's hand tightened its grip around Charlie's shoulder. They continued to bellow their hellos. The *Indicateur* fell off my knees. Bent down to pick it off the floor, heard Dick's voice, cool and disappointed.

'For you, Marion.'

'For me?'

'England.'

Marion jumped up to snatch the receiver from Dick. Charlie, incredulous and open-mouthed, hovered by her side, then gradually retreated to his chair.

'Yes? . . . it *is* me . . . Ellis? Ellis, darling . . . what? . . . oh, *no* . . .' Long pause. 'Where did it . . . when . . .?'

'I don't know why I guessed at once what had happened. Saw a clearly etched picture. Long before Marion uttered the next syllable.

'*Your* doctor? . . . when . . . how many did he take?'

We were all composing ourselves to respond suitably to Marion's news, when Charlie Raeburn lost his head.

'It's for *me*!' he yelled at Dick, 'I *know* it's for me. You're trying to shield me. She's talking to the surgeon . . .'

He flew across the room to wrest the receiver from Marion. Antje jumped up, tried to restrain him, held on to a silk shirt-tail, upset the chessboard. The onyx figures clattered down on marble, rolled away in all directions. Dick was guiding Charlie, still struggling and protesting, to a sofa.

By now, Marion had put down the receiver. She stood quite still, arms folded across her chest.

'Have you got a cigarette?' she asked me.

I lit one, got up, placed it between dry lips. She started to cough. Dick poured out a brandy. She drank it, still refused to sit down.

'If Ellis hadn't turned up on his way home . . . he'd been to the pictures . . .'

'What's happened?' Antje whispered to Dick, who ignored her. I placed one arm around Marion, muttering, kissing her temple, begging her to sit down.

'They're pumping out his stomach,' she said tonelessly. 'Ellis suspected something, called a doctor. They had to break down the front door. I'll have to fly back tomorrow. If Barry asks . . .'

She still didn't cry, but her shoulders had started to shake.

'I'll look after Barry,' I said. 'You leave Barry to me.'

Even now, nobody mentioned Joe's name. For a long time nobody could think of anything to say at all: no phrase, no word, that had not suddenly become taboo. Antje enfolded Marion in an embrace. Dick gazed at his feet, embarrassed.

The first one to speak was Charlie, crawling about on the floor, picking up scattered chessmen, carefully replacing them in a little wooden box.

'If you're booked back to London on a night excursion flight,' he told Marion, 'don't fly back in the afternoon. Costs the earth.'

Marion and I slept in the same bed that night. No other arrangement was possible. She lay on her side of the double bed, I lay on mine, a deep dark hollow between us. Antje brought us two glasses of some malted Dutch liquid, which I suspect Dick had drugged. Drank it to the dregs, asking no questions, not of Antje, not of each other.

When I woke up, Marion was already dressed and packed, keeping herself occupied by helping Antje to prepare lunch. Dick, having volunteered to take Marion to the airport in the afternoon, used up the morning (gratefully, I suppose) to drive Charlie to Grasse. Having heard nothing from the doctors, Charlie suspected a conspiracy, told Dick that he would camp at the hospital until Irene had recovered sufficiently to confirm his theory.

Coming down in my swimming trunks, I was in time to see them off. Jumped into the pool to splash about with Barry and Leonore. Told myself I was doing the only useful thing circumstance allowed: playing the sane and happy father.

Neither of the children were expert swimmers. I loaded

them on my back, swam with my burden from the deep to the shallow end, then back again.

When Dick returned, we all sat down to a bleak *al fresco* lunch. Like actors, walking through unrehearsed roles, we haltingly steered our way through blocked-out moves, improvising dialogue, repeatedly faltering. Neither Irene's condition, nor Charlie's devotion to her, could be articulated in case a loose phrase led to the forbidden subject of Joe.

We nibbled at our food (pâté, hard-boiled eggs, a dreadful oily ratatouille), the kids prattled, all of us grateful to them for monopolising the talk. I noticed for the first time that Leonore and Barry had become firm friends, sucked up some obscure relief from this observation. Dick didn't speak at all. He finally rose from the table, extracted a *Nice-Matin* from the back-pocket of his jeans, tossed it across at me, and curtly announced that he was taking a shower. He would be ready to drive Marion to the airport in twenty minutes.

Antje, terrified to be left alone in the emotional smog, heaped dishes on a tray, clattered after him into the house. The children rushed down the steps of the terrace, threw themselves back into the pool, squealing.

I looked down at the folded *Nice-Matin*, was about to turn to the sports section, when my eye caught the paragraph Dick had wanted me to find. Under the heading, *Cahiers du Festival*, I read the brief announcement that the Critics' Selection Committee had made their final choice the previous evening. There followed a list of chosen films, countries of origin placed in brackets. My eyes ran down the list, stopped at Angleterre. Title in front of brackets: *Les Nuits Bleues*. Stared at this for a few seconds, unable to speak. My heart pounded as it had done briefly the previous night.

'What,' I managed to ask Marion, 'was the name of Roger Arnold's film?'

'What? Oh. He kept changing his mind about that,

darling.' Relieved we were talking again. 'Originally he wanted to call it *Number One*, but Hammond talked him out of that. Finally they agreed on *Busted* . . .'

'Ah,' I grunted, '*Busted*. Nice title.'

'Only in the end this distributor wouldn't wear *Busted* either. Darling, would you credit it? Can't even remember the title of my own film. *White* something . . .'

'*Blue Nights?* That it?'

'That's it. *Blue Nights*. Whatever that might mean.'

'Congratulations,' I said.

I tossed the folded newspaper across the table, watched her eyes wandering all over the page, could tell the precise moment when she found the paragraph, read the title. She frowned. I interpreted: How can I react to this without hurting George? I was touched.

'Didn't even know they'd entered it,' she said. Numbed.

I picked up a fork, placed it close to my right eye. Through the gap in the prongs, I peered at the children scrambling about in the pool. After Marion had come round the table to kiss the top of my head, and gone into the house, I unfolded *Nice-Matin*, feverishly searched for football tables. Roger Arnold, Festival King. Hearing about Joe's attempted suicide hadn't hurt half as much.

The Blacks closed in, made a meal of me. Gobble, gobble, gobble. Serves you right, George, trying to play the swinging bloody amateur at your time of life! Not just a failure, George, but a fraud. *They Made Me a Criminal*, John Garfield (Warner Bros. 1939). Gobble, gobble, gobble. Taking money from the Network under false pretences. Income-tax evasion. Swearing lying affidavits. If Melud pleases, the Queen's Proctor has had to intervene in this case. Steel doors slamming shut. Walk to the scaffold. *A Place in the Sun* (George Stevens, 1951). Bankrupt. Trapped. No way out. Tell it to the Judge. This gun is loaded, see? If I go, I'll blow you all skyhigh. Jimmy Cagney. Beautiful.

Dick had come out again, storing Marion's suitcase in the back of his Buick. Marion took her leave. I embraced her with excessive formality.

'Do whatever you think is right,' I told her.

'We'll see, darling, we'll see. I'll ring Barry tonight, tell him.'

'I'll look after Barry, not to worry.'

'Oh, darling, I do wish you were coming with me . . .'

'I've told him his Daddy has caught 'flu . . .'

Noticing Marion's imminent departure, the kids had climbed out of the pool. Barry offered his mother a wet embrace.

'Come on, Marion,' Dick said. 'You'll miss the bloody plane.'

After they had driven off, I went into the house, came out again two minutes later with a virgin pack of Dick's cigarettes and the *Indicateur Européen Cook*. Antje, I was relieved to note, had gone off in the car with Dick and Marion.

Alone then. Just me. And *them*. Ripped off my shirt, lit a cigarette. The heat prickled pleasantly on my back. I opened the Guide. Ceremoniously. *Orient Express?* No, going the wrong way. Istanbul?

Screaming assailed my ears. I looked up, shaded my eyes against the sun. Barry and Leonore were running towards me, supple and dripping, shiny little seals.

'We've thought up a play, Daddy!' Leonore cried.

'Can we do our play for you now, Uncle George?'

Back in the old routine. Just me. And them. Father. Relax. Inhale deeply. Dissolve that dumpling.

'Who's in it?'

'Just the two of us. But you've got to watch it by the pool, Uncle George.'

Right. Followed them down to the side of the swimming-pool. No, *not* Istanbul. Too far.

'Who directed this epic?' I asked them. 'Got to have a director.'

'Me,' Leonore cried. 'Action!'

'You see, we're on this desert island . . .'

'First we'll do the commercial,' Leonore commanded. First they did the commercial. Lovely sexy Oxo Cubes. Then the play proper began.

'The title of our play,' Barry announced, 'is *The Isle of Desires* . . .'

Yegods, *The Isle of Desires*! (Son of a screenwriter!) They had jumped into the blue water, yelling instructions.

'We're in this shipwreck, see?'

'Lost at sea, get it, Daddy?'

'Got you.'

They paddled about in the shallow end, acting exhaustion.

'Land Ahoy!' Leonore cried, bringing her palm up to her brow.

Screams of delight. Magic island. Isle of Desires. They were clambering up the edge of the pool.

'Now we're on the Isle of Desires,' Barry explained in an authoritative bass voice. 'My mate and I can recognise it from pictures we've seen of it.'

'Somewhere on this island,' Leonore elaborated, 'we shall find the magic tree.'

She, too, affected a deep voice. They were sailors.

'If we find the magic tree, all you have to do, you rip off a piece of it, and then you make a wish and it comes true. See, Daddy?'

'Don't explain it, you fool. *Act* it!'

They stalked about the garden, shading their eyes, searching for the magic tree. They met cannibals. They killed the cannibals, cutting their throats. They met Indians, shot them, threw them into the pool. They squatted down, rubbed pebbles together, made a fire, cooked Beefburgers, patted their bellies. Strengthened, they raced around the pool to find the magic tree.

They found it. Me. I was their Magic Tree. Their

audience of one became their only prop. Granting all wishes.

First they danced around me, hollering. Then they knelt down at the foot of the tree. They kissed my feet.

'It only works,' one sailor explained to the other, 'if you kiss the roots first.'

They began to rip pieces of bark off me. And wishing. Rip. A great castle. Rip. A Rolls-Royce. Rip. A treasure chest. Barry got angry, because Leonore was spoiling the play, giggling too much.

'Now we've got to cut some more bits off the tree to take home to our children,' Barry announced.

'All your twigs and branches, Daddy. Off with them!'

'Stop calling him Daddy, you nit. He's a tree!'

Laughing uproariously, they set about amputating my feet and my hands, then my legs and my arms, lastly my head. They'd begun to forget I was a wish-granting tree. Dismembering a father was more fun anyway. Holding up armfuls of my limbs, they danced around me in triumph. All their desires would be granted now; their children's wishes, too.

This was supposed to be the end of the play. Intoxicated by all the activity, they couldn't stop. Leonore came up quite close, face flushed.

'Stand up, Daddy,' she ordered.

I stood up, stared at her matted red hair.

'And now,' proclaimed the bearded sailor, 'I'm cutting off your magic leaf. Also known as your Willie. A good luck charm for my daughter.'

Using her invisible knife, she carefully trimmed off my Willie, strung it along a necklace, hung the captured talisman around her neck. Barry had not anticipated this encore, rolled about on the ground, clutching his plump little stomach. Unable to control his jubilation.

'There,' Leonore said. 'Now I can have anything I want, and so can all my children. The End.' ·

'You've done this magic tree of yours a very serious

injury,' I complained. They couldn't hear me. Leonore, exultant, had already pushed Barry back into the pool, jumped in after him.

So I jumped too. Water in my nostrils, my throat. I came up for air, their yelling was close to my ears. My brain was marvellously clear. I knew what I would do, what I had known all along I would do. Could smell burning. Liberation. Swam to the deep end, hoisted myself up on my elbows.

'Hey, kids,' I called out to them. 'Out you come now. Got a nice surprise for you.'

Not Cagney, no.

While Barry and Leonore towelled each other dry, I quietly slipped upstairs, ran a bath, soaked my body in Badedas, shaved off my Chinese Warlord moustache without mishap. Packed my suitcase, then Leonore's. Telephoned Cannes station for a taxi, took the receiver off the hook, searched for Barry's passport. Then, with extreme care, I packed his bag too. Called the children upstairs, told them to change into their best clothes, spread out on their beds. While they got on with this, I sat down to compose a note for Dick.

Not Cagney. Something more contained, introverted, intact was required. I gazed into the dressing-table mirror, narrowed my eyes, exercised a tiny muscular tick just above the right cheek-bone, drew back my top lip taut against my upper teeth. Snarly lisp. Perfect.

Pithily, I scrawled:

Thanks for everything, pal. For the real situation see Cook's Continental Timetable.

Signed it *Bogey*, pinned it on one of Dick's youth-enhancing T-shirts, which Antje had hung up in the kitchen to dry.

The taxi arrived: bloody Mercedes, driven by a Corsican gangster, filling in time between blackmailing film-stars. Get in, kids. Wave goodbye to the Villa Rameau. Forever.

At the railway station, we asked the Corsican black-mailer to wait. Carried our bags to the *consigne*, slipped the cloakroom ticket into my wallet, right beside my hoard of travellers cheques.

'We'll pick up the bags before the train leaves,' I lisped.

'Are we really going on a sleeping-train, Daddy? Really—really?'

'You heard me,' I snarled.

'Where exactly *are* we going?' Barry wanted to know. 'Mummy said she was ringing up.'

'Daddy *told* us, you fool. On a sleeping-train!'

'Has she gone to London to have her baby?' Barry enquired of Leonore. She shrugged.

'You don't know the place, son.' I put an arm around Barry, brushed back his silky black hair. 'Name wouldn't mean a thing to you. Gotta trust your Uncle George.'

At my command, we transformed ourselves into knights. Blue, black and white knights charged out of the station into blinding white sunlight, lances poised.

The Corsican was waiting. Got into his Mercedes, drove to Dick's travel-agent on the Boulevard Carnot.

'Stay in the car,' I instructed, Bogey again.

To the absent travel-agent's Girl Friday (Lauren Bacall) I introduced myself as *un ami anglais du Monsieur Bligh*. Expensively scented, wearing a plain white smock and an unconvincing platinum wedding ring, Baby Bacall plonked down a fat railway guide, opened it. We pored over the guide, heads almost touching across the counter. My booking (one single, two halves, three second-class sleepers) required complicated negotiations. Calls were made to the Wagon-Lits office in Nice; train connections had to be checked and double-checked. Miss Bacall couldn't even pronounce our destination. Projected casual efficiency and hygienic eroticism. We would be obliged to change trains twice, she had the impression. There were easier routes if we started in the morning. Nothing doing, baby. I kept glancing through the travel agency's window, making sure that the Corsican bandit hadn't made off with my charges. Inside my clean white collar I began to feel a prickle of sweat. *The Big Sleep* (Warner Bros., 1946).

Finally all the tickets were assembled. Using my Diners Club Card, I signed for them, flouting Her Majesty's Government's foreign currency regulations. Lauren Bacall accepted my signature without question. What was one crime among so many?

The gangster drove us to the beach. (The Carlton, where else?) I paid and dismissed him. We booked mattresses, lay down to soak up the fading strength of the afternoon sun. I drank Pernod, the children sipped Coca-Cola through straws. I bought a beach ball, inflated it, got them to join me in a game of football by the water's edge. Exhaust their energies. From time to time I looked at my wristwatch.

As the flat cloudbanks started to roll up again from the mountains, we got dressed and paid our bill. In the golden blaze of the dying day, we strolled along the Croisette towards the glittering harbour, with its gleaming yachts and white sails. I gave the children their tea at a large self-service restaurant near the port, favourite of Leonore's from That Other Time. Watched them eat spaghetti and fruit salad, had never seen them happier. My head was filled with light and air. I was reminded of that silver morning in front of the Martinez. No mistakes this time, love. None.

Back to the station. A porter collected our bags and disappeared, pushing his little iron trolley out of sight. To Leonore's relief, he turned up again at the far end of our platform. The sky had turned a comforting dark blue. The moon, full and brilliant, cast a ghostly glow upon the roofs of the surrounding villas.

Bought the latest *France-Football*; a volume of Andersen's Fairy Tales in English for the children.

Over the loudspeaker came muffled exhortations from the station announcer. The train drew in very slowly, whined to a halt. Now. It was happening. With all the well-oiled efficiency I had promised myself. Follow the pleasure fantasy, follow it through to the end of the night.

A beery Wagon-Lits attendant prosaically checked his list, appropriated our tickets and passports. I helped the kids up the steps of the coach. We walked along the corridor, found our compartment. It smelled of disinfectant and oranges. The porter installed our luggage. I tipped him. 'I bags the top sleeper,' Leonore insisted.

Barry climbed up to the middle bed. I took possession of the bottom bunk, lay back, lit a cigarette, opened my *France-Football*. Slowly the train began to jerk out of the station. In the narrow compartment, the kids clambered up and down the olive-coloured ladder, scraping their shins, pressing noses against glass.

Lights flashed by. Fulfilment.

The Wagon-Lits attendant knocked, opened the door, asked us if we desired anything. I ordered three bottles of Perrier, let the children totter out into the corridor to explore the entire length of the train, read *France-Football*.

When they returned, red-cheeked, with perspiring upper lips, I persuaded them to get undressed and slip between crisp sheets. They experimented with the light-switches and drank Perrier. I kissed them, first Barry, then Leonore, carefully tucked them in. Reclining on my bottom bunk, I opened Andersen's Fairy Tales.

'Lovely up here,' Leonore confirmed from very far away.

'I'll read you a story,' I told them. 'Then you must get some sleep. We'll be changing trains quite early in the morning.'

'Oh, Daddy, it's super.'

'Isn't it?'

I glanced down the table of contents. *The Snow Queen*. That was the one. Bogey had been dismissed long ago. No further need for him. For anyone. Just me. And them. Called for silence and began:

'Well, now, let's begin and when we come to the end of the story we shall know more than we do now . . .'

'Can't hear you, Daddy, train's rattling about. Speak up.'

'I know it,' Barry called down from his middle bunk 'About those two Scandinavian kids. Kay and Gerda. Soppy name for a boy, Kay.'

I read on: *'There was once a wicked demon—one of the worst—the Devil himself! One day he was in a really good humour, because he made a mirror which had the power of making everything good and beautiful reflected in it disappear almost to nothing, while all that was bad and ugly to look at showed up clearly and appeared far worse than it really was . . .'*

My voice—not Bogey's, not Scott Fitzgerald's, not Dracula's. Went on reading, while part of my mind remained fixed on that opening paragraph. A devil's mirror: Marion and my unborn child abandoned. Barry and Leonore kidnapped. Joe driven to suicide. Linda frozen in her ice-cube. Dick's career railroaded into a blind alley. My friends' weaknesses exploited for gain.

Into the Unknown. Free at last.

'Louder, Daddy, louder,' Leonore called from her top bunk, her own voice reduced to a sleepy whimper.

The train gathered speed. I read on. Louder. Louder. Over the night train's sostenuto roll and rumble. Fairytale.

'. . . they flew over forests and lakes, over land and sea, while below them the cold wind shrieked, the wolves howled, the snow sparkled, and over it flew the black screeching crows. But above them the moon shone large

and bright, and Kay gazed upon it all through that long, long winter night. During the day, he slept at the Snow Queen's feet...'

I paused, heard no protest; only the even breathing of two sleeping children, the clatter of wheels over rails. I closed the book, switched off the reading light. A mellow blue haze illuminated the compartment. I rose silently, opened the door slightly, stepped out into the corridor.

During the day, he slept at the Snow Queen's feet ...

I unclipped one of the blinds covering the corridor windows, pushed it up as high as it would go. Then I pulled down the window itself, leaned out. Felt my face fanned by draughts of welcoming night air. Violet jerseys. Over a gravelly pitch. With puddles. Soon now. The train roared on, through the calm darkness. Soon, soon, quite soon.

I pulled my head back, pushed up the window, swayed in the corridor to the rhythm of the wheels, arms outstretched, palm flat against glass, other hand touching the door-handle of our compartment. No mistakes. Nothing irrational in my actions. Nearly £500 in travellers cheques tucked away in my wallet. Me. George Kane: Gifted, reliable director of television drama, with a Guild Award to prove my talents. Could work anywhere. Not that it really mattered.

Guarding them as they slept. Me. George Kane. Intact.

After a while I turned, opened the compartment door, very quietly slipped inside. Lay down on my bunk and closed my eyes.

Are you still cold? she asked him and kissed him on the brow. Her kiss was colder than ice: it went straight to his heart, and his heart was already halfway to being a lump of ice. He felt as if he were about to die—but only for a moment, and then everything was all right again —and he no longer noticed the cold all around him.

On the following pages

are details of some recent Arrow Books

that should be of interest:-

THE BLOODY SUN AT NOON

by George Beare

The Persian Gulf: sweating south under a scorching sun; a dhow. On board, an oddly assorted collection of people: the skipper, Stallard, a man with murder in his past; La Rosa, petty gangster and pimp; Abdulrahman Davidson, philosopher and spy; Cynthia Godwin, journalist; Madeleine, beautiful and available, at a price.

Ashore: desert, flies, heat, corruption. And oil. Oil that was the cause of all the action, the violent deaths. Oil that brought together sophisticated techniques and primitive gut reactions.

RING IN THE NEW

by Phyllis Bentley

The West Riding: setting for the earlier novels in the Oldroyd saga – the novels that were so successfully televised as the Inheritance trilogy.

Now the story is continued. The old, closely-knit world of the textile families has changed. When old Henry Morcar dies suddenly, a new generation comes into its inheritance.

Old problems appear in new forms. Syke Mill is threatened by a take-over bid. The leader of a protest march is the descendant of a Luddite rioter. Social conditions change but picture of the West Riding and its people is as authentic as ever.

THE ONLY WAR WE'VE GOT

by Derek Maitland

'It's the Only War We've Got. Think about it.' (*Col. Wendel C. Mayer.*)

'A Fantasmagorical, Action-Packed, Glittering Cavalcade, Presenting the Very Best in Entertainment Brought to You at Great Expense by a Star-Studded Cast of Thousands. The Greatest Show on Earth – The Vietnam War.
You May Laugh; You May Cry. You May Die Laughing.'

An Hilarious, but Thrilling Tale of Death, Corruption, Romance, Sex, Politics, Greed, Ambition, Hatred, Drugs, Atrocity and Accident, set in the exotic Far East.
Vietnam: Land of Mystery and Adventure.

'Brilliant, moving first novel, about the Vietnam War.' (*Manchester Evening News.*)

'Takes devastating aim.' (*Times Literary Supplement.*)

A CHILD AT ARMS

by Patrick Davis

In February 1943 Patrick Davis went to war. He was eighteen when he reported to the Great Central Hotel, Marylebone. By November 1943 he was a subaltern in the 3rd Gurkhas. The next year he met his enemy, the Japanese, for the first time.

He had been posted as a novice to a battle-scarred battalion of Gurkhas in Burma who 'had fought for about as long as troops can fight and remain a recoverable unit'. But they had recovered and soon they were back in action, taking part in the desperate series of battles in which Field-Marshall Slim's Fourteenth Army drove the Japanese back across the Irrawaddy and laid the foundations for the famous march to Rangoon.

And all the time he was taking stock, noticing the process by which he became a soldier, learning to understand his Gurkha troops and to be accepted by them. Learning the techniques of fighting and charted the mental changes that took place in himself. Discovering in action the ability to be brave, and then discovering that a man's stock of courage can be expended. Realising that the war must still go on, even when that has happened.

CROWN AND MITRE

by Robert Neill

'Mr Burnaby, who had escaped from prison that afternoon, thought he must be going mad.'

Very strange his escape had been – he had just walked out unhindered. But the madness was London's, not Burnaby's. He had walked out into one of the most troubled and bewildering episodes in British history. Cromwell was dead and the future all uncertainty. Now: the infighting, the wheeling and dealing that was to end in the return of King Charles II, the Restoration of the Monarchy.

And at the very heart of the negotiations was to be Burnaby, the former rebel, taken in arms against the Commonwealth of England.

STAND ON ZANZIBAR

by John Brunner

They'll tell you that the whole human race could be put on the 147-square-mile Isle of Wight. They couldn't move of course, just stand there. True? Maybe in 1918. Now you'd need the 221-square-mile Isle of Man.

By 2010, something larger; something like 640-square-mile Zanzibar. By 2010 there are more than 7 billion people crowding the world. A world of acceleratubes, Moonbase Zero, intelligent computors and mass-marketed psychedelics. A world where a quiet man can be turned into a human machine, programmed to kill.

A terrifying world because all the elements are already discernible in this world now.

WHITE FANG GOES DINGO

by Thomas M. Disch

'When the Masters had first manifested themselves to mankind, they had insisted that they be given complete authority over all electric plants, dams, dynamos, and radio stations. Without in any way interfering with their utility from a human stand-point . . . the Masters transformed this pre-existent network into a sort of electro-magnetic pleasure spa.'

The Masters were beyond human comprehension – seemingly some form of pure electro-magnetic phenomenon. They chose not to enslave mankind. They made pets of them.

These stories of Thomas M. Disch cover a wide range, but each shows a wittily imaginative mind at work, questioning the nature of future societies, deftly exploiting the consequences of new technologies. Often outrightly funny, always the light yet perceptive play of the intelligence.

George Kane: television director and domestic refugee. In flight from his wife, in perpetual pursuit of other women.

Obsessive and schizoid, seeing all life as a collage of old movie fragments. A man sunk so deep in his medium that he can only surface, spluttering wildly, at intervals to note despairingly that 'real life' is just as fragmented and hopeless. Then he sinks into his private world of film and sexual confusion. George Kane: self-mocking and bitterly funny about sex.

'A brilliant novel'

'It's a lovely novel … Worrying, probing, erotic here and there, always wonderfully funny'

United Kingdom 35p
Australia $1·10
New Zealand $1·10
South Africa 85c

ISBN 0 09 004960 8

a Pelican Original $1 45

The Vikings

Johannes Brøndsted